WORDS FROM THE HEART

"So Lady Katherine told you I was here," she said. "I should have guessed. She is always so sure she knows what is best for other people."

"It seems to me she's not the only one," said Raymond with a sidelong look. "Caroline, you seem convinced I ought not to care for you. But I do care for you—I *love* you, in fact. You are the woman of all others I love and want to marry. It will be a source of misery all my life if you refuse me."

"You can't know that," she said. "People change, Raymond. Feelings change. I am sure you would end up regretting it if I agreed to become your wife. To most of society, I'm Caroline Sedgewick, the most celebrated jilt in England. Why would you want to tie yourself with such a woman?"

"Because I know she is not the most celebrated jilt in England but, rather, a most misunderstood young woman," said Raymond. "Because she is honest, and witty, and altogether delightful company. Because I never fail to enjoy myself when I am with her. And because I love her with all my heart. Is that not sufficient reason?"

Books by Joy Reed

An Inconvenient Engagement

Twelfth Night

The Seduction of Lady Carroll

Midsummer Moon

Lord Wyland Takes a Wife

The Duke and Miss Denny

A Home for the Holidays

Lord Caldwell and the Cat

Miss Chambers Takes Charge

Catherine's Wish

Emily's Wish

Anne's Wish

The Baron and the Bluestocking

Lord Desmond's Destiny

Lord Yates and the Yankee

Mr. Jeffries and the Jilt

Published by Zebra Books

MR. JEFFRIES AND THE JILT

Joy Reed

ZEBRA BOOKS
Kensington Publishing Corp.
http://www.kensingtonbooks.com

ZEBRA BOOKS are published by

Kensington Publishing Corp.
850 Third Avenue
New York, NY 10022

First Printing: August 2003
10 9 8 7 6 5 4 3 2 1

Printed in the United States of America

One

The Honourable Mr. Raymond Jeffries had never had a high opinion of watering places. As he stood on the terrace of his aunt's home, however, looking over the tiled roofs of Shelton-on-Sea, he found himself agreeably impressed.

"It's a pretty enough place," he said, adding pessimistically, "but I daresay it's filthy cold in wintertime."

"There's no place in England that isn't filthy cold in wintertime," said his aunt, who had accompanied him onto the terrace. "That's why I winter in Italy as a rule. Or in Greece. The pleasantest winter I ever spent was in a farmhouse on one of the Greek isles. There was sunshine every day, all the olives and goat's milk cheese you could eat, and plenty of hills to scramble up whenever you got tired of just sitting and admiring the scenery."

Raymond regarded her indulgently. Mehitabel Jeffries looked a thoroughly ordinary English spinster, but in fact she was anything but ordinary. Left with ample means at an early age, she had been able to fully indulge her own tastes, which included a most unladylike penchant for travel and adventure. By the time she was in her thirties, she had achieved a real celebrity for her exploits, and by the time she was fifty, she was a near legend, having visited not only the Continental capitals but more exotic locales such as Egypt and the Holy Lands. Recently she had published a book about her experiences, which had further enhanced her celebrity. But celebrity had done nothing to alter Miss Jeffries's severe, elder-maidenly mien, or her frank and forthright speech. Her next remark to her nephew was typical of this last-named quality.

"And let me tell you, Raymond, I won't hear of your finding fault with Shelton-on-Sea. It's as pretty a place as you'll find in England, and so I tell you. I don't doubt it *is* cold here in winter, but it's not winter now, it's June. To hear you going on about the cold in such perfect weather!" She gestured toward the bay full of dancing whitecaps. "It puts me out of patience. Makes you sound like a tiresome creature who's above being pleased."

Raymond laughed. "No, indeed," he said. "On the contrary, I have been very much pleased by Shelton-on-Sea, Aunt. It's big enough for diversion without being so big as to become merely another, inferior Brighton. And the city in general has been laid out in a very good style."

"I think so too," said his aunt, nodding with satisfaction. "After breakfast, we'll go around to the pump room. It's not quite the eighth wonder of the world some folks would have it, but it beats Bath all hollow, and most of the Continental watering places too."

"Pump room?" inquired Raymond, arching a quizzical eyebrow. "I thought one swam in the waters of Shelton-on-Sea, not drank them. You held out sea bathing as a lure to get me here, as I recall."

"Aye, so I did," agreed his aunt. "But you know

there's those who hold that it's healthy to drink seawater as well as bathe in it. Dr. Briar, our local leech, claims to have worked some miraculous cures with seawater drafts. It was he who convinced the city fathers we ought to have a pump room so as to be able to take the waters in style."

Raymond's mouth was puckered in an expression of distaste. "Pray do not imagine for one moment that I will dose myself internally with saltwater, Aunt," he said. "Not though you should assure me it is a veritable fountain of youth and a panacea for all ills."

"Oh, I'd never do that," said his aunt, looking amused. "I tried drinking it once when I first came here, and between you and me, once was enough. Still, there's plenty of folk that drink the stuff on a daily basis and swear it's done 'em a deal of good. But I think it's all a humbug myself. We'll go to the pump room merely to be sociable and not because we want to muddle our insides with saltwater."

"You relieve me, Aunt," said Raymond, smiling. "But pray do not feel obliged to be sociable on my behalf. The only society I want, or am likely to find agreeable here, is your own."

Instead of looking gratified by this speech, Miss Jeffries looked annoyed. "There you go again," she said. "That's the kind of remark that puts me out of patience, Raymond. How do you know what kind of society you'll find here, or whether you'll find it agreeable?"

Raymond smiled again, a cynical smile. "I know what the common run of humanity is," he said. "Even in London, in what is termed the best society, fools and bores abound. I wouldn't expect to find the situation any better at a seaside watering place. If anything, I should expect to find it worse!"

His aunt shook her head. "Do you know what the problem with you is, Raymond?" she said, answering rhetorically. "You've been spoiled, that's what. You inherited your grandmother's money early on, so you've never wanted for that, and you've got your mother's good looks, so that everyone's praised and flattered you from the time you were in leading strings. And because it's known you'll step into your father's title someday, every toady in the *ton* has been making up to you these ten years, until it's no wonder you're sick of your fellow men and women. If you were a younger son with your way to make in the world, I'll wager you'd take a different view of life."

This diatribe, far from offending Raymond, merely made him throw back his head and laugh. "How I might view life in such a situation is quite beside the point, Aunt," he said. "I am as I am, and you must take me as you find me."

"Well, it's as I said before: I find you uncommonly spoiled," said his aunt sternly.

"Spoiled is such an ugly word," complained Raymond, a smile dancing about his lips. "Could you not rather say discriminating in my tastes?"

"No, I couldn't," returned his aunt. "If you were merely discriminating, I'd have nothing to say to it. You're a Jeffries, after all, and our family's always had the reputation of being particular. But I tell you plainly that you carry it beyond what's rational. Pretty soon you'll be so nice that nothing will be good enough for you, and then where will you be?"

"I don't know," said Raymond, smiling again. "Not at Shelton-on-Sea, at any rate. I've already said I like the look of the place. Can you not be satisfied with that and not expect me to embrace its populace as well?"

"No, for there's some decent society here, though you might not think it. We have weekly balls at the Assembly Rooms during the summer months, not to mention concerts, picnics, and all manner of other diversions."

Raymond murmured a polite approbation, but inwardly he felt nothing but dismay at his aunt's words. When even parties at Carlton House were a dead bore nine times out of ten, he could not view with any eagerness the prospect of attending a series of assemblies patronized by a lot of provincial dowagers and valetudinarians (for so he reckoned the populace of Shelton-on-Sea to chiefly consist of). It stood to reason there could be no persons of note among them, certainly no one he would have chosen to associate with voluntarily. Such persons would have gone to Brighton instead, or to some other fashionable resort, not to a quiet place like Shelton-on-Sea. His aunt, to be sure, had chosen it when she might have gone anywhere, but his aunt was an Eccentric with a capital E and not to be taken as any kind of general indicator. No doubt she, who could find diversion even in a weeklong journey in a French *diligence*, had found enough to amuse her here by the seaside.

But he, the discriminating Raymond Jeffries, asked for something more than merely a weekly assembly and an occasional concert or picnic. He wanted wit, humor, intelligent conversation—in a word, he wanted society that would stimulate him rather than bore him. *"And God knows that's hard enough to find even in London,"* he reflected ruefully.

Although Raymond tried to conceal these reflections from his aunt, it was evident she perceived some part of them. Once more she shook her head.

"You look as though I'd proposed to plunge you into the midst of a howling desert, Raymond, rather than bring you among decent folk whom you'd like if you gave them half a chance," she said. "Emily Renquist is here, and Admiral Humphrey and his wife, and Sir Brandon and Lady Hardcastle. And there's a plenty of pretty girls too," she added with a significant smile. "You used not to be above liking a pretty girl."

"No," agreed Raymond cautiously, "although it rather depends on what you mean by pretty. Sometimes I have found the term used in a—how shall I put it?—a somewhat elastic manner."

"And, of course, any girl who wasn't a Diamond of the First Water wouldn't be a fit companion for Raymond Jeffries," agreed his aunt caustically.

"Not at all," protested Raymond, but his aunt shook her head.

"It's no use trying to gammon me, Raymond. It's obvious you're as particular where women are concerned as in everything else. Otherwise, you wouldn't still be single at the age of thirty in spite of all the snares laid for you."

"Possibly," agreed Raymond, "but it is also possible the fact I am still single is owing to that precise circumstance, Aunt. All the snares laid for me may have given me a distaste for being caught in the first place."

Although he spoke the words lightly enough, his aunt gave him a searching look. "It's like that, is it?" she said. "I should have guessed, to be sure. It's a shame the way women will chase after a man who's got a good income—not to mention a handsome face and a future title."

"Well, it's not for me to talk of shame," said Raymond, smiling ruefully. "But I can say from experience that they can be both enterprising and persistent."

"I daresay. Still, I find it hard to believe you haven't found a lady yet whom you were minded to take to wife. Whatever happened to that pretty Hampstead chit you were squiring about a couple of Seasons ago?"

Frowning, Raymond made an effort at recollection. "She's married now, I believe. I am sure I heard she was engaged a year or so ago, though I can't remember to whom."

"Well, it's evident you aren't breaking your heart about it," said his aunt dryly. "And what about Belinda Entwhistle's daughter? I thought for certain that would be a match."

Raymond smiled faintly. "I thought the same thing at one time. But it came to nothing in the end. She's a nice enough girl, and I wish her well, but—"

"But in the end, she was found unworthy to become Mrs. Raymond Jeffries," finished his aunt with another ironic smile.

"I didn't say that," said Raymond. For the first time there was a hint of sharpness in his voice. "I didn't say that at all. Perhaps it's I who was unworthy of her."

His aunt was unimpressed by this statement. "That's flummery, Raymond, and you know it," she said. "The whole reason you've never found a girl who suits you is that you're too particular. You expect perfection, and there's no such thing in this world—certainly not where women are concerned. Or men either." She laughed. "By heavens, I begin to think you and Miss Sedgewick ought to make a match of it! By all accounts, there's nothing to choose between you where being particular's concerned."

"Indeed?" said Raymond. "And who is Miss Sedgewick?"

"Miss Sedgewick—Caroline Sedgewick. Old George Sedgewick's daughter." When Raymond merely looked blank, his aunt shook her head impatiently. "You must be acquainted with her, Raymond. She was presented in London a few Seasons ago and had quite a little success by all accounts."

Raymond, after much frowning recollection, finally recalled a lady by the name of Sedgewick. "I seem to recall she was engaged to that old bore Scroggins," he said.

"Yes, she was," said his aunt. "But she jilted him only a few days after the engagement was announced. Then last Season she went and got engaged to young Rob Cullen—and now she's jilted him too. Sophia Cullen isn't half in a taking about it. And there was another fellow besides that Miss Sedgewick was engaged to too—a young army officer, I think it was. So that's three fellows she's thrown over, and no sign that she's any closer to the altar than before. That's why I said the two of you ought to get together, Raymond. To all appearances, she's as particular as you are."

Raymond, frowning, begged not to be compared with Miss Sedgewick. "I have not been engaged even once, let alone three times, Aunt," he said. "I think any comparison between the lady's behavior and mine quite unwarranted." As an afterthought, he said, "Are you sure it is the same Miss Sedgewick we are talking about? The girl I remember was rather plain—reddish hair, and nothing out of the ordinary for looks."

His aunt nodded. "That sounds like her," she said. "Though I'm not sure I agree with you about her being plain. It's true she don't have the kind of looks that bowl you over at first glance, but she's a taking enough girl in her way."

Raymond felt assured his aunt was mistaken. He was certain that if Miss Caroline Sedgewick had been at all a taking girl, he could not have failed to notice it. "At any rate, she seems to have done pretty well for herself," he observed aloud. "Engaged to three men, and one of them old Scroggins! I wouldn't have supposed the devil himself could bring Scroggins to the point."

His aunt opined that it had probably been Emilia Hurston's doing, between which lady and the devil there was little to choose in terms of principle. "You know it was Emilia who sponsored Miss Sedgewick when she made her bows. They're some sort of relatives, I believe. And there's nobody more alive to the main chance than Emilia, or with fewer scruples about getting what she wants. She'd be quite capable of maneuvering a man into marrying a protégée of hers, even such an old fox as Scroggins."

"Thanks for the warning," said Raymond with a grimace. "I'll take care to keep out of her way if she should dangle Miss Sedgewick in front of me. But no doubt I am safe so long as I am staying in Shelton-on-Sea."

His aunt shook her head, smiling. "No, there's no safety for you here, Raymond," she said. "Though I don't suppose you're in any danger from Miss Sedgewick, any more than from Miss Hampstead, or Miss Entwhistle."

Raymond was too taken up with his aunt's previous statement to feel this barb. "You don't mean to say the Siren is actually staying here?" he exclaimed. "I would have thought Shelton-on-Sea too small a covert for the kind of game Emilia Hurston hunts."

His aunt shook her head. "Emilia isn't sponsoring Miss Sedgewick any longer," she said. "They parted ways a while back, not long after Miss Sedgewick threw over Lord Scroggins. Indeed, I wouldn't be surprised if there weren't a connection between the two events. Emilia can't have been pleased to see such a prize slip through her fingers."

"Miss Sedgewick appears not to have done badly for herself even without her relatives' help," said Raymond, smiling. "You mentioned she was engaged to Robert Cullen. He's a warm man by all accounts, if not so deep in the pockets as Scroggins. Still, you said she threw him over too."

"Yes, she did, and quite recently. Sophia Cullen was livid about it. And she was even more livid when Miss Sedgewick showed up a few weeks ago here at Shelton-on-Sea. She said it made her sick to see her walking the streets, smiling and smirking and pretending to be a pattern card of propriety, after what she had done to her son."

"If I know Robert Cullen, he won't be long in making a recovery," said Raymond cynically. "In fact, I think he's recovered already. I saw him just a few weeks ago handing La Bella Verlucci into her carriage outside the opera house."

"I doubt Sophia knows about that. In any case, she would regard it as quite beside the point. To her mind, Miss Sedgewick publicly sullied the honor of her son by jilting him, and she will never forgive her."

"And as a result, she has no doubt done her best

to make Miss Sedgewick's stay in Shelton-on-Sea highly uncomfortable," said Raymond with a short laugh.

"No doubt she would like to," agreed Miss Jeffries. "But it happens Miss Sedgewick is staying with Lady Katherine Baddington and so beyond Sophia's touch. It irks her to no end to see Miss Sedgewick taken up by people of such fashion as Lady Katherine."

Raymond received this news with interest. "So the Baddingtons are here, are they?" he said. "You did not tell me *that,* Aunt. Shelton-on-Sea must be a more popular place than I reckoned if such fashionables as Lady Katherine have taken it up."

"Aye, she and her husband have a house here in one of the new squares. I should have remembered to mention it before, Raymond. No doubt it would have recommended the place to you far more than the fact that Emily Renquist or Admiral Humphrey live here."

"Oh, I wouldn't say that," said Raymond. "I'm not one of Lady Katherine's particular admirers, though I'll admit she's a charming woman."

"Yes, she is. Mr. Lindensmyth, who keeps the Assembly Rooms, is *aux anges* to have her here. It's no wonder, of course, for it's a great recommendation to be able to say that Lady Katherine Baddington is a patroness of his rooms."

Raymond said dryly that he had no doubt of it. "And as a result, every mushroom and Cit in town patronizes his rooms too, so they can tell their friends that they attended an assembly with Lady Katherine," he said. "That's one of the things I dislike most about places like this, Aunt. I'm surprised Lady Katherine is willing to put up with it. She has the reputation of being a rather discriminating woman."

"She not only appears at our assemblies, she seems to enjoy 'em. But there, I daresay she's not as nice as you are, Raymond."

Miss Jeffries spoke these last words with such exaggerated deference that her nephew could not help smiling. "Perhaps I *am* too nice in my notions, Aunt," he said. "It's a failing of mine, I admit. But I am willing to attend your assemblies if you like. Where Lady Katherine goes, I certainly should not be afraid to follow."

His aunt said approvingly that this was a sensible attitude. "There's an assembly tonight, as it happens," she said. "I didn't mention it earlier, since you got in only last night. I thought perhaps you might prefer to rest today after traveling so far."

Raymond looked both pained and amused. "I hope you do not think me so frail as to be knocked up by a six-hours' ride in a comfortable carriage," he said. "Especially when you yourself think nothing of traveling all night over roads Mr. McAdam would shudder at! If I did not know better, I might suspect you invited me to Shelton-on-Sea merely to bolster up my failing health with seawater, applied both internally and externally."

His aunt, laughing, disclaimed such intention. "In any case, I've already told you that seawater wasn't meant to be taken internally, in my opinion. Bathing in it's well enough, but drinking it—no! Still, I don't mean to prejudice you," she added with a teasing smile. "When you've seen our pump room, who knows but you'll decide to try a course of the waters yourself?"

Raymond declared himself in no danger of such a

decision but said he was very ready to see the pump room. His aunt, with a glance at the old-fashioned watch at her waist, said they might as well go now, as it was full late enough for the *habitués* of the place to have gathered. Accordingly, they donned their hats and outer wraps and set off for the pump room, Raymond assuring his aunt that in all proceedings related to drinking seawater he was content to remain merely a spectator.

Two

The building that housed Shelton-on-Sea's pump and assembly rooms had been designed in the classical style, with a white stucco facade and rows of Corinthian pillars. Even Raymond had to admit it made a fine appearance, though he prophesied all the stucco would soon flake away in the salt air.

"Hush, ingrate! If stucco's good enough for the Prince Regent, it's good enough for you," his aunt told him sternly. And indeed, with the blue of a June sky overhead, set about by urns of bright flowers and enlivened by a group of young ladies in light muslins who stood chattering on its steps, the building looked so attractive that Raymond forbore from further criticism.

Inside, its rooms proved equally attractive. There was a vestibule with retiring rooms for ladies and gentlemen; this vestibule opened into the pump room proper, a large apartment made light and airy by a row of windows looking out on a central courtyard. Along one side of the room ran a marble counter where seawater was served forth at twopence a glass by pretty, pink-cheeked maids who looked a testimony to the health-giving properties of their own wares. Raymond wondered that anyone would indulge in the folly of buying seawater when the whole of the bay lay free for the taking, but he supposed there might be some difference between the beverage served forth by the maids and raw water taken from the ocean; he hoped so, at any rate. Having a dilettante's interest in science, he had once had the privilege of peering through a microscope at a drop of seawater, and after seeing what unappetizing creatures made their home therein, he could not like to think anyone would drink it in its natural state.

Still, if the city fathers of Shelton-on-Sea were misguided in promulgating the health benefits of seawater, Raymond had to admit they had at least done the thing properly. The marble counter; the pretty maidservants in their caps and aprons; even the beverage itself, served forth in cut-glass goblets, made taking the waters seem both an elegant and appealing pastime. It was evidently a popular pastime too. Although he noted many in the pump room who, like him and his aunt, eschewed seawater as a beverage, there were at least as many who were clasping cut-glass goblets from which they now and then took a sip, albeit with no very apparent enjoyment.

The hour was still early in Raymond's estimation, but already there was a crowd in the pump room. He had to wait some minutes at the counter before he could obtain cups of tea for his aunt and himself. He spent the time looking about him at the other pump-room patrons. He could see now he had been mistaken in supposing Shelton-on-Sea inhabited solely by dowagers and valetudinarians. There were plenty of these to be seen, of course, but plenty of younger people as well.

A cluster of girls in white dresses and pink bonnets stood near the door, engaged in a conversation enlivened by much giggling. Opposite them was a matching cluster of young gentlemen in high collars and tasseled boots, making even more noise than their feminine counterparts. A pair of elegant-looking young matrons sat with their heads together, discussing fashions with the enthusiasm of true votaries, while a youthful couple, obviously newly married, stood bashfully receiving the congratulations of their friends and acquaintances.

Raymond found amusement in watching all these goings-on, but his chief interest, unacknowledged even to himself, was in trying to identify Caroline Sedgewick among the ladies present. What his aunt had told him concerning Caroline had interested him mightily, and he thought he would like to see the Siren who had raised so much havoc among his own sex. His remembrance of her in London was hazy, so hazy he could not be certain whether she was among the young ladies in the pump room, but on the whole he thought not. There were one or two young ladies with fair or sandy hair, but they were plump rather than slim, and he remembered Caroline as definitely slim.

It was a point against her in his opinion. He had no liking for skinny women. Indeed, he found himself wondering if his aunt might be mistaken about its being the same Caroline Sedgewick. He found it impossible to believe that the young lady he recalled could have attracted one earnest suitor, let alone three.

In any case, Caroline did not appear to be present. Having reached this conclusion, Raymond returned his attention to the counter and waited patiently until he was able to secure the attention of one of the maids and, in due course of time, two cups of tea. Carrying these carefully in his hands, he made his way through the crowd to where he had left his aunt seated on an upholstered settee.

She was still there, but during the time he had been gone she had acquired a companion. A willowy matron with chestnut curls and large light eyes was seated beside her, speaking volubly in a low, throbbing voice. Both ladies looked up as Raymond approached. His aunt rose with a welcoming smile to accept the cup he held out to her. "Raymond! My dear, I am sorry you should have been put to so much trouble merely to get me a cup of tea. It's always very busy in the pump room of a morning, but today it seems positively mobbed."

"I wondered if it was always so busy," said Raymond. He did not relish the idea of fighting his way through the crowd once more, but knowing his duty as a gentleman, he bowed politely to the willowy matron and asked his aunt, "Shall I fetch another cup for your companion?"

The willowy matron at once disclaimed any wish of drinking tea. "I could not dream of putting you to so much trouble," she said earnestly. "Such a dreadful squeeze! I don't believe I've ever seen the pump room so crowded."

"Raymond, you are not acquainted with Mrs. Cullen, are you?" said his aunt. "I know you mentioned knowing her son, but I did not think you had met her before. Sophia, this is my nephew, Raymond Jeffries; Raymond, this is Mrs. Robert Cullen."

Mrs. Cullen put out a hand in a purple kid glove and seized Raymond's in an almost painful grasp. "Are you indeed a friend of Robert's?" she cried. "It is a privilege to meet you, sir!" In a more melancholy tone, she added, "Dear boy, he has need of friends in these dark days."

As it happened, Raymond was no friend of Robert Cullen. He had always regarded Cullen as a coxcomb with underbred manners, but in deference to his mother he murmured something polite and conventional about their being members of the same club. This seemed to satisfy Mrs. Cullen. Grasping his hand still tighter, she said, "Have you seen Robert lately? Is he well? As soon as I heard what that Miss Sedgewick had done, I made immediate plans to leave Shelton-on-Sea and rush to his side. But Robert would not hear of it. Poor boy, I am sure he wants his mother's care, but he would not allow me to cut short my holiday to wait on him."

Remembering in what company he had last seen Robert Cullen, Raymond could well believe this. "He seemed to be keeping his spirits up when last I saw him," he said in what he trusted was not too ironic a voice. "But of course that was several weeks ago."

"Several weeks ago? But that, perhaps, was before he received the blow. You must know that woman—that dreadful woman"—Mrs. Cullen pronounced the words with pronounced bitterness—"jilted him only two weeks ago this day."

Raymond looked at her speculatively. He could not recall the exact date on which he had seen Mr. Cullen handing Signorina Verlucci, principal dancer in the opera-ballet and notorious high-flyer, into her carriage, but he was quite sure it was more than two weeks earlier. This fact seemed to cast a new and interesting light on the whole Sedgewick-Cullen affair. Still, Raymond thought it better not to give voice to such private reflections. Instead, he addressed Mrs. Cullen in a warmer tone than he had used before. "I am sure you must want a cup of tea, ma'am. Will you not allow me to fetch one for you?"

Mrs. Cullen again protested she could not dream of putting him to so much trouble. "Although I do like a cup of tea in the morning," she added with a wistful look at the cup in his hand.

Raymond at once presented it to her, saying he had not drunk any of it and did not want it in any case. After a little more demur, Mrs. Cullen accepted it, and she and Miss Jeffries reseated themselves on the settee, making room for him beside them.

Raymond was now definitely intrigued by the subject of Robert Cullen's broken engagement. Accordingly, he was very pleased when Mrs. Cullen, having refreshed herself with several sips of tea, took up the subject once more. "As I was saying just now, it was two weeks ago this day that Miss Sedgewick jilted Robert. Poor fellow, he puts a brave face on it, but I can tell from his letters he is most unhappy. It makes it so much worse that Miss Sedgewick should be actually here at Shelton-on-Sea, bold as brass and apparently quite at ease about her own conduct."

"Her behavior does seem rather equivocal," said Raymond. "Particularly since my aunt tells me she has been twice engaged before and had broken those engagements as well."

"Yes, so I understand. Indeed, even when Robert first spoke of marrying her, I had doubts about the match. Not only because she had jilted a couple of suitors before, but you know her portion is nothing out of the ordinary and her birth no more than genteel. Robert might have looked much higher for a bride if he had chosen. But nothing would do but he should marry Miss Sedgewick. And now you see what has been the result!"

Raymond and his aunt both nodded sympathetically. Mrs. Cullen, wiping a few fugitive tears from her eyes, said it was her earnest hope Robert would soon recover from his disappointment. "I expect he soon will," said Raymond, thinking of La Bella Verlucci. "Er—did Miss Sedgewick happen to give any reason for breaking the engagement?"

Mrs. Cullen shook her turbaned head decidedly. "No, she did not. Robert says it came as a complete surprise."

Raymond felt highly skeptical about the extent of Robert Cullen's surprise. But if Caroline's reasons for jilting him involved La Bella Verlucci, then he could see why he had chosen not to relate them to his mother. "So Miss Sedgewick gave no reason at all for breaking the engagement?" he asked again.

"Oh, I believe she gave some sort of excuse—the usual thing, you know, saying she had decided they would not suit."

Miss Jeffries shook her head. "That seems to be true, at any rate," she said. "Seeing how unstable Miss Sedgewick's character is, she would hardly suit any respectable man. In my opinion, your son has had a lucky escape."

"Yes, but unfortunately he doesn't see it that way. The woman has him quite infatuated, upon my word. He persists in seeing no fault in her and says he was to blame for everything."

Raymond pricked up his ears at this. He felt more than ever certain his private surmises were correct. Aloud, however, he said merely, "That shows a generous and forgiving spirit," which earned him an approving smile from Mrs. Cullen.

"Indeed, Robert is the best and most generous of men," she said. "That is why it is so difficult for me to see Miss Sedgewick flaunting herself here when he is breaking his heart in London. From her behavior, you wouldn't think she had a care in the world, let alone that she had just injured one of the noblest men in England. Oh, there are times when I can scarcely restrain myself from going up to her and telling her what I think of her conduct."

Mrs. Cullen's voice was quite fierce as she made this statement. Her frail hands in their purple kid gloves were clenched into tight fists as though she anticipated giving Miss Sedgewick more than opinion by way of chastisement. Raymond nodded gravely, but inwardly he was amused. He had already written Mrs. Cullen down as a foolish woman, for any woman who could consider a loose-living coxcomb like Robert Cullen the noblest of men must necessarily be a fool. Likewise, the fact that she was airing such a personal grievance before a new-met acquaintance did not argue any strong sense of discretion. It seemed remarkable to him that living in the same town as Caroline, she had not already confronted her and taken her for task for her wrongdoing.

"I am sure it must take great self-control on your part to keep from approaching Miss Sedgewick," he agreed with just the faintest shade of provocation in his voice. "Especially as it happens you are actually seeing each other on what must be almost a daily basis. That seems quite a coincidence, by the way. Surely she would not have purposely chosen to come to a place where she must needs meet the mother of the man she has just jilted?"

"Oh, I daresay she did not know I was here at Shelton-on-Sea," said Mrs. Cullen. "I came just a few weeks ago upon a whim, having heard it was a more exclusive place than Brighton—yes, and a good deal cheaper too. But even if Miss Sedgewick had known I was here, I doubt it would have stopped her. You must know she is as bold as brass, and cares what nobody says about her. And as long as she is with Lady Katherine, she is safe enough. No one would dare insult her while she is staying with the Baddingtons," finished Mrs. Cullen with some bitterness.

This answered most of Raymond's questions. It appeared that Mrs. Cullen, for all her maternal outrage, was nonetheless unwilling to risk offending such a leader of society as Lady Katherine Baddington. "It's surprising that Lady Katherine is willing to patronize Miss Sedgewick, " he commented. "Of course Lady Katherine is not what one would call a straitlaced woman, but even so I would not have supposed she would tolerate a companion who has made herself as notorious as Miss Sedgewick reportedly has done."

To Mrs. Cullen, however, this anomaly was easily explained. "No doubt Miss Sedgewick has told Lady Katherine a lot of lies," she told Raymond. "I expect she had some plausible story about why she decided to jilt Robert. I have no doubt Lady Katherine knows little, if any, of the real facts of the case. If ever I have the chance, I intend to drop a word in her ear, just to let her know what kind of viper she has been nourishing in her bosom. So far, however, there has been no opportunity."

Raymond could not suppose any such opportunity would be soon forthcoming. Neither could he regard with anything but amusement the image of Miss Sedgewick's being nourished as a viper in Lady Katherine's celebrated bosom. But he wrested his thoughts away from these entrancing side issues and returned to the matter at hand. "I take it Miss Sedgewick is not actually here today?" he asked, glancing around the pump room. "I saw her in London only once or twice, but I think I would recognize her."

"No, she is not here," said Mrs. Cullen with another vigorous shake of her turbaned head. "Indeed, she is seldom in the pump room of a morning. No doubt she stays out so late cavorting with Lady Katherine and her friends that she does not rise until late in the afternoon."

Raymond forbore to point out that this practice was nothing remarkable among fashionable Londoners, including Mrs. Cullen's own son. He merely nodded and said, "I suppose Miss Sedgewick might also be sea bathing at this hour. My aunt tells me many people prefer to take their dip early, on first arising."

Mrs. Cullen allowed this was possible, though in a grudging tone. It was clear she preferred to think of Caroline engaged in some disreputable vice. "But I have seen her sometimes on her way to the bathing machines of a morning," she added. "Emily Renquist pointed her out to me the other day, when we were upon the balcony of her hotel room. It just goes to show what a heartless creature Miss Sedgewick is, that she should be able to enjoy herself with sea bathing while Robert is miserable in London."

Again Raymond nodded. He was beginning to

tire both of Mrs. Cullen and the pump room. Or perhaps it was merely because he now knew Caroline Sedgewick was not there. In any case, he seized upon this pause in the conversation to suggest to his aunt that they might walk down to the shore and inspect the bathing machines with an eye to taking a dip later in the day. His aunt agreed, and they bade Mrs. Cullen adieu. When they left, she was already busily recounting her and her son's grievances to a retired colonel of the guards, whom she had seized on as her next victim.

Three

"What a tiresome woman," remarked Raymond as he and his aunt left the pump room. "Now I've met her, I understand why Robert Cullen has such a high opinion of himself. She clearly thinks him the most remarkable fellow that ever drew breath."

"Yes, she does," agreed his aunt. "But you know that's nothing unusual, Raymond. Most mothers do tend to favor their own offspring." She threw him a direct look. "Besides, you are not making allowances for her state of mind. She is very distressed right now because she considers that Miss Sedgewick has injured Robert. And quite rightly too, in my opinion. Miss Sedgewick appears to have behaved very badly."

Raymond nodded, although he was conscious of mixed feelings on the subject. While in agreement that Miss Sedgewick had no business jilting three fiancés in a row, he nevertheless could not help feeling that anyone who dealt Robert Cullen a set-down could not be a wholly bad person. This was the more true because she had a legitimate grievance in the shape of La Bella Verlucci. Some part of this feeling he sought to express to his aunt. "There's no doubt that Miss Sedgewick appears to have behaved badly by Mr. Cullen, but appearances can be deceiving,

Aunt. I don't believe for a minute that the account we got from Mrs. Cullen was unbiased."

"No," agreed his aunt. "And if it were not for the circumstance of Miss Sedgewick's previous engagements, I would be inclined to grant her the benefit of the doubt. Any girl might enter into an engagement with good faith, then find she had made a mistake. But for her to do so three times in a row—no, I think you will be hard put to defend that conduct, Raymond. It seems to argue a sad instability of character, to say no worse of it."

This being undeniably true, Raymond thought it better to change the subject. He asked his aunt to tell him a little about the buildings they were passing. She accordingly pointed out the theater, a florid building in pink stucco, and beside it a large hotel with wrought iron balconies. "Emily Renquist has rooms there," she said. "You are acquainted with Emily, are you not? A fine woman but a bit of a busybody. That's why she prefers staying at the hotel to renting a house of her own. Not only can she keep apprised of all new arrivals into town, she has a fine view of the shore. The hotel overlooks it, you see, and Emily has a telescope—to watch the shipping, she says. But I think she watches the esplanade and bathing machines more than the ships. Remember how Mrs. Cullen mentioned Emily seeing Miss Sedgewick going out to bathe the other day?"

Raymond did remember and looked with interest at the hotel with its tiers of balconies. "The shore must be quite close if Miss Renquist can see it from her rooms," he said. "I can see nothing of it from here."

"No, because that row of shops opposite blocks the

view. But when we come to the corner opposite the pastrycook's, we will be able to see it. That is Bayview Street, which leads directly down to the esplanade."

Surely enough, when they had turned the corner opposite the pastrycook's, they had a clear view of the bay ahead, dotted with whitecaps and sparkling in the sun. The esplanade was not merely a strip of grass along the shore as in other watering places, but a broad covered walkway whose roof was supported by slender columns leaving open the view both seaward and shoreward. Miss Jeffries explained that the roof had been added at the local ladies' request, because the trees planted at intervals along the esplanade were too small as yet to provide much shade. "It makes a pleasant place to walk on even the warmest days," she told Raymond. "On a fine Sunday, almost the whole town comes here to stroll, and gossip, and see who has got a new hat, and who is walking out with whom."

In the ordinary way, Raymond would have turned up his nose at this kind of provincialism, but standing on the esplanade, looking out at the sparkling waters of the bay, he thought he could tolerate it, even to the point of appearing at one of the Sunday walking parties.

Just then he caught sight of the row of bathing machines beyond the esplanade. This gave his thoughts a new direction. "I'd like to see the bathing machines, if I may," he said. "I've never been sea bathing, and I must confess your letters have given me a curiosity to try it."

His aunt laughed. "Well, you won't be able to gratify your curiosity in one of those machines," she said. "Those are for the ladies! The gentlemen's machines are around the other way, beyond the esplanade. I have been told there is an area for bathing without machines as well—though of course I wouldn't know about that," she added primly.

Raymond grinned, understanding that this was a reference to the fact that while ladies swathed almost the whole of their persons in voluminous bathing dresses, gentlemen bathed in nothing at all. "I'll make inquiries when we get back to the house," he said. "No doubt one of your servants will be able to direct me to a reputable bathing machine." As he and his aunt retraced their steps along the esplanade, however, he threw a look over his shoulder at the row of ladies' bathing machines. He could not help wondering which one was patronized by Miss Sedgewick, and if she made a practice of coming there often.

His curiosity on this subject had to remain unsatisfied, but in regard to the subject of sea bathing in general, Raymond was very soon able to satisfy himself as to its being a most interesting and agreeable pastime. His aunt's butler proved willing not only to direct him to a suitable bathing machine but to lead him thither and even take charge of the negotiations with the attendant. As a result, Raymond spent a very enjoyable hour swimming about in the surf. As he dried himself afterward with the towel provided by the attendant, then lay down in the sand to warm himself, he decided there might be something in the benefits of sea bathing after all. He felt relaxed yet stimulated, with a sense of well-being that permeated his whole body. It seemed to him he had not felt so well in years.

As he lay basking in the sun, he began to think the week he had allotted for his stay in Shelton-on-Sea might not be sufficient after all. There was no reason why his visit could not be extended to a couple of weeks, or even a couple of months. The place was much better than he had expected: larger, more elegant, and altogether very attractive. He would tell his aunt so, and if for any reason she found it inconvenient to put him up for more than a week, he could easily remove to the hotel.

Thoughts of the hotel led him again to thoughts of Caroline Sedgewick. With amusement, he reflected that she could have no idea of the interest her every move excited. Even the mere fact of her visiting a bathing machine was being held against her as if it had been a crime. It was easy to see that all the old cats at Shelton-on-Sea had gotten their knives into her.

But of course old women liked nothing better than to tear apart the reputation of a pretty girl. Only Caroline Sedgewick was not a pretty girl—was she? On this point Raymond found himself more and more uncertain. He felt sure he would have remembered if she was anything out of the common way, but his very uncertainty as to the details of her appearance made him wonder if perhaps there was more to her than he remembered. It seemed as though there must be if she had been able to cajole three men into making her offers of marriage.

Altogether, Raymond found himself quite eager to renew his acquaintance with Caroline. It had been a disappointment not to see her in the pump room that morning, but it sounded as though she usually attended the evening entertainments at the rooms—flaunted herself there, as Mrs. Cullen had put it. Likely he would see her that evening if he attended the assembly with his aunt. There was a pleasant excitement in the idea. Normally he would have yawned at the thought of a public assembly in a provincial watering place, but on this occasion he found himself positively stimulated by it.

Must be the sea bathing, he told himself. *It's got my blood going, so even the thought of romping through a dozen country-dances with a parcel of nobodies seems like a pleasant exercise.*

It may have been sea bathing that made him look forward to the exercise of dancing that evening, but that hardly explained the care with which he dressed himself for the assembly, or the attention he gave to the polish on his dancing pumps and the set of his neckcloth. And it was likewise not sea bathing that made him look eagerly around as he entered the Assembly Rooms that evening on the arm of his aunt.

A quick survey of the rooms brought him only disappointment, however. There were one or two young ladies whom he recalled seeing in the pump room, but by that very token he knew they could not be Caroline Sedgewick. Raymond was vexed—almost absurdly vexed, as he reflected. After all, it was not as though Caroline were a celebrated beauty, a famous wit, or an acclaimed *artiste.* His sole interest in her was curiosity, and it must be a vulgar sort of curiosity that centered on a young woman whose only claim to fame rested in the distinction of her having jilted three men in a row.

A very vulgar curiosity, Raymond told himself sternly. He straightaway resolved to put Caroline out of his mind. But even as he moved about the room with his aunt, shaking hands with her friends and expressing himself glad to make their acquaintance, he kept a weather eye on the door.

When at last Caroline did enter, he was among the first to see and recognize her.

She came in very quietly, looking about her with calm self-possession. Raymond recognized her at once, despite having had no previous clear memory of her face. It was not a beautiful face, but it was, Raymond thought, a distinctive one. There was character in it, for one thing, a character centered mainly in the firm little chin and the green eyes deep set beneath delicately arched brows. Raymond wondered that he had never been previously struck by Caroline's eyes. They were a very clear, bright green—a brighter, clearer green that he ever recalled seeing before.

But though Caroline Sedgewick's eyes might be remarkable, the rest of her was markedly less so. Her hair wasn't exactly red, but it was more red than anything else, a gingery shade midway between blond and brown. Her figure, too, left much to be desired. This was the more obvious because Lady Katherine had entered the room behind her and stood beside her now, laughing and talking with her usual animation. Beside Lady Katherine's glowing brunette beauty and Junoesque figure, Miss Sedgewick looked thin, plain, and ordinary. But though Raymond's eye registered this fact with unerring precision, it was at Caroline Sedgewick he went on looking.

She had turned to Lady Katherine and was addressing a remark to her, smiling as she spoke. Raymond, surveying her critically, decided a smile did much to enliven her rather ordinary face and features. Her dress, too, though not so eye-catching as Lady Katherine's scarlet silk, had been chosen to enhance her good points. She was dressed all in white, net over satin with ruchings of lace and clusters of white rosebuds. A circlet of matching rosebuds crowned her tawny head, and the deep green of its leaves seemed to intensify the green of her eyes. Raymond, surveying her with a connoisseur's eye, had to own the effect was pleasing. Clearly he had made an oversight in previously dismissing Caroline's charms. She might not be a beauty, but attractions she undoubtedly had, and it was remiss of him not to have noticed them before.

He had just reached this conclusion when Caroline, looking up from her conversation with Lady Katherine, happened to catch his eye. For a moment her face reflected surprise and something like consternation. Then she lifted her chin and returned his gaze with a long, hard look—almost a hostile look.

Raymond quickly averted his eyes and felt himself flush as he did so. It had not occurred to him before that in subjecting Caroline to such an intense scrutiny, he was guilty of a breach of manners. But the look on her face as she returned his gaze had made him realize it in a hurry. In truth, it had made him feel something very like shame, and shame was not an emotion Raymond Jeffries was in the habit of feeling. He was not a saint by any means, but he had always prided himself on the correctness of his behavior, and to be found wanting in this area made him feel unaccustomedly gauche.

"This is what comes of indulging vulgar curiosity," he told himself sternly. Still, now that Caroline had caught him staring, he felt he might as well put a good face on it. Without reflecting whether it was contrition that moved him or only another manifestation of vulgar curiosity, he strolled over to where she stood.

"It is Miss Sedgewick, isn't it?" he said with a bow.

Caroline gave him a slight curtsy in return. "Yes, it is," she said. Her eyes were even more brilliantly green when seen up close, but at the moment they were fixed on Raymond with an expression of wary inquiry.

"I hope you will forgive me for staring just now," he continued with an apologetic smile. "Perhaps you may have forgotten the circumstance, but I believe I have had the pleasure of meeting you before."

"Yes, at the Barnstables' ball," agreed Caroline at once. "I remember the occasion quite well. I am surprised that you do, however."

Her voice was low, musical, and attractive. There was a quality in it that made Raymond look at her sharply, however. Almost he thought she must be mocking him. But he could think of no reason Caroline Sedgewick should mock him, Raymond Jeffries. He had not exchanged a dozen words with her before today, and as far as he knew he had never done anything to offend her, apart from his earlier faux pas, for which he had just apologized.

While he was still trying to make up his mind what, if anything, Caroline meant by her words, Lady Katherine swooped down on him with cries of delight. "My dear Mr. Jeffries! To find you here at Shelton-on-Sea! It's a pleasure I would not have dared hope for. And to actually be attending one of our assemblies too! We are honored indeed."

As Raymond reflected dryly, one would have supposed she was his dearest friend rather than a mere nodding acquaintance. It was Lady Katherine's way to be eternally delighted with everything and everyone, however, and Raymond could not deny it was a pleasant way, even if he knew it meant nothing in particular. So he shook hands with her and inquired after her husband.

Lady Katherine's lovely face assumed a look of pretended sorrow. "Oh, in the card room, of course—where else? Like most of your sex, he prefers cards to dancing. Caroline and I might sit and cool our heels on a bench all evening if we depended on *him* to partner us. Mightn't we, Caroline?"

"I do not think Mr. Baddington would put us to such an extremity as that," said Caroline, smiling faintly. "But I for one should be very loath to accept a dancing partner who was wishful to be engaged at cards."

Lady Katherine laughed gaily and told her she was much too scrupulous. "For my part, I will dance with any man whom I can beg or bully to stand up with me," she said. "And since I find you here, Mr. Jeffries, you will do nicely as my first victim. Or are you going to follow Mr. Baddington's example and flee to the card room?"

This speech, as Raymond reflected, was pure Lady Katherine. There was no other woman in the *ton* who would so brazenly have asked a man to dance with her. Yet there was something in Lady Katherine's manner that robbed her words of their impertinence, especially since she had given him a ready-made excuse should he wish to decline her invitation. So he responded good-humoredly, "By no means, Lady Katherine. I would be very honored to stand up with you."

Lady Katherine responded with protestations of gratitude, asking Caroline if she did not think him the most accommodating of men. This made it natural for him to turn to Caroline also and say, "I would be very honored if you would dance with me as well, Miss Sedgewick."

Caroline hesitated noticeably before replying. To Raymond, used to quick and delighted acceptances when he asked a lady to dance, this was a definite insult. The speech that followed her hesitation only increased his sense of affront. "You are very good, Mr. Jeffries," she said. "But I think I must decline your invitation. Although you have flung yourself into the breach on Lady Katherine's behalf, you need not do so on mine. I would not dream of begging or bullying you to dance with me."

Raymond hardly knew how to respond to this speech. It was true that Lady Katherine had more or less prompted him to ask Caroline to dance, but she had certainly not compelled him to do so, and in any case, he had the distinct impression that it had been his intention to dance with her all along. Still, he could hardly say all this aloud. Besides, as Raymond reminded himself, she had given him to understand that it was beneath her dignity to beg or bully him into dancing with her. That being the case, he was not about to turn around and do the same thing by her.

So he gave Caroline a low bow, preparatory to expressing his regret at her refusal. But Lady Katherine, who had been looking at him keenly, forestalled his words. "Caroline, don't be a goose," she said. "Can't you see you are offending Mr. Jeffries?" Turning to Raymond, she continued. "You must know Caroline has the greatest dislike of imposing on anybody. But you honestly do wish to dance with her, don't you? I am sure that you do, Mr. Jeffries—I can *see* that you do."

"Dear Kate, he could hardly say otherwise, since you have asked him," said Caroline. A reluctant smile was twitching her lips, and her smile deepened as she turned to Raymond. "Indeed, sir, I do not mean to offend you. I truly appreciate your invitation, only I was in some doubt as to the propriety of my accepting it. You know Lady Katherine did suggest your dancing in the first place. And in any case, I am not sure I should be dancing at all."

"Now, *that's* nonsense," interjected Lady Katherine warmly. "Why shouldn't you dance as well as the rest of us?" Turning again to Raymond, she addressed him in a lowered voice. "Miss Sedgewick is the dearest girl in the world, but she has some notions I can call only nonsensical. There is no reason in the world she should not dance the second set with you. If she tries to fob you off with some kind of excuse, I advise you to pay her no heed, but to simply *compel* her to dance. It's the only way to deal with her, I have found."

Raymond could not help smiling at this speech. An answering smile was hovering on Caroline's lips. "Indeed, sir, it would appear we are both under compulsion," she told him. "Lady Katherine is the dearest girl in the world, but when she gets a notion in her head, one might as well argue with the wind. That being the case, I will accept with pleasure your invitation to dance, as being at once the quickest and easiest way to settle the matter."

Smiling, Raymond gave her a low bow. "I gladly bow to your superior knowledge, Miss Sedgewick," he said. "The second set, then?"

"The second set," she agreed. They shook hands solemnly upon the bargain, while Lady Katherine beamed approvingly upon them both.

Four

When Raymond led Lady Katherine out for the first set, an approving murmur rose from the spectators in the Assembly Rooms.

Everyone agreed it was only right that the son of a viscount and the daughter of an earl should lead off the dancing. Mr. Lindensmyth, the elderly gentleman who acted as master of ceremonies, beamed upon them as they took their places at the top of the floor. Mr. Jeffries's aunt smiled and nodded to see her nephew comporting himself so correctly; so did the other elderly ladies present; and behind their fans, the young ladies agreed that Lady Katherine gave herself really intolerable airs, but that Mr. Jeffries could have chosen no other partner without giving offense. Accordingly, they fixed their hopes on dancing with him later in the evening. The orchestra played their liveliest tune; the dancers went through the steps with grace and spirit; and all was right in the social universe of Shelton-on-Sea.

When the second dance began, however, and Raymond led out Caroline, approbation gave way to consternation.

"It cannot be!" exclaimed Mrs. Cullen, her eyes nearly starting out of her head. Miss Jeffries, sitting beside her, said nothing but watched the pair with an expression of grave disquiet. All around her, people were raising quizzing glasses and craning their necks to get a better view.

"Looks as though Miss Sedgewick's marked out her next victim," remarked a young dandy with a low whistle. "Who *is* that fellow? Don't think I've seen him before."

"Oh, that's Raymond Jeffries, Lord Baywater's son," said the gentleman beside him. "Wouldn't have expected to see *him* here. He's devilish exclusive, like all the Jeffrieses. Thinks he's too good to mingle with the rest of us scaff and raff, don't you know."

"Don't seem to thinks he's too good to mingle with Caro Sedgewick, at any rate," observed the first gentleman with a laugh. "Who'd have thought it?"

Indeed, this was a sentiment shared by the greater number of the assembly-goers. They could scarcely believe that Raymond Jeffries, who might have danced with any lady present, should choose to distinguish a semi-scandalous creature like Caroline Sedgewick.

Raymond, out on the floor, did not at first remark the furor he was causing. He was too busy trying to make Caroline smile. Although she had made no demur when he had claimed her for the second dance, she had appeared strained and uneasy; and Raymond, without understanding her mood, had nonetheless felt it his duty to lighten it.

"If you could bring yourself to smile, Miss Sedgewick, I would take it as a great compliment," he whispered as they went down the line together. "As it is, everyone must be wondering what I am saying to you to make you look as though you were being led to the gallows."

Caroline gave him a mirthless smile. "Not the gallows exactly," she said. "More like the pillory."

Raymond was just about to inquire what she meant by this, when a voice, not too loud but audible nonetheless, spoke out behind him. "The hussy! Look at her, the shameless hussy! Got her claws in him already."

At these words, a tide of crimson rolled over Caroline's cheeks. Raymond turned sharply to see who had spoken, but the speaker, whoever he or she was, had already melted into the crowd. He encountered a number of eyes fixed on him, however, some with curiosity, some with avidity, and some with what appeared to be simple pity. "Ah," he said with comprehension.

Caroline gave him another mirthless smile. "Now you understand, Mr. Jeffries," she said. "When I said I would rather not dance with you, it was no reflection upon you personally. It was rather a wish to spare you the opprobrium of standing up with the most notorious woman in Shelton-on-Sea."

Raymond went through a figure or two before replying. "The most notorious woman in Shelton-on-Sea," he repeated in a musing voice. "I suppose you might qualify as that. In London, of course, such notoriety as you have achieved would hardly signify, but here, no doubt it would serve to give you a certain distinction."

Caroline regarded him with astonishment. "I *beg* your pardon?" she demanded.

Raymond obligingly repeated his remarks. "Notoriety, like nearly everything else, is a comparative concept," he explained kindly. "What earns you the title of the most notorious woman in Shelton-on-Sea would be hardly noticed were your conduct held against that of someone truly notorious—say, for example, Letty Lade."

Caroline stared at him an instant, then began to laugh. She laughed until the tears ran down her face. "I don't know whether that makes me feel better or worse, Mr. Jeffries," she said between gasps of laughter. "Certainly I hope I am less abandoned than Lady Lade! But at the same time, to hear you denigrating my own hard-earned notoriety makes me feel quite indignant!"

Raymond joined in her laughter. "It's often that way," he said. "Human nature being what it is, we generally find something on which to pride ourselves, even if it is something undesirable."

"And if we cannot achieve legitimate fame, then infamy will do as the next best thing," said Caroline with a rueful sigh. "Dear me! You have quite taken the wind out of my sails, Mr. Jeffries. If I lament my sad lot now, you will think I am merely putting on airs to make myself interesting."

"Not at all," said Raymond. "I can see it must be difficult for you here. But at any rate, you seem to have a firm friend in Lady Katherine." In a more diffident voice, he added, "I hope I have proved by my behavior tonight that I am not afraid to stand your friend either."

Caroline smiled crookedly. "I ought to be much obliged, I am sure," she said. "Indeed, I *am* obliged, both to you and to Lady Katherine. But I am afraid neither of you quite realizes the awkwardness of my position."

"How do you know?" countered Raymond.

"Because you would not act as you have if you did realize it," said Caroline. "Lady Katherine is very insistent that I go everywhere with her and hold my head high, as though I had nothing to be ashamed of, while you have made me conspicuous by singling me out among all the women here tonight to dance with. It's very kind of both of you to stand by me so publicly, but frankly, at the moment I would rather be buried in the deepest obscurity."

"But burying yourself in obscurity is the very worst thing you could do," said Raymond. "Lady Katherine is quite right to counsel you against it. If you hid yourself away at this juncture, it would look as if you had something to be ashamed of."

"But perhaps I do have something to be ashamed of," said Caroline. She regarded him with steady green eyes. "In that case, would you not counsel me to take myself apart and perform appropriate penance for my wrongdoing?"

Raymond gave her a long, meditative look. "I have always been given to understand that penance, to qualify as true penance, ought to be in some degree uncongenial," he said. "And you have said you would prefer to bury yourself in obscurity. In that case, I should think there could be no better penance for you than to appear at public assemblies such as this one and to dance all the dances with me."

Once more Caroline's laugh rang out. "Hoist with my own petard, by heaven!" she said. "I always heard you were a clever man, Mr. Jeffries, and I see that rumor has not lied." She gave him a look that was half smiling, half reflective. "So you consider that dancing with you qualifies as penance?"

"Yes, for you have said you find it uncongenial," said Raymond gravely. "And it is remedial too, which ought to be a feature of any penance whenever possible."

At these words, Caroline looked faintly surprised. "How do you mean?" she asked. "It's true that dancing with you has made me more conspicuous than I like. But you are wrong in thinking I find it uncongenial. Dancing with you could never be that, you dance so very well." She gave him a shy smile. "As for its being remedial, I think you will be puzzled to prove that, Mr. Jeffries!"

"Oh, but the inference is obvious," said Raymond, returning her smile. "By dancing with me, you are making reparation to the sex whom you are presumed to have injured."

At these words, however, Caroline looked affronted. "No! Oh, no!" she said, shaking her head vigorously. "You misunderstand me, Mr. Jeffries. I owe nothing by way of reparation to your sex."

Raymond was taken aback by her vehemence. "No?" he said. "I regret to say that public opinion has it otherwise, Miss Sedgewick. But it would not be the first time public opinion was mistaken."

Caroline's only response was a short, bitter laugh. This was unsatisfactory to Raymond, who had hoped she might expand on her remark. When he came to think of it, however, he realized that such an event was highly unlikely. Given the circumstances, she had been much more forthcoming than he ever would have expected, considering they had hardly exchanged a dozen words before tonight. On reflection, Raymond realized he had been unusually forthcoming too. He was usually much more reserved with strangers, but tonight he and Caroline had been laughing and talking as though they were old friends. It was quite amazing when he thought about it. He never remembered feeling such an instant rapport with anyone, certainly not with a young lady of dubious reputation with whom he would hardly have expected to find two ideas in common.

Caroline was looking up at him, studying his face as though trying to read his thoughts. That she had done so with some success was proven by her next remark. "I suppose it is natural you should talk of my making reparation to your sex," she said. "I have no doubt Mrs. Cullen has been telling everyone how badly I behaved. And since she is one of your aunt's friends, you have no doubt heard the whole story ad nauseam."

There was a bitterness in her voice that roused all Raymond's sympathies. "No," he said. "I have heard Mrs. Cullen's account, but I would never consider that the whole story. Especially since I am in some degree acquainted with Robert Cullen."

Caroline gave him a startled look. "I wonder what you mean by that," she said.

"I mean that in my opinion, Mrs. Cullen has a very partial and mistaken notion of her son," said Raymond, returning her gaze steadily. "And so it would not surprise me if she were partial and mistaken in other things too."

Caroline contemplated him a moment longer, then drew a deep sigh. "You cannot know what a comfort it is to hear you say that," she said. "I have been so used to getting nothing but blame, from everybody but Lady Katherine."

"Well, *I* would not blame you either," said Raymond, "not, at least, without hearing your side of the story." Realizing too late this sounded like a bid for her confidence, he hurried on, flashing an apologetic smile. "But indeed, I wouldn't blame you, whatever your motives were. I don't think any person can adequately judge another's motives. Especially when it comes to what is commonly called an affair of the heart."

"An affair of the heart," repeated Caroline in a melancholy voice.

She said nothing more for a moment or two, and Raymond feared she was offended. He could hardly wonder if she was, for he could not think how he had come to speak of her personal affairs so freely. "I don't mean to be impertinent," he said apologetically.

Caroline looked at him with surprise, as though she had been thinking of something else. "Impertinent?" she said. "You're not impertinent. I don't think you could be that if you tried."

"Well, I am very glad you think so," said Raymond. "But I assure you I would not normally presume to speak concerning someone's personal affairs on so slight an acquaintance."

"I wouldn't suppose you would," agreed Caroline. "Certainly you have not that reputation."

"Ah, but you cannot always believe what you hear concerning people's reputations," said Raymond gravely.

Caroline stared at him, then laughed again. "Indeed you cannot! Yours, for instance, has not done you justice at all." She smiled at him. "I had always heard you were very correct, very reserved, and very nice in your notions—"

"And you have found me none of these things," said Raymond with an understanding nod. "Very disappointing, I'm sure."

Again Caroline's laughter rang out. "Indeed, sir, you are determined to willfully misunderstand me!" she said. "But no, I think you understand me very well indeed." She gave him another of her quick, shy smiles. "That's what I meant when I said your reputation had not done you justice. I had heard you were clever, but not that you were so amusing, or so sympathetic."

It was Raymond's turn to be silent. It was quite true he had not the reputation of a sympathetic man, and in his heart he did not think he really was one, for such a term implied a certain lack of discrimination, a quality no Jeffries could condone. But he could not deny he felt sympathy for Caroline Sedgewick. Indeed, he was not certain he did not feel something more than sympathy. When she had smiled at him and said, "I think you understand me very well indeed," there had come over him a feeling that was not merely sympathetic understanding but a compound of admiration, respect, and esteem so powerful as to leave him feeling quite stunned.

He still had enough of his natural reserve left not to betray these feelings, however. When he spoke, it was merely to express regret that the dance was almost over. "Will you do me the honor of standing up with me again?" he asked.

Again Caroline flashed him a smile—that same smile that had smitten him so powerfully a moment before. "No," she said. "I give you the word with no bark on it because I know you will not misunderstand me, Mr. Jeffries. I have enjoyed dancing with you very much, and I would enjoy doing so again if the circumstances were different. But unfortunately I must face the pillory of public opinion if I go on making myself so conspicuous. And though it might do my character a deal of good for the space of one dance, I tell you frankly that I shrink from enduring it a second time."

Put like this, Raymond could not dispute her decision. Indeed, he himself felt that it would be neither wise nor prudent for him and Caroline to take the floor together a second time. Yet his inclination was to damn wisdom and prudence and dance with her just the same.

What the devil is the matter with me? he asked himself in alarm. He was not used to finding his own feelings so intractable. As a rule, they ran smoothly in harness with common sense and discretion. It was a shock to find them now so widely at variance.

Raymond had no time to meditate on this phenomenon, however. The dance was over, and since Caroline had refused to dance with him again, he had to lead her back to her seat. She thanked him formally, and he thanked her in turn for standing up with him, but they had no time to do more, for Lady Katherine had come hurrying up at that moment and had whisked Caroline away, ostensibly to introduce her to some people who had just come in. As Raymond strolled back to his own place, he reflected indignantly that if Lady Katherine were not an earl's daughter, he should consider her quite rag-mannered.

His mood was not improved when his aunt greeted him reproachfully. "Raymond, I was quite surprised to see you standing up with Miss Sedgewick," she said. "Whatever did you mean by it?"

"Mean by it?" said Raymond coldly. "Merely that I asked her to dance and she accepted. Why should that surprise you?"

His aunt regarded him sternly. "Raymond, do not be a chucklehead," she said. "You know what comment it must cause, your singling her out in such a way. If you had heard Sophia Cullen going on and on about it—"

"I have no interest whatever in Mrs. Cullen's remarks," said Raymond more coldly than ever. "She has already shown herself a fool, and as such her opinions have no weight with me."

There was a pause before his aunt spoke again. "I don't know that I'd dispute with you there, Raymond," she said in a milder voice. "Perhaps it would not be too much to call Sophia a fool. But you must know it was not only she who was talking. We were all surprised that you would distinguish Caroline Sedgewick out of all the young ladies present."

"Then it seems you are easily surprised," said Raymond with some heat. "Why should I not dance with Miss Sedgewick as well as any other young lady? She is more presentable than most of the young ladies here tonight—aye, and more conversable too."

"So she may be," said his aunt, eyeing him with curiosity, "but she has also made herself notorious by jilting three men in a row. When a girl does a thing like that, naturally people will talk about her."

"Naturally," said Raymond. "But that does not mean I must take an interest in their talk."

"Raymond, you reason like a fool," said his aunt in exasperation. "Do you not see that if you dance with Miss Sedgewick, then you, too, are going to be talked about?"

Raymond was silent. His aunt went on, dropping her voice a little as she spoke. "Indeed, I am sure it will be all over town tomorrow that you stood up with Miss Sedgewick," she said. "Not that anyone can make very much of that, but still you should take care how you go on in the future. Already Mrs.

Cullen is saying she must have bewitched you in order to get you to dance with her!"

Miss Jeffries spoke these last words with a smile, making it clear she put no credence in the idea. Raymond, however, felt an unpleasant lurch in the pit of his stomach. He did not really believe Caroline had bewitched him, but he had to admit there had been something very strange and uncharacteristic in the way he had behaved. Somehow she had gotten around his usual reserve and made him laugh and forget himself in a way he had never done before.

But of course witchcraft had nothing to do with that. Raymond shook his head to clear it of this unwelcome thought. "You may tell Mrs. Cullen that Miss Sedgewick has not bewitched me," he said. "The idea is nonsensical."

"Well, of course it is," said his aunt, looking surprised once more. "I daresay you were only being kind to the girl. I remember your saying you thought Robert Cullen a conceited ass, and so it stands to reason you would take her part. But you know you cannot touch pitch without defiling yourself, and you cannot consort with a girl as notorious as Miss Sedgewick without making yourself the subject of talk. Unless you wish to be spoken of in a way you would find highly distasteful, you had best leave the knight errantry to others."

Oddly enough, Raymond did not like this speech any better than Miss Jeffries's previous one. It was better to be thought a knight errant than to be thought bewitched, but in fact he had been moved by neither knight errantry nor bewitchment when he had asked Caroline to dance. He had done so because it had seemed the natural, normal, reasonable thing to do, and in dancing with her he had enjoyed himself very much. To have the impulse degraded to an act of charity annoyed him more than he could well express.

Still, he could see that his aunt's remarks had been kindly motivated. No more than she did he like the idea of being the center of gossip. It was a thing no Jeffries could endure. Of course his social position was secure enough to withstand any amount of talk, but he could see it might be better if he gave the gossips no further ammunition. "I have been in Shelton-on-Sea only twenty-four hours, and it seems I have already caused a scandal," he said lightly. "Tell me, would it be thought scandalous if I dance the next set with my aunt?"

His aunt laughed. "With me! My dear boy, I am sure there are partners more to your liking than an old woman like me." At Raymond's insistence, however, she took to the floor with him and performed a country dance in a manner that he swore put all the younger belles to shame.

He was not wrong in thinking this would ameliorate his former conduct. Several elderly ladies who had been eyeing him askance now began to smile on him once more. The younger ladies began to hope he might, after all, get around to dancing with them later in the evening, and even Mrs. Cullen, who had been looking upon him coldly since the second dance, came over to wish him a good evening. Since she followed up her greeting by warning him against Caroline in a very earnest and unnecessary manner, however, this was not a concession he appreciated.

"I know you will forgive me for speaking so freely," she told him, fixing her large light eyes on his face.

"But when I saw you dancing with *that woman,* my heart turned to ice. Indeed, Mr. Jeffries, you ought not to risk it. Lady Katherine no doubt suggested you dance with her—she is always getting up such schemes, hoping to get society to swallow Miss Sedgewick along with herself. But I have already told you that I think Lady Katherine mistaken in Miss Sedgewick's character. In my opinion, it would be better to have nothing to do with her, even if it means offending Lady Katherine. You have already heard how Miss Sedgewick behaved by my poor Robert. If such a man as he could be deceived in her, what then the risk for you, Mr. Jeffries? I believe Miss Sedgewick to be a very dangerous and abandoned young person, and I give you this warning in good time, lest you, too, be caught in her web."

This was a disagreeable speech to Raymond, who could not decide whether he was most offended by its general tone of impertinence or by Mrs. Cullens's comparing his judgment unfavorably with her son's. In any case, his sole reply was a low bow and a curt "Much obliged, ma'am, I'm sure." This satisfied Mrs. Cullen, however, who went away feeling she had done her duty, and Raymond's annoyance soon subsided.

If one became angry at fools every time they behaved foolishly, he reflected ruefully, *one would never have done being angry.*

So he set himself to get what enjoyment he could out of the rest of the evening. He still wished he could dance with Caroline again, and indeed was not wholly without hope he might yet do so. She had objected to the singularity of his dancing with her twice in a row, but he reasoned that if he danced with a few other ladies first, he might ask her to dance again later without its appearing such a singular event.

Accordingly, he gladdened the hearts of the young ladies of Shelton-on-Sea by asking Mr. Lindensmyth to introduce him to some of them, then by dancing with each of them in turn. They all seemed like nice girls, and some of them were pretty girls too, but there was a dreadful sameness to their niceness and prettiness. To Raymond one seemed much like another, so much so that he had a difficult time keeping their names straight and did in fact mistakenly call one fluffy little blonde Miss Timms, whose name was Miss Thompkins. This was an error that might well have had fatal consequences seeing that Miss Timms was a rival belle and Miss Thompkins's bitterest enemy. Miss Thompkins readily forgave his mistake, however, when he asked her to dance with him a second time, reckoning triumphantly that this circumstance would put her head and shoulders above her rival.

In truth it was not solely Miss Thompkins's injured feelings that motivated Raymond's second invitation. It occurred to him that Caroline would be less liable to feel he was making her conspicuous if he had already danced twice with another girl. But his stratagem backfired, for just as he was taking the floor again with Miss Thompkins, he saw Caroline and Lady Katherine gathering up their wraps and making their way to the door.

Raymond was filled with consternation. He had wanted to dance with Caroline again, or if he could not do that, he wanted at least to talk with her some more. Now he was prevented from doing either. All he could do was smile and nod at her from his place on the floor. It appeared that Caroline did not see him, however. She merely put her shawl over her shoulders and went quietly out of the room with Lady Katherine.

The evening was rather flat after that.

Five

In the carriage, Lady Katherine reached out to pat Caroline's knee.

"Poor darling," she said sympathetically. "I hope your headache is not very bad. It's such a shame you are not feeling well. You looked as though you were having such a good time earlier, before your headache came on."

Caroline gave her a look in which affection was mingled with exasperation. Long acquaintance had made her familiar with her friend's methods, and she knew the casual tone in which Lady Katherine had spoken masked an insatiable curiosity. She also knew that Lady Katherine's curiosity, once aroused, could not rest until satisfied, and that any evasion on the part of her victim would merely cause her to prosecute in her inquiries in a different fashion. As a result, Caroline thought it better to come to the point at once. "I suppose you are talking about my dancing with Mr. Jeffries," she said.

"Well, I did just wonder," said Lady Katherine, widening her beautiful dark eyes in an innocent way. "I had no idea the two of you were so well acquainted."

"We aren't," said Caroline. "I never met him but twice before in my life."

She remembered both occasions perfectly. The first, which had taken place in the spring of the previous year, had come about through the agency of her aunt Emilia. Caroline blushed now to recall how energetically Aunt Emilia had pursued Raymond's acquaintance. She had practically forced him to be introduced to her niece. And it had been apparent Raymond was not at all impressed. He had acknowledged the introduction in his usual well-bred fashion, but he had also made it clear that Miss Caroline Sedgewick was nothing to him and never would be. Considering the matter objectively, Caroline could hardly blame him. Even then her aunt's efforts to find her a husband by hook or by crook had deeply embarrassed her. It was unfortunate that she had done nothing about the situation until it had come to a head.

The second occasion on which she had met Raymond was at a party she had attended with Lady Katherine. They had run against each other in the passage, and he had given her a nod of recognition. Such recognition was more than Caroline would have bargained for. By then she had broken with her aunt and was deeply ashamed of having ever been associated with her at all. So she had merely returned Raymond's nod with a smile and bow and registered the gesture in her memory as an example of unmerited good fortune on her part and unmerited good nature on his.

Although those two occasions were the only occasions she had formally met Raymond, she had seen him on many other occasions. He was a person of note in London and a frequenter of most of the fashionable venues. She had often seen him at the theater and opera or riding in the park. She had always taken special notice of him, partly because he was such a striking-looking man, and partly because, in her heart of hearts, she had long cherished a secret and wholly unrequited admiration for him. This admiration she knew to be ridiculous, for she was sure Raymond Jeffries would never look twice at her—at least not more than twice, as events had proved. But at the same time, she could see no harm in admiring him, assuming it were done from a distance and without hope of a return. Because Raymond Jeffries really *was* an admirable man—not merely admirable in looks, but intelligent, well read, and well mannered. It had been a harmless enough employment for her affections, as Caroline reflected. She wished with some bitterness that they had always been so harmlessly employed.

But all that was past now, and at the moment her most urgent concern was to divert Lady Katherine's suspicions. So Caroline repeated firmly, "I never met Mr. Jeffries but twice before in my life."

"Truly? But the way you were talking and laughing, Caro darling! One would have supposed you were the closest of friends."

Caroline shook her head. "I promise you, I have met him only twice, and only once to speak to," she said. "I doubt we have exchanged a dozen words before tonight."

Lady Katherine smiled a disbelieving smile. "Well, you certainly exchanged more than that tonight," she said. "I can't remember when I last saw you so animated. Or him either, for that matter. Upon my word, I don't believe I ever saw Raymond Jeffries laugh out loud before, as he was doing tonight. You must have been uncommonly witty to amuse him so much."

"I don't believe I was, really," said Caroline. In a reflective voice she added, "Perhaps he had merely been drinking too much champagne."

Lady Katherine gave her another disbelieving smile. "Perhaps," she said. "But if you ask me, it was you and not the champagne, Caro dear. He seemed greatly taken with you."

Caroline flushed up to the roots of her hair. "Please don't," she said. "That's ridiculous, Kate, and you know it. Raymond Jeffries would never think of me in that way."

She had been telling herself this same thing all evening. Since she had admired Raymond so long, it was only too likely that his attentions might go to her head. She had imagined she was keeping her head very well, up till the moment she had seen him lead out Miss Thompkins for a second dance. Then it had been demonstrated to her just how weak was her hold on her own emotions. She had felt such jealousy and resentment toward Miss Thompkins, and such despair and depression on her own account, that she had pleaded a headache and come away so she might not have to watch them going through the figures. For this weakness, Caroline scolded herself as a fool.

What does it matter whom he dances with? she told herself sternly. She reminded herself that she, too, might have danced with him twice if she had cared to. But she had thought it better to refuse his invitation, for she had made herself conspicuous enough by dancing with him even once. There was no need to compound the error by doing so a second time.

She could not doubt now it had been an error to dance with Raymond. If she could be such a goose as to become jealous and possessive after one dance with him, then clearly she had no business dancing with him at all. Besides, here was Kate rallying her on having made a conquest of him merely because she had made him laugh a couple of times. She, Caroline, knew very well there was nothing in it. But if Kate believed there was, then other people might too, and the last thing she needed was for the gossips to find more reason to talk about her. She drew a deep sigh.

Lady Katherine, unimpressed alike by sigh or denial, went on talking. "Say what you will, Caro, I think he *was* taken with you," she said. "I saw the way he looked at you. I think he would have danced with you again if you had given him any encouragement."

Caroline sighed again. "Have it your own way, Kate," she said. "Of course I am such a femme fatale that he had no choice but to succumb to my charms. Next time we meet, he will no doubt propose marriage, and then I can see if my fourth engagement will be any more successful than my first three."

Lady Katherine looked sympathetic once more. "Poor Caro!" she said, reaching out to pat Caroline's knee again. "You have certainly been very unlucky. But you mustn't let a few bad experiences put you off. I am sure if you find the right man, you will settle down as happily as Rufus and I."

Caroline could not help smiling at this statement, in spite of her agitation. When the beautiful, wealthy Lady Katherine Delville had insisted on marrying Mr. Rufus Baddington, a man of undistinguished birth and small fortune, society had raised its collective hands in horror. Even Caroline, who had reason to know worldly wealth and estate were not everything, had thought them a mismatched pair.

Mr. Baddington was slow, deliberate, and a man of few words. Lady Katherine was quick, impulsive, and almost as great a talker as Sally Jersey. Yet in spite of these disparities, they had done very well together.

This Caroline knew firsthand, for she had lived some months now in their household. One could not be deceived when one lived with people day in and day out. Their affection showed itself in small ways—in Mr. Baddington's always making sure Lady Katherine had her favorite red roses to carry when she went out at night, for example, and in Lady Katherine's employing a woman cook whose plain English cooking her husband preferred to the more fashionable French cuisine. She might rally him about preferring cards to dancing, and he might shake his head at her giddy ways, but they were clearly happy together in spite of their differences.

This was a thought both to comfort Caroline and to fill her with despair. On the one hand, such criticism as Lady Katherine had endured at the time of her own engagement had made her sympathize when Caroline's engagement to Lord Scroggins had been first announced and then retracted within the space of a few days. Caroline still shuddered to recall the misery of those days. Her aunt, furious at her for having rejected such a desirable suitor, had declared she would not harbor her beneath her roof a day longer. Caroline's other relations had likewise washed their hands of her, telling her she had brought disgrace on the family name and should have known her own mind before accepting Lord Scroggins's suit. Caroline would have been in dire straits indeed had not Lady Katherine stepped forward at that moment to offer her the protection of her home.

Lady Katherine was peculiarly fitted to sympathize, for she not only knew what it was to make an unpopular match, she knew what it was to refuse a popular one. There had been a marquis, a childhood acquaintance, whom all her friends and family had urged her to marry and whom she had refused in favor of Mr. Baddington. Caroline was grateful for Lady Katherine's sympathy, but though her friend might share her feelings up to a point, there was a point at which their experiences diverged. As Caroline reflected gloomily, Lady Katherine was married to Mr. Baddington, the man she truly loved and who truly loved her back. She, Caroline, had nobody—although there had been a time not so long past when she had thought otherwise. But that incident, too, had ended in disaster, and it was all Caroline could do to keep from weeping when she recalled its particulars.

Lady Katherine seemed to guess her thoughts, for she reached out to pat Caroline's knee once again. "Forget Robert Cullen," she said. "I know it's difficult, but you did the only thing you could. Soon it will blow over. Indeed, I think most people have forgotten it already."

"Mrs. Cullen hasn't," said Caroline gloomily. "I saw her glaring at me across the room tonight."

Lady Katherine dismissed Mrs. Cullen with a wave of her hand. "Of course *she* has not forgotten. It's not to be supposed she would soon forget your snubbing her darling son. But everybody else has, Caro; I'm sure of it. Why, it's been at least a week since anybody has spoken of it in my hearing."

Caroline nodded, but inwardly she felt cynical. She was not surprised to hear that people avoided discussing the subject around Lady Katherine, but away from her she was quite certain they had no such reticence. Mrs. Cullen would see to that. Caroline knew Mrs. Cullen made a point of speaking most volubly and bitterly about her behavior, and she knew also there was no way she could silence her that would not make matters worse. Bad as it was to be thought a heartless jilt, it was better by far than being known as a credulous fool.

But perhaps she was already known to be a fool. Caroline frowned, remembering Raymond's words that evening. He had seemed to think she had had justification in jilting Robert Cullen. But surely he could not possibly know what her justification was? Caroline felt uneasy. She knew how quickly gossip spread in fashionable circles. It was quite possible that the details of Robert Cullen's misbehavior were more widely known than she supposed. Still, it did not seem likely that Raymond had been referring to the same details she was thinking of. He had, after all, made that joke about her owing reparation to the male sex. But in fact the boot was quite upon the other foot, as Caroline reflected. And it had never been more so than where Robert Cullen was concerned.

"Reparation," Caroline told herself bitterly. Raymond's using such a word in connection with her engagements would have been funny if it had not been so ironic. Caroline did not feel she owed the male sex any reparation whatever. No one, she reckoned, could have been more unfortunate in her dealings with the opposite sex. Or perhaps it was merely that she was a fool. Caroline sometimes suspected this was the real truth of the matter, for certainly she had behaved like a fool in each of the three instances that had linked her name publicly with three different men.

The first had been folly, but folly of a comparatively forgivable kind. Caroline had known James de Very from the time she was a small girl. They had been neighbors, growing up in the same neighborhood and encountering each other at social functions all their lives. But it was not until James, newly enlisted in a cavalry regiment, had received word that he and his regiment were shipping over to Spain to fight under Wellington that Caroline had learned he cherished any warmer affection for her than friendship.

She could still remember the night James had told her of his love. They had been at a party together and had gone out onto the terrace in search of fresh air. James had told her then of his just-received orders. When she had expressed dismay at his going to Spain, he had caught her hand in his. "Do you truly care, Caro?" he had asked, gazing into her eyes. When Caroline had said that of course she cared, he had seized her hand in a yet tighter grasp and poured out his feelings for her—feelings Caroline had never suspected him of harboring until that moment. He had ended by making a formal proposal for her hand in marriage.

Caroline, only seventeen at the time, had been touched and flattered by James's proposal. Even so, she had hesitated. Young and inexperienced as she was, she had felt instinctively that though she did care for James, it was not the same as being in love with him. But how to express this to a man who was going forth to fight, perhaps even to die? Besides, James was so very eloquent, so passionate in his devotion. In spite of herself, she was swept along by the romance of it all. By the time he went off to Spain, a notice had appeared in all the papers stating that

Miss Caroline Sedgewick, only daughter of George Sedgewick, Esq., was engaged to marry Lieutenant James de Very of His Majesty's Cavalry.

No one had made any serious objection to the match. Caroline's mother had died years before, and her father had made no more demur than to say she was rather young to think of marriage. Most of her relatives thought it a respectable if not brilliant match, and her friends united in thinking it very romantic and exciting. And in fact it *was* romantic and exciting, at least at first. James had written her regularly from Spain, long letters full of his love for her and his plans for their future. But over the course of the next two and a half years, the letters had become less frequent. When at last she received word that James had sold out his commission and was coming home, she was shocked to find that far from anticipating his return, she was actually dreading it.

Caroline had been horrified by her own inconstancy. She reminded herself that she had plighted her troth to James, and that it was her duty to fulfill that troth. But the first time she had encountered him after his return, he seemed not the James to whom she had pledged her love so long ago but, rather, a stranger. When he bent to kiss her, she had shrunk from him—an actual physical shrinking that he could hardly have helped noticing.

He said nothing about it at the time, but over the next week or two Caroline began to suspect he, too, had suffered a change of heart. He spoke no more of his love for her or his plans for their future. He squired her to several events around the neighborhood but without any visible enthusiasm, and though his treatment of her did not amount to discourtesy, it likewise did not speak of any great tenderness.

Finally, gathering her courage, Caroline had broached the subject frankly. She told him that she had felt a difference in his manner and asked if he wished to be released from their engagement. At first he had evaded the question, telling her he meant to stand by his word, but when she confessed the reservations she herself had been feeling, he had looked relieved and admitted he shared them. It had ended by their shaking hands and agreeing to be merely friends.

"You're a great girl, Caroline," he had told her as he leaned down to kiss her on the brow. "I hope you'll be very happy, whomever you end up marrying. I can't tell you how much I appreciate how you've behaved in this. There's not a girl in a thousand who'd have been as honest as you, by Jove."

A notice had been posted to the papers, stating that the marriage between Miss Caroline Sedgewick and Lieutenant James de Very would not take place after all. On the whole, it had caused very little sensation. Both James's relations and hers had taken news of the breakup philosophically, and at the age of twenty Caroline had found herself free once more, a few years older and a good deal wiser, as she thought.

Shortly after this, her father had died. His estate had devolved upon a male cousin, and Caroline had been sent to live with her aunt Emilia, a sister-in-law of her late mother's. Of all the periods in Caroline's life, this was the one that loomed blackest in her memory. Not only had it been made painful by the death of her father, she and her aunt had proved as incompatible as oil and water. Aunt Emilia held that the first duty of a young lady was to get herself married as soon as possible to the man of greatest wealth and highest estate she could compel to marry her. She likewise held that it was the first duty of that young lady's relatives to assist her in this endeavor by both fair means and foul. There was not so much to suffer the first year, for even Aunt Emilia could not campaign too openly on behalf of a young lady in deep mourning, but as soon as Caroline had exchanged her blacks for black ribbons, the quest to find her a husband had begun in good earnest.

Caroline had found the whole process excruciating. Left to herself, she thought she would have enjoyed her first London Season, but to know she was there only because her aunt hoped she might catch the eye of some eligible man made her feel like a filly on the block at Tattersall's. And she was not even a particularly promising filly. London was full of girls who had come there for the purpose of getting husbands, many of them richer and better connected than she was and most of them—it seemed to her—very much prettier. Her aunt agreed, telling Caroline that she was already as good as on the shelf and that she needed to put herself forward more if she wanted to catch a husband. It had been a surprise to both of them when Lord Scroggins stepped forward to offer his hand and heart.

Lord Scroggins was in every way an eligible parti. He had a barony in Sussex that carried with it a handsome property as well as fortune enough to keep it up properly. Unfortunately, Caroline could not like him. It was not that he was an ill-looking man—on the contrary, he was quite good-looking—but he had a supercilious personality that no amount of good looks could make up for, in Caroline's opinion at least. She had tried to explain this when her aunt scolded her for refusing his proposal, but her aunt had told her that beggars could not be choosers and that she might think herself lucky that Lord Scroggins meant to persevere.

Persevere he did, much to Caroline's discomfort. Having made up his mind to marry her, he found it incomprehensible that any young lady in her senses could refuse him. It would have been particularly incomprehensible in Miss Caroline Sedgewick, a girl with no particular fortune and only a moderate degree of good looks.

Indeed, there were times when Lord Scroggins wondered if Caroline was really worthy of the honor he meant to bestow on her. Yet something about her had captivated him from their first meeting, and in the end he always decided he would rather have her with her modest portion and moderate good looks than a prettier, wealthier girl. For one thing, there was an honesty and candor about her that one did not often encounter in young ladies, accompanied by a most refreshing intelligence. It was Lord Scroggins's experience that intelligence usually went with a scheming nature, not with honesty and candor. Nobody could have accused him of possessing honesty and candor himself, but he could quite appreciate those qualities in other people. He accordingly made up his mind that Caroline Sedgewick was the woman he wanted to marry.

Caroline was distressed to find him so determined. She had found it hard enough to refuse him the first time, and now she found herself having to do it on a weekly basis. There was no escape from these interviews, for her aunt would not let her refuse to see him when he came to call. Caroline knew her aunt was still hoping she would change her mind and marry him. She also felt certain that Aunt Emilia was doing everything she could to soften her niece's refusals in order to keep Lord Scroggins—as she gracefully put it—"on the hook." Still, though Caroline was distressed by this state of affairs, she was not particularly worried by it. After all, neither Lord Scroggins nor her aunt could force her to marry, as she reminded herself. She was twenty-one now and her own woman as far as the law was concerned. She needed only to be resolute in her refusal, and sooner or later Lord Scroggins must give up and go away.

Alas, she had reckoned without her aunt's lack of principle. One morning, coming down to breakfast, she had turned unsuspectingly to the list of marriages and engagements in the *Morning Post* and read there of her own engagement to Lord Scroggins.

The scene that had followed had been a truly dreadful one. She had immediately sent for Aunt Emilia and demanded to know if she had anything to do with the announcement. Aunt Emilia had at first hemmed and hawed, but finally she admitted to inserting the announcement, telling Caroline she ought to be grateful that somebody, at least, was looking out for her interests. When Caroline had told her angrily that she wanted no part of a marriage with Lord Scroggins, Aunt Emilia had grown angry too. She had scolded Caroline, then burst into tears and wept over her ingratitude, then scolded her again until her voice ran out. The burden of her refrain was that Caroline must go through with the engagement now it had been announced. She had already jilted one man, as people knew, and if she jilted another she would find herself quite outside the pale of decent society. Moreover, she would have to pack her bags and leave that minute, for there was no way she, Aunt Emilia, could shelter any longer a girl who had shown herself so singularly ungrateful for her efforts on her behalf.

It was a source of some pride to Caroline that she had been strong enough to withstand these threats. She had packed her bags, ordered her aunt's servants to find her a hackney cab, and had been on the verge of setting off alone into an inhospitable world, when Lady Katherine had appeared on the scene.

Lady Katherine's purpose in calling that afternoon had been to offer Caroline her best wishes on her engagement. They had met only a few weeks before at a party, but Lady Katherine had taken a great fancy to Caroline and had distinguished her since with various small attentions. When she had read the announcement of Caroline's engagement to Lord Scroggins, she had been much surprised, for she knew he was pursuing Caroline, but she had gathered the pursuit was contrary to Caroline's wishes. Thus it was mainly curiosity that brought her to Aunt Emilia's house that day. But if it was curiosity that brought her there, it was kindness that made her spring to Caroline's defense as soon as she learned what had transpired. She had told Aunt Emilia her opinion of her in a few pithy words, loaded Caroline and her baggage into her phaeton, and conveyed her to her own home, where Caroline had dwelt ever since.

As Aunt Emilia had predicted, there had been repercussions from this affair, but on the whole the repercussions had been fewer and milder than Caroline had dared hope. Lord Scroggins was not a popular man, and most people thought Caroline's jilting him a very good joke. True, there was a portion of society who shook their heads and said she was a fickle girl who did not know her own mind, but most of society were inclined to look indulgently on her fickleness, especially since Lady Katherine was seen to be taking her up. So overall, Caroline found her situation actually improved through jilting Lord Scroggins. She was no longer with Aunt Emilia but with a friend who never embarrassed her by pushing her forward or forcing her to consort with men she disliked. She could pick and choose her own friends, her own engagements, and her own clothing. The tarnish her reputation had acquired through her two abortive engagements actually enhanced her in some people's eyes, for a girl who was so difficult to please posed an irresistible challenge to men bored by too many easy conquests. This, at any rate, was Caroline's conclusion, viewed from her present cynical perspective. It seemed the only way to explain why a beau like Robert Cullen had singled her out over the superior claims of half the girls in London.

No one could have been more surprised than Caroline when Robert had first begun to notice her. There were people who called him Adonis Cullen, and the name was not unfitting. He was tall and magnificently built, with wavy dark hair and brilliant dark eyes that always seemed to sparkle with laughter. Neither were good looks his only asset, for his birth was irreproachable and his fortune more than genteel. Caroline thought, and still thought, that with such attributes he might have aspired to almost any woman in London barring perhaps the royal princesses.

Yet for some reason he had settled on her, Caroline Sedgewick. It had seemed inexplicable at the time. Indeed, when he had first begun to notice her, Caroline had supposed his intentions must be dishonorable if he had any intentions at all. It was not until he had made her a formal offer of marriage that she had begun to take him at all seriously. Even then she had brushed aside his first proposal, fearing it might be a joke that everyone was in on but herself. But it had proved not to be a joke. He had continued to court her, singling her out at parties, showering her with gifts, and showing in every way that his feelings were sincere as far as they went. That they did not go far enough was a fact Caroline did not discover until a good deal later, after she had consented to marry him.

The fact was, as Caroline admitted to herself, that Robert had simply swept her off her feet. He had seemed so much like the man of her dreams in nearly every respect that she had been won over against her own better judgment. Given her previous experiences with love and courtship, she had feared that her heart was blighted and that she would not be able to return a man's love even if she found one worthy of loving, but Robert had shown her these worries were needless. Her heart was not blighted but merely barricaded. Once she had let down her guard, there had proved nothing wrong with her feelings at all. By the time he had proposed to her a second time, she had begun to return his love with a fervor so intense that it made her quite blind to every other consideration. She had agreed to marry him, and soon all society knew that Miss Caroline Sedgewick was engaged to Mr. Robert Cullen.

For some months following her engagement, she

had continued in a state of blind infatuation. It had been easy to ignore the small signs that might have told her Robert was unworthy of so much feeling. When a young lady at a party had taken her aside and told her that a friend of a friend had seen Robert with a dancer from the opera under suggestive circumstances, Caroline had supposed the friend imaginary and the young lady's words mere jealous spite. It stood to reason all girls must be jealous of her, who was lucky enough to be the acknowledged fiancée of Robert Cullen. When another friend mentioned seeing him with La Bella Verlucci, Caroline had brushed this aside too. But when, coming home early one night from a party that had proved rather flat, she had seen Robert and Signorina Verlucci sitting side by side in Robert's carriage, she had been unable to deny the evidence of her own eyes. And when she had actually seen Robert take the signorina in his arms and kiss her as passionately as ever he had kissed Caroline, that was the last straw as far as she was concerned.

She had not reached that conclusion all at once, to be sure. For twenty-four hours she had struggled to find an excuse for what she had seen: some explanation that would reason away her hurt and anger and leave her free to love Robert once more. But no excuse or explanation would suffice for a betrayal so complete. She knew Robert had had dealings with the muslin company, but he had assured her that was in the past, and that since meeting her he had turned over a new leaf. Now it appeared that his assurances had been false. Having faced that he was false in one regard, Caroline saw plainly that none of his other assurances could be relied on either.

That left her two alternatives, both equally dreadful. She could either go ahead and marry him knowing he was a faithless liar, or else break the engagement. The latter alternative made her shudder, for it stood to reason society would not look lightly on a young lady who had broken three engagements. Even worse would be the pain of having to acknowledge, both to herself and society, that she had bestowed her heart on an unworthy object.

Yet Caroline knew herself well enough to realize she could never be happy with Robert now that she knew him to be untrue. Happiness was out of the question no matter what she did, but this was a case where half a loaf was worse than none at all. Still, the necessity of breaking her third engagement was a bitter thing for her. She had been so cautious about letting herself love in the first place, but once she had done so she had loved with all her heart. Now she had to try to pick up the pieces of her heart and go on despite an overwhelming conviction that all happiness in life was ended.

Lady Katherine had been a great help during this time. Finding Caroline in tears when she came in that evening, she had insisted on knowing the whole story, and she had agreed there was nothing to be done but break the engagement. "There's girls who wouldn't mind if their husband kept mistresses, but you're not one of them," she had told Caroline. "I always had doubts about you and Robert Cullen. He has a dreadful reputation where women are concerned. They say a reformed rake makes a good husband, but *I* think otherwise. Once a rake, always a rake, has been my experience. And you're such an idealist, Caro. Whoever you marry will have to be a perfect paragon if you're to stay in love with him, and

Robert Cullen could never be that, no matter how he tried."

In spite of her misery, Caroline had been wryly amused by these words. No one could be less of an idealist than she was, as she reflected bitterly. The experiences she had been through had made her much more a cynic than an idealist. But she had kept these thoughts to herself. "I must break the engagement as soon as possible," she had said aloud. "Would it do to merely write Robert, do you think, or must I see him?"

Lady Katherine had thought writing would suffice. "If it were anyone else, I would say you ought to see him and tell him in person," she had told Caroline. "But Robert Cullen doesn't deserve such regard. Most men would at least break with their mistresses until after the wedding, but it's just like Robert to think he could eat his cake and have it too."

Caro had essayed a weak laugh. "I am just as glad he didn't break with Signorina Verlucci if he meant to take up with her again eventually," she said as she drew pen and paper toward her.

"Of course, darling. As I said, you're an idealist. That's another reason it's better to break the engagement in writing. If you saw Robert, it's ten to one he would find some way to explain his conduct, and though you wouldn't really believe him, you might want to so badly, you'd let him talk you over. And then you'd just end up getting your heart broken all over again. Take my word for it, darling, it's much better to make a clean break now and put this whole nasty business behind you."

Caroline was sure Lady Katherine was right, and the letter had accordingly been written. After it had been dispatched by one of Lady Katherine's footmen, Caroline had gone to the window and stood gloomily looking out at the square, where the first light of dawn was beginning to show through the trees. "It's going to be miserable, seeing Robert around town these next few weeks," she said. "I don't suppose I can escape him, no matter how careful I am. And there will be such a lot of talk about my breaking our engagement."

"Yes, and that's why I think it better to get right away from London," Lady Katherine had said briskly. "Mr. Baddington and I always go to the shore when the Season ends, and there's no reason we can't advance our plans by a few weeks. I'll write notes canceling all my engagements, and then we'll go right away instead of waiting until after the King's birthday. You'll like Shelton-on-Sea, Caroline. It's not a big place like Brighton, but that's all to the good in the present situation. Nobody we know is likely to be there, and a few weeks of fresh air and sea bathing will set you right up. By the time the summer's over, you'll have forgotten all about Robert Cullen."

Unfortunately this prophecy had not come to pass, for almost the first person they had met on coming to Shelton-on-Sea was Mrs. Cullen. Still, as Lady Katherine had pointed out, her presence was no real cause for distress. "She might give you a few dagger looks, but she can't eat you, Caro dear. Trust me for that! If she tries to cause trouble, I'll soon put her in her place, for she was only one of the Lancashire Peabodys before she married Harold Cullen, and everyone knows they are a very inferior branch of the family."

Lady Katherine had been as good as her word,

and nobody had been allowed to annoy or insult Caroline to her face. But the gossip that went on behind her back was a different matter. Caroline had learned to dread the silence that followed her entrance into a room, and the exchange of glances that took place whenever she moved or spoke. Even worse were those occasions when some particularly bold critic publicly denounced her as a jilt or hussy, as had happened that very evening when she was dancing with Raymond.

Caroline's cheeks burned, recalling the mortification of that moment. There was no one she would rather not have had witness such an incident than Raymond Jeffries, whom everyone knew to be the most fastidious of men. Of course he had been very nice about it, but that was merely because he was too much of a gentleman to be otherwise. Caroline was sure he must have been shocked and disgusted to find himself associating even temporarily with a woman whose behavior left her liable to such reproaches. And though there was no sense in it, she found this idea weighed more heavily with her than the memory of the reproach itself.

Six

Raymond left the Assembly Rooms that night with a sense of dissatisfaction.

He was still pleased with Shelton-on-Sea, but the party that evening, after getting off to such a promising start, had somehow devolved into a most dull and stupid affair. He did not go so far as to connect this phenomenon with Caroline's early departure, but as he readied himself for bed that night with his valet's help, he reflected how unfortunate it was that he had had no opportunity to speak to her after their dance. She was a most entertaining girl, and there were many things he would have liked to say to her. He wondered if she would appear at the pump room the next morning. His aunt had said Caroline did not usually visit the pump room, but that did not mean she *never* did. Raymond's feelings on the subject were not so acute as to make him resolve to go there merely on the chance he might see her, but as he got into bed he reflected that *if* he awoke early the next day, and *if* his aunt wished to go to the pump room, then he might as well accompany her.

He did wake early, as it happened, and his aunt did wish to go to the pump room. But after he had escorted her there and established her comfortably on her favorite settee, it did not take him long to determine that Caroline was not present. Raymond was disappointed—absurdly disappointed, he told himself. There was no reason it should matter whether she was there or not, especially when there were so many other young ladies ready to fill in the void. Miss Thompkins smiled upon him, and so did Miss Timms, and Raymond was kept busy for some minutes returning their greetings. When he was at leisure to look around once more, he received a shock. Caroline was still nowhere to be seen, but Mrs. Cullen had just come into the pump room, and beside her, looking his usual handsome and conceited self, was Robert Cullen.

For a moment, Raymond was actually guilty of the vulgarity of staring. It was not until his aunt dug her elbow into his ribs that he was brought back to a sense of his surroundings.

"What is it, Raymond?" she asked. "Why are you standing there gawking like a looby?"

"I beg your pardon, Aunt," said Raymond, pulling himself together. "I did not mean to stare. It's only that I am surprised to see Robert Cullen here. When we spoke with Mrs. Cullen last night, she said nothing about her son's coming to visit her."

"No more she did," agreed Miss Jeffries. She followed his gaze to where Cullen stood at his mother's side. "So that's Robert Cullen, eh?" she said. "A handsome buck. I had thought Sophia was exaggerating a trifle when she went on and on about how good-looking he was, but I see now she wasn't."

Raymond felt a sense of irritation. Of course Robert Cullen was undeniably a handsome man, but still he resented the admiration in his aunt's voice. "I wonder what the deuce he's doing here," he said in a dissatisfied tone. "It seems odd he should come to Shelton-on-Sea."

His aunt smiled. "Do you think so?" she said. "To my mind, nothing could be more natural."

"Why is that?" demanded Raymond a trifle sharply.

His aunt smiled again and shook her head. "Why, because of Caroline Sedgewick, of course," she said. "Likely he knows she is here. He probably means to try his hand at winning her back." She gave a little chuckle. "*That* wouldn't please Sophia, not after all the things she's said about Miss Sedgewick! She might have hated her jilting Robert, but she would hate even worse for him to make up with her now."

Raymond was silent. The idea of Robert Cullen winning Caroline back did not please him either. In fact, he found he resented it with quite a surprising warmth. "I don't suppose there's the least chance of Miss Sedgewick taking up with Robert Cullen again," he said firmly.

His aunt shook her head and smiled in a maddening way. "You can't know that, Raymond," she said. "Lovers' quarrels are a common enough thing, after all. Miss Sedgewick might have broken with Mr. Cullen, then come to regret it. She's such a fickle creature, I'm sure there's no telling what she might or might not do from one minute to the next."

Again Raymond was silent. He strongly disliked his aunt's using the term "lovers' quarrels" in connection with Caroline and Robert Cullen, and he likewise took exception to her calling Caroline fickle. Much as he would have liked to argue, however, he knew he had no arguments that would carry any weight with her. His aunt would hardly accept Caroline's own words as evidence, and neither was she likely to accept his opinion of her as a frank, friendly, well-principled young lady. When he thought of it, he had to admit the duration of one dance was hardly sufficient to gain a complete knowledge of Caroline's character. But so convinced was he that he was right and his aunt wrong that he had trouble keeping his tongue between his teeth.

His aunt, meanwhile, was still talking. "It will be interesting, at any rate, having both Miss Sedgewick and Mr. Cullen at Shelton-on-Sea," she said cheerfully. "Ought to put the cat regularly among the pigeons. *If* Mr. Cullen knows Miss Sedgewick is here—and I am sure Sophia must have told him. Yes, surely she must have. Only see how he is looking around the pump room!"

Indeed, there was a noticeable anxiety in Robert Cullen's gaze as he looked around the pump room. At the same time, however, his face wore its usual affable smile—the smile of a man who believes himself irresistible. Raymond regarded him with distaste, but it was apparent that his distaste was by no means general. Both Miss Timms and Miss Thompkins were gazing at him with admiration, and so were half the other young ladies in the room. Raymond felt Cullen was quite aware of their admiration, though he pretended to be busy looking around the room for Caroline.

"What a coxcomb," said Raymond internally. Aloud, he said, "I suppose I must go over and pay my respects. Do you care to come with me, Aunt? You may as well see firsthand why I consider Robert Cullen a conceited ape."

His aunt laughed and said she would not mind making Mr. Cullen's acquaintance. They walked over to where he and his mother stood talking to a couple of elderly ladies.

Mrs. Cullen swung around eagerly at their approach. "Mr. Jeffries!" she said. "I am so happy to see you. Robert has come to stay with me, and it will be so nice for him to have a friend here." With a significant look, she added, "I have told him that he must not expect to find such congenial company *everywhere* we go."

Raymond noted with interest that these words brought a faint color to Robert Cullen's face. He shook hands cordially, however, and wished Raymond a good day in a friendly voice. His greeting to Miss Jeffries was very cordial too. Raymond was disgusted to see his usually levelheaded aunt quite fluttered by this meaningless gallantry. To himself, he reflected bitterly that even the most sensible women lost their heads when a handsome rogue smirked and threw them a few compliments.

"I'll go fetch us all something to drink," he said shortly, and went off to the counter, glad of an excuse to escape the sight of Robert Cullen's face for a few minutes.

The wait at the counter turned out to be longer than a few minutes. Business in the pump room was brisk, and there was a long line of patrons waiting to purchase tea, coffee, and seawater. During his wait, Raymond was able to reason himself back into something resembling his usual composure. Still, when his turn came to purchase beverages for his party, he took malicious pleasure in ordering seawater for Robert Cullen. "I am sure you want some restorative," he said gravely as he handed Robert the goblet of grayish water. "It appears to me you're looking a bit fine-drawn."

Mrs. Cullen immediately supported this statement, saying that she, too, thought Robert looked unwell. "You drink that right down," she said commandingly. "I am afraid you are inclined to be consumptive, Robert. Dr. Briar says seawater is a sovereign remedy against consumption."

Raymond had hard work not grinning as Cullen, having given the goblet a dubious inspection, took a sip, choked, and pulled a face. Mrs. Cullen would not allow him to leave off drinking, however, and the sight of him sipping away with obvious distaste was enough to restore Raymond to his former good humor. "How do you like Shelton-on-Sea?" he asked. "I suppose you have not visited here before?"

"No," said Cullen, taking another minuscule sip of seawater. "This is my first visit." His tone implied it would be his last if he had any say in the matter.

"It's my first visit too," said Raymond conversationally. "My aunt has been praising the place for years, but I never had occasion to come here before. No doubt your situation is much the same." He scrutinized Cullen with seeming casualness. "I suppose your mother persuaded you to pay her a visit?"

"Er—yes," said Cullen with a sideways look at his mother. "That was the way of it, Jeffries. Thought I'd come down and see what the place was like, don't you know."

Raymond felt certain this was a lie. The look and hesitation that had accompanied Cullen's words said as plainly as possible he had other reasons for coming to Shelton-on-Sea. Indeed, there was something in his look that made Raymond suspect he might have confided those reasons had his mother not been standing nearby. He was thus not wholly surprised when, a few minutes later, Cullen proposed they walk to the other end of the room, under the pretext of inspecting some snuffboxes and other trinkets displayed for sale there. Raymond accompanied him willingly enough. Little as he cared for Cullen's company, he could not help being curious to know what he wanted to say.

The first thing Cullen did once he was out of eye- and earshot of his mother was to empty the contents of his goblet into a nearby potted plant. "Damme, what a place," he said with a shudder. "Imagine making a fellow drink such a tipple at this hour of the morning! It's barbaric, that's what it is." With a grimace, he added, "I need a shot of brandy to take the taste out of my mouth."

"You'll have to make do with tea," said Raymond. "They don't sell spirituous liquors in the pump room."

Repeating that Shelton-on-Sea was a barbaric place, Cullen went to the counter to order a cup of tea. The pretty, dark-haired maid who waited on him looked him up and down with interest, and Cullen returned her look with one of reciprocal interest. "Nice little bit," he said in a low voice to Raymond. "Pretty gel, and a neat ankle too. I wouldn't mind having a touch at her, hey, Jeffries?"

In an aloof tone, Raymond suggested they had been going to look at snuffboxes. "Oh, aye," said Cullen, picking up his tea and moving toward the trinket table once more. Lowering his voice, he added, "But just between you and me, Jeffries, that was only an excuse. I wanted to talk to you away from Mother."

"Oh, yes?" said Raymond. "What did you wish to talk with me about? The maidservants' ankles?"

Cullen burst out laughing. "Lord, no!" he said.

"Mean to say, I like a pretty girl as much as the next fellow, but that's not why I'm here at all." With a more sober look, he added, "Mother said you were dancing with Caroline last night—Caroline Sedgewick. I wondered if she said anything about me."

"Then you know Miss Sedgewick is here?" said Raymond.

Cullen made a gesture of impatience. "Of course I know," he said. "Good Lord, you surely didn't think I came here for Mother's sake! A pretty spot in which to spend one's summer." He looked disparagingly around the pump room. "If it weren't for Caroline, I'd never have set foot in this godforsaken place. Tea and seawater!" Regarding his tea with a distaste only slightly inferior to that with which he had regarded the seawater, he added, "My mother wrote and told me Caro was here, and so of course I came at once."

"Why 'of course'?" inquired Raymond. "I had understood the two of you were no longer engaged."

Cullen looked gloomy, and it seemed to Raymond he looked slightly embarrassed as well. "It's true enough we're not engaged at the moment. But it was all a mistake—a foolish misunderstanding. I'm sure once I explain the matter to Caroline, she'll see what a mistake it was." With a slight cheering of manner, he added, "She's had time to cool down by now. I don't expect it'll be hard to talk her over."

"Indeed," said Raymond coldly.

Cullen nodded, seemingly unaware of the chill in his manner. "Indeed, yes," he said. "You'll say I'm a fool to go to so much trouble, but Caro's an exceptional girl. She's something quite out of the common way, by Jove."

"Indeed," said Raymond again. His tone was as discouraging as before, but Cullen went on, quite heedless.

"I never thought I'd fall for any girl as I've fallen for Caro. There's plenty of girls handsomer than she is, and richer too, but damme, it's me for Caro, and nobody else. Crazy thing, ain't it? I always swore I'd never be leg-shackled, but before I'd known Caro two months I found myself asking her to marry me. And though you mayn't believe it, Jeffries, I've never regretted it."

"No?" said Raymond. With a pointed look at the dark-haired maidservant, he added, "But there, I don't suppose your devotion is single-minded enough to hamper you in your other dealings with the fair sex."

Cullen grinned, showing all his handsome teeth. "You may well say so! But that's nothing to the point, Jeffries. A bit of fun is one thing, and marriage quite another. Indeed, that's what I've got to make Caro understand. It seems she saw me one night when I was out with Lucia Verlucci and naturally she cut up rough. The most damnable thing! If only I could have talked to her at the time, I'd have made her see there wasn't anything in it. But I haven't set eyes on her since it happened. She sent a note along the next morning saying she wished to end the engagement, and since then she's been playing least-in-sight."

Raymond was regarding him attentively. "You're saying there wasn't anything between you and Signorina Verlucci?" he asked.

Once more Cullen's laugh rang out. "Oh, I wouldn't go so far as to say *that,*" he said. "What I mean is, it was nothing *serious.* A fellow's particular is one thing, you know, and his fiancée quite another." In a voice of dissatisfaction, he added, "I wouldn't have thought Caro was such a fool. It's not as though she's a green girl straight out of the schoolroom. Mean to say, there was all that business with her and Scroggins before she met me. If I was good enough to overlook that, you'd think she'd be able to overlook me and Lucia."

Raymond gave him a cold smile. "It doesn't sound to me as though the situations are quite the same," he said. "From what I understand, Miss Sedgewick was engaged to Lord Scroggins, not conducting an illicit liaison with him. And that engagement was over and done with before she took up with you."

Cullen shrugged his shoulders impatiently. "Oh, aye, that's true enough. But still it seems to me Caro ought not to kick up a dust. Mean to say, if I'm willing to marry her, what's her grievance? I never offered to marry Lucia, or any of my other particulars."

"Your contention, then, is that Miss Sedgewick should be so overcome by the honor of marrying you that she should be willing to overlook your alliances with Signorina Verlucci and any other women you might care to bestow your attentions upon?" said Raymond. He tried hard to keep the sarcasm out of his voice, but he must not have quite succeeded, for Cullen gave him a sharp look.

"I wouldn't put it quite like that," he said. "But Caro ought to appreciate that I'm giving up something to marry her. Mean to say, my mother didn't half like the match, and of course after what's happened, she likes it even less. But I don't intend to let that stop me. I still want to marry Caro, and I'm perfectly sure she still wants to marry me. It's nonsense to let a little thing like Lucia come between us."

Raymond regarded him as he might have a two-headed snake. "You seem very sure Miss Sedgewick still cares for you," he commented.

"Oh, aye, I think so," said Cullen with a self-satisfied laugh. "It don't become me to say so, perhaps, but she was dashed fond of me. I'm sure she regrets throwing me over. With luck, I'll get a chance to talk to her today. Mother mentioned she goes down to bathe most days. I'm planning to take a stroll toward the shore in a little bit, and with luck I can catch her on the way to or from the bathing machines. If only I can see her and talk to her, it's ten to one she'll be wearing my ring again before the day's over."

Regarding his confidently smiling face, Raymond felt a sense of revulsion. He had always thought Robert Cullen a conceited ape, but now he saw he was twice as conceited and apelike as he had formerly supposed. "You think it will be settled as easily as that, do you?" he said in a voice he strove to keep dispassionate.

"Yes, I should think so," said Cullen with another self-satisfied laugh. "And I'll tell you, it can't be settled too soon for me! The sooner I shake the dust of this place from my feet, the happier I'll be. Seawater, for God's sake! I never heard of such idiocy."

Raymond hardly heard him. His brain was busy forming a resolution. It was iniquitous that Robert Cullen should waylay Caroline while she was on her way to bathe. He felt quite sure she did not even know her former fiancé was in Shelton-on-Sea. Someone ought to warn her. *He* ought to warn her. He would go and warn her this very minute.

"I need to speak to my aunt," he said, and left Cullen gaping after him with his mouth half open.

Miss Jeffries, on the other hand, expressed no particular surprise when Raymond explained he needed to run an errand. "That will be quite all right, Raymond," she said graciously. "Take as much time as you like. You needn't bother to return for me. My house is only a step away, and no one makes a fuss here if a woman goes abroad without an escort. That's one of the things I like about living in Shelton-on-Sea."

His mind relieved on this score, Raymond hurried out of the pump room. He did not know where Lady Katherine's house was, but inquiries of a passing chairman soon produced the necessary information. The Baddingtons' house was a place of some grandeur, located on the highest hill of Shelton-on-Sea with a fine view of the harbor. Raymond, a trifle out of breath from having climbed the hill in a hurry, rapped firmly upon the door. "I wish to see Miss Sedgewick," he told the servant who opened the door. "There is a matter of some importance I wish to discuss with her."

The servant took his card but seemed in some doubt as to whether Caroline was at home. "I will make inquiries, sir," he said. "If you will please step into the parlor?"

Raymond obediently stepped into the parlor, a good-sized apartment decorated in the Eastern mode with brasses and a profusion of Turkish carpets. In the ordinary way, he did not care for this kind of fashionable extravagance, but there was an exuberance in the room's decor that spoke plainly of Lady Katherine's own personality and made it charming in spite of its excesses. He was just surveying a brazen Buddha, a tolerant smile on his lips, when Lady Katherine herself appeared in the parlor doorway.

"It *is* you," she exclaimed. "Whoever would have thought it?"

This was not what Raymond would have considered a civil greeting, but he rose to his feet and wished Lady Katherine a good morning. "I would like to speak to Miss Sedgewick if she is here," he added politely. He had already said as much to the servant, but Lady Katherine's evident surprise at finding him there made him conclude his message had not been relayed.

Lady Katherine, however, nodded as though she knew all about it. "Oh, yes," she said. "But I have told the servants I am to see all callers for Miss Sedgewick first. She doesn't know you're here yet."

"No?" said Raymond politely. He thought this an odd way to proceed, but courtesy forbade him from voicing his opinion aloud.

Lady Katherine seemed to know what he was thinking, however. "Of course you think that very odd," she said, flashing him her brilliant smile. "But, you see, I was not sure if you really *were* Raymond Jeffries. Now I have seen you, of course there is no objection to your seeing Caro. I'll tell her you're here."

"Tell her who's here?" inquired a low-pitched feminine voice, and the next instant Caroline herself stepped into the room.

She, too, seemed surprised to see Raymond. Stopping just inside the door, she gave voice to an astonished "Oh!"

"It's Mr. Jeffries," Lady Katherine told her unnecessarily. "He has come to call on you."

Caroline said, "Oh" again in a bewildered voice. But a smile was spreading across her face, and after a moment she came forward to offer Raymond her hand. "I am very pleased to see you again, Mr. Jeffries," she said. "Won't you please sit down?"

The warmth of her welcome almost made Raymond forget his errand. Indeed, he had already started to seat himself before he recalled why he was there. "Look here," he said. "I'd enjoy very much sitting and talking to you, but this isn't really a social call. I came because there was something I thought you ought to know."

The smile on Caroline's face was immediately wiped away, to be replaced by a look of suspicion. "Yes?" she said. "What did you think I ought to know, Mr. Jeffries?"

Raymond was just about to reply, when Lady Katherine beat him to it. "Robert Cullen!" she exclaimed. "He's here at Shelton-on-Sea. Isn't he?" she demanded of Raymond.

Raymond, feeling deflated, admitted she was correct. "So you already knew Mr. Cullen was here?" he asked Lady Katherine.

She shook her dark head vigorously. "No, I didn't know," she said. "But I was sure he would turn up sooner or later."

"Oh," said Caroline. The color had rushed to her cheeks, staining them a rosy pink. She pressed her hands against them as though trying to cool them. "What on earth is Robert doing *here?*"

Lady Katherine gave her an affectionate smile. "Looking for you, darling, of course," she said. "I wonder you need ask."

"But I would not have supposed he wished to see me again!"

"Well, *I* would have," said Lady Katherine. "He's that sort of man, Caro darling. Quite a common sort, actually. The more unobtainable a thing appears to him, the more he wants it. And vice versa, of course," she added reflectively.

Caroline seemed not to hear these words. She was still pressing her hands to her cheeks, her expression distraught. "Robert here!" she said. "I can't see him. I *won't* see him."

"Of course you won't, darling," said Lady Katherine soothingly. "I'll have the servants tell him you're not at home. Thank heavens we were not taken by surprise! I think you must agree it was very kind of Mr. Jeffries to come and give us warning of his intentions." She smiled warmly at Raymond.

This brought Caroline's eyes around to Raymond at once. "Yes, it *was* kind," she said. "I am much obliged to you, sir."

Raymond, embarrassed, disclaimed his actions as nothing. "I merely thought you ought to know Mr. Cullen was here," he explained. "He spoke of—ahem—accosting you on the way to the bathing machines. I did not think it was fair you should be taken off your guard."

As he spoke, he was aware that Lady Katherine was looking at him speculatively. In the ordinary way this would have irritated him, but at the moment he was too taken up with Caroline's emotions to give anything else much heed. "Perhaps I might make a suggestion?" he continued. "If you merely have the servants deny you, that will keep Mr. Cullen at bay, but it also means you must keep to the house all day."

Caroline nodded. "That's true," she said. "But what else can I do? I simply can't run the risk of meeting Robert."

Raymond cleared his throat. "You could come riding with me," he suggested. "My curricle is at my aunt's, and if I sent a message, one of the servants could bring it round in a trice. It's a lovely day for a drive."

"Yes, it is," agreed Lady Katherine at once. "Much too lovely to spend sitting indoors, Caro darling. I think you should go with Mr. Jeffries. The fresh air will do you good."

"I don't know," said Caroline. She was looking at Raymond with doubt in her eyes. "It's very kind of Mr. Jeffries, but I hate to put him to so much trouble."

"It's no trouble," Raymond assured her. "I was going for a drive anyway." Although this was not strictly true, it *was* true that he wished to go driving with Caroline. Fixing his eyes on her, he said earnestly, "Do come, Miss Sedgewick. I would enjoy having your company very much."

"I doubt I will be much company," said Caroline with a short laugh. Before she could say anything more, however, Lady Katherine intervened.

"You had much better go, Caro," she said. "I'll fetch your bonnet and pelisse. Mr. Jeffries, here are pen, paper, and ink. If you write a message to your aunt's servants, one of my footmen will carry it around for you." To Caroline, who still appeared inclined to protest, she said firmly, "No, darling, not another word. Far better to go driving with Mr. Jeffries than spend all day skulking indoors. Even you must see that."

Apparently Caroline did see it, for she made no further protest. Lady Katherine went upstairs to fetch Caroline's bonnet and pelisse, while Raymond wrote a note to his aunt's servants. The note was entrusted to one of Lady Katherine's footmen, who set off down the hill at a brisk pace and reappeared moments later in the curricle being driven by Raymond's groom. Raymond dismissed both servants, and a few minutes later he and Caroline were seated side by side in the curricle, clattering along the cobblestone streets of Shelton-on-Sea.

Seven

Within the environs of Shelton-on-Sea, there was enough traffic to require Raymond's full attention. Once they had passed the outskirts of the town, however, he was able to relax and steal a look at his companion.

Caroline sat slumped on the seat beside him, her face shaded by a wide-brimmed hat. A breeze off the bay ruffled the folds of her white muslin dress. In one hand she held a parasol, an elegant trifle of white silk with a heavy fringe. It and the bonnet kept Raymond from getting a clear view of her face, but what he saw was not encouraging. There was a downward droop to her lips and a brooding look in her eyes, as if her thoughts were elsewhere.

Presently she seemed to become aware of his regard, for she turned her head and made an effort to smile at him. "Forgive me, Mr. Jeffries," she said. "I am afraid I am not very good company today. I did warn you, but Kate was so intent on getting me out the door that my protests went unheard."

"Why should you think you are not good company?" asked Raymond.

Caroline gave him a look that held both pain and amusement. "I don't know. Perhaps because I haven't said two words since I got in your carriage!

Indeed, Mr. Jeffries, I feel quite certain I will contribute nothing to your pleasure today. You had much better take me back to Lady Katherine's house and find someone else to go driving with you."

"Of course I will do so if that is *your* desire," said Raymond. "But if you are proposing such a scheme on my account, then please don't bother. I am very well suited as I am."

"How could you be?" said Caroline, looking honestly perplexed. "I don't see why you should wish to bother with me when I am so obviously in a foul mood."

Raymond smiled at her. "Perhaps I have the headache and prefer a quiet companion," he said.

Caroline stared at him a moment, then laughed. "Indeed! Well, that is most convenient," she said. "But I would beg you to take care, lest you exchange your malady for mine. In my experience there is nothing so contagious as a foul mood."

Raymond assured her he was willing to take the risk. Again Caroline surveyed him with a mixture of amusement and perplexity. "I wish I understood you," she complained. "I know this talk of having a headache and preferring a quiet companion is all gammon. Why should you be so kind to me?"

"Why should I not?" returned Raymond. "It is very little I am doing. And even that little I am doing as much for my own benefit as yours."

"So you say, but I take leave to doubt it. Why did you invite me to go driving with you? Was it merely because you felt sorry for me?"

There was an edge in Caroline's voice as she asked this question. Raymond threw her an amused look. "Certainly not," he said. "I am happy to take credit for chivalry when it is due, but it would be neither honest nor honorable to claim it when it is not. I asked you to go driving with me because I had a pleasant time dancing with you last night and wished to enjoy more of your company."

"Oh," said Caroline. After a moment, in a shy voice, she added, "I enjoyed dancing with you too." Another moment passed, and then, as though the words were wrenched out of her, she added, "I saw you dancing later with Miss Thompkins. You seemed to find her enjoyable company too."

"Miss Thompkins," repeated Raymond reflectively. "Miss Thompkins. Oh, yes, that is the little blond girl who giggles incessantly. Or is that Miss Timms? I called one by the other's name and had to dance with her twice by way of reparation, but I'm embarrassed to say even now I'm not sure which is which. They seemed quite interchangeable."

Caroline stared at him. "That's ridiculous," she said. "You can't possibly have mistaken Miss Timms for Miss Thompkins. They are both very pretty girls, but there the resemblance ends, for one is blonde and the other the darkest sort of brunette!"

"Well, they seemed tediously alike to me," said Raymond. "If it hadn't been for dancing with you, I'd have considered the evening a dead waste."

Caroline gave him another incredulous look. After a long pause, she said, "Mr. Jeffries, I hardly know how to take such compliments. You are far too generous, upon my word. But I thank you very much for your kindness. It was kind, especially, for you to come to Kate's house this morning and give me warning of Robert's being in town. It would have been very unpleasant for me to meet him unawares."

"Yes, I thought it might be," said Raymond.

Again there was a longish pause. Finally, in a voice that strove for lightness, Caroline said, "Mr. Jeffries, forgive me for harping on the same theme, but I cannot help wondering what moved you to do such a thing. Surely you must have had some motive besides kindness?"

Raymond hesitated, then nodded. "Strictly speaking, I did," he said. "I suppose most of us, in choosing a course of action, have motives that are mixed. In this case, I did wish to help you, but I will also admit that my feelings toward Mr. Cullen may have had some bearing on my decision to come to your aid."

Caroline gave him a long, searching look. "I see. You do not like Robert?" she asked.

This question put Raymond in a spot. It was true that he heartily disliked Robert Cullen, but he felt uncomfortable saying so in front of Caroline, who had once been his fiancée. Of course she had broken the engagement, but it might be she still had feelings for him; her questioning him so closely certainly looked like it. That being the case, Raymond thought it best to avoid giving a direct answer. "I don't know Mr. Cullen very well," he hedged. "Hardly enough to have formed an opinion on whether I like him or not."

Caroline's clear green eyes held irritation. "That's nonsense, Mr. Jeffries," she said. "You are merely being kind again. In my experience, one decides almost instantly whether one likes or dislikes a person. And from the tone of your voice when you speak of Robert, I would gather that you do not like him in the least."

She paused, looking at Raymond. So open and honest was her gaze that he was compelled to be open and honest in return. "Very well," he said.

"Since you will have it, I'll confess that I don't particularly care for Mr. Cullen."

Caroline nodded gloomily. "I thought so," she said. "It's all of a piece with everything else."

Raymond could not tell from these words whether he had offended her or not. On the whole he thought not, but there seemed no doubt that his response had made her unhappy. "I'm sorry," he said apologetically.

"For what?" she asked, fastening her clear green gaze on him once more.

"For saying what I did about Mr. Cullen."

"But why should you apologize for that? I asked your honest opinion."

"Yes, you did. But it occurs to me I might have been more tactful in giving it."

"I don't care twopence for tact," said Caroline with some violence. "I wanted to know what you *felt.* Now you have told me, and it only confirms my own opinions."

As she seemed quite upset, Raymond was reluctant to question her further, but he wanted badly to know what she was talking about. "Er—if I might ask—what opinion have my words confirmed?" he asked.

"That Robert Cullen is an intolerable bounder," said Caroline dejectedly. "And that I was a fool ever to become engaged to him."

"Here, now, I never said *that,*" said Raymond hastily. "Upon my word, I never said anything about your being a fool."

"No, but I am sure you must have thought it. It goes hand in hand with your feelings about Robert Cullen."

"Not at all," said Raymond decisively. "I am willing to believe you were honestly deceived in Mr. Cullen's character."

"But that makes me none the less a fool," said Caroline, her voice gloomy. "If I had not been, he never would have deceived me in the first place. *You* would not have let yourself to be deceived by him," she charged with a challenging look at Raymond.

"Perhaps not, but our situations are rather different," he said, smiling. "I am a man, and you are a young lady. Mr. Cullen has nothing to gain by misrepresenting himself to me, but it is far otherwise with you. I can readily believe he made himself very agreeable"

"Well, he did," said Caroline, her voice gloomier than ever. "But still I was a fool to let myself be taken in."

"If so, you are in good company. I know many people who hold him in high esteem. And even I, who am frankly prejudiced against him, must own he can be charming when he wishes."

"Yes," agreed Caroline, looking a degree more cheerful. "That's true."

"Of course it's true," said Raymond. "Even my aunt, whom I regard as the most sensible of women, was blushing and bridling like a schoolgirl this morning when he was talking to her in the pump room."

"Was she?" said Caroline with interest. "That *does* make me feel better. I have always thought your aunt a most intelligent woman."

"She is," said Raymond. "I will make it a point to introduce you to her the next time we meet."

Caroline's expression instantly became gloomy once more. "I am afraid Miss Jeffries would not care for such an introduction," she said. "She does not at all approve of me."

"That is only because she does not know you," Raymond assured Caroline. "If she did, I am sure she would be glad to make your acquaintance. Particularly if she knew the circumstances surrounding your engagement to Robert Cullen."

"Indeed," said Caroline with a startled look. "I had not supposed those circumstances were generally known. May I ask what you have heard about my engagement to Mr. Cullen?"

Raymond saw, too late, that he had been indiscreet. "It's not a question of what I have *heard,*" he said hesitantly. "It's rather a question of what I *saw.*"

"I see," said Caroline. After a moment she drew a deep sigh. "I can guess, I suppose. You saw Mr. Cullen some evening, accompanied by a lady who was not me, with whom he seemed to be on excellent, not to say intimate, terms."

"That's it," said Raymond, relieved not to have to spell the matter out. "That's it exactly."

Caroline sighed again. "And when was this?" she asked. "When did you see him with his—his *chère amie?*"

"It was something over three weeks ago, I think. I haven't, of course, mentioned the matter to anyone else. But when my aunt told me you had broken your engagement, I thought there might be a connection between the two events."

"Yes," said Caroline in a hollow voice. "There was a connection." She drew another sigh. "I must say, I had hoped nobody but me knew about Robert and his *chère amie.* That is naive, of course, but still I had hoped."

"Well, if it's any consolation, I don't think very many people *do* know about it," said Raymond.

"Otherwise it would not have created such a flurry when you broke your engagement with him."

Caroline attempted a smile. "You may be surprised to hear it, Mr. Jeffries," she said, "but there are quite a number of people who would consider it ridiculous to break with a man merely because he keeps an opera dancer or two. Particularly a wealthy man like Robert Cullen. My aunt Emilia, for one, would never have done scolding me for it."

"No doubt there are some people who would criticize," said Raymond. "But I think any right-minded person would honor you for your scruples. The fact that you did not allow mercenary motives to outweigh the promptings of your heart does you only credit in my opinion."

Caroline turned to look at him. "Truly?" she said.

"Yes, truly," said Raymond, meeting her gaze directly. "Indeed, Miss Sedgewick, if the circumstances of your engagement to Mr. Cullen were more widely known, I think you would find yourself an object of most people's sympathy. I know you have endured a certain amount of public criticism over the breaking of your third engagement." Caroline smiled weakly. "But that would not be the case if people knew why you had broken it. Some might still criticize, of course, like your aunt, but I think most would sympathize."

Caroline was silent a moment. Finally she drew a deep sigh. "I daresay you are right," she said. "But the plain fact is I would rather have people's criticism than their sympathy!" She made a brave attempt at a smile. "You will call that pride, no doubt, and you would be right, Mr. Jeffries. But still I would rather be called a jilt than have people know I broke my engagement because my fiancé was faithless to me."

Raymond was silenced by this speech. He was a proud man himself and could easily see Caroline's point of view. Indeed, he only wondered that he had not seen it before.

Caroline, however, misinterpreted his silence. "You disapprove, of course," she said. "I don't know that I blame you. It's only another example of my folly, as I very well know. But I simply cannot bring myself to tell the world at large why I broke with Robert."

"It happens that I *don't* disapprove," said Raymond. "I quite understand your feelings and sympathize with them too. But, no, I'm forgetting. You don't want sympathy," he added, giving her a quick smile. "So I will merely say instead that I understand and approve."

Caroline laughed. "I don't mind *your* sympathy, Mr. Jeffries," she said. "It is rather the sympathy of people who pretend to be sorry and are really delighted to see me discomfited that I resent." She smiled back at him. "Indeed, it has been quite pleasant to tell my woes to a confidant who is so—well, so sympathetic."

She could not help laughing as she spoke these words, and Raymond joined in her laughter. "The shortcomings of the English language!" he said. "There ought to be a means to distinguish between real sympathy, which is based on understanding, and the sense in which it is ordinarily used, in which it merely denotes pity." He smiled at Caroline. "But at any rate, we seem to understand the distinction even if we cannot express it!"

"Yes," agreed Caroline, twirling her parasol in a gloved hand. "I think we understand it very well."

Raymond thought she looked embarrassed. To spare her, he shifted his attention back to the road but went on watching her out of the corner of his eye. "I am honored that you would consider me worthy of your confidence," he said. "As I mentioned before, I had suspected you were justified in your conduct toward Mr. Cullen, but I am glad to have it confirmed by your own lips."

Caroline did not look as pleased by this speech as he had expected. "I would hardly call that confirmation, Mr. Jeffries," she said. "You cannot be sure I am not misrepresenting myself just as Robert misrepresented himself to me."

Raymond smiled. "Miss Sedgewick, your candor is admirable, but your logic is at fault," he said. "Don't you see that the very fact of your mentioning such a possibility is the strongest proof against it? You would hardly be planting doubts in my mind if your intent was to deceive."

A sparkle had appeared in Caroline's eye. "But perhaps I am more deceptive than you give me credit for," she said. "I might think, 'This is Mr. Jeffries, who has the reputation of being a clever man. That being the case, he might question a straightforward assertion of honesty. But if I preempt him by calling my own motives into question, then his suspicions will be allayed by my seeming candor!'"

Raymond laughed. "If you are as clever as that, Miss Sedgewick, then I am happy to be deceived by you," he said. "But I do not believe it. After dancing with you last night, I came away convinced that whatever you may have done in the past, your conduct must have been perfectly justified."

The smile that had been hovering on Caroline's lips vanished at these words. "As to that, I hardly know," she said with a sigh. "Certainly I've done nothing I did not *think* justified. But there is a distinction, unfortunately. Still, I thank you for your words, Mr. Jeffries. To win your approval must count for something."

She was silent after this, and Raymond concluded she meant to say no more on the subject. To say he was disappointed would have been an understatement. He had hoped she might speak further concerning her past, but she evidently felt that while he might deserve some explanation of her conduct in regard to Robert Cullen, her conduct in regard to her other fiancés was none of his affair.

Raymond had to admit such a feeling was justified. Still, he was disappointed. Caroline had seized his imagination in a remarkable way, considering how brief their acquaintance had been. He found himself wanting to know everything about her, and in particular he wished to know about her previous engagements. He had been speaking the truth when he said he felt she must have been justified in her past conduct, but though he might feel assured on this point, the logical, dispassionate part of his mind wanted corroboration. He wanted to *know.* And the fact that Caroline evidently did not mean to tell him made him feel remarkably frustrated.

He hid his frustration as best he could, however, and began to speak of other things. He asked her how she liked Shelton-on-Sea and whether she made a practice of sea bathing. Of course he already knew the answer to this, but Caroline responded readily enough, and for some minutes they discussed sea bathing with the animation of fellow enthusiasts. The conversation then turned to the practice of seawater drinking, and here, too, he found Caroline of the same opinion as himself. So colorful was she in describing her first—and last—taste of seawater that he was emboldened to describe how he had induced Robert Cullen to partake of the waters that morning. Caroline laughed until the tears ran down her face.

"Mr. Jeffries, that does me more good than a full course of the waters as prescribed by Dr. Briar," she said. "I am not a vengeful woman, I hope, but the idea of Robert drinking a glass of that horrible stuff and trying to look as if he liked it does my heart good. I don't suppose you did it with my interests in mind, but I thank you for it all the same." With these words, she leaned over and kissed him on the cheek.

Raymond felt the blood roll up under his skin. He had a confused impression of warmth despite the stiff breeze blowing off the bay, and there was a buzz in his ears like the pounding of the surf, only louder. After a moment, he risked a glance at Caroline. She was sitting on the curricle seat, looking out at the passing landscape. She seemed quite unaware of the conflagration raging in his veins. It was true there was a touch more color in her cheeks than had been there before, but that was likely the effect of the sun and sea breezes.

Raymond felt a little dizzy. His hands kept their grip on the reins, and his eyes continued to scan the road ahead for hazards and oncoming traffic, but he was not feeling the leather between his fingers or seeing the level surface of the roadway bordered by flowering hedgerows. Instead, he was feeling again the touch of Caroline's lips on his cheek and seeing the light in her eyes as she leaned over to kiss him. As kisses went, it had been a mild affair; indeed, it could hardly have been milder, considered from a dispassionate viewpoint. That made it all the more shocking that it should have affected him so profoundly.

But though Raymond had been shaken to the core, he had spent too many years among the *ton* to let his face betray his feelings. He had always prided himself on his sangfroid; and now, even though his *sang* felt anything but *froid,* his face wore its customary expression of impassive good breeding. "There is no need to thank me, Miss Sedgewick," he said, "I'm sure you are most welcome." And he felt satisfied that no casual auditor, hearing him speak, would have suspected he had just fallen deeply and irretrievably in love.

Eight

Caroline, without seeming to, was studying Raymond from beneath the brim of her hat.

She still found it hard to believe she was sitting beside him. It was as though the Prince Regent himself should take her driving—except that she would have been less nervous about driving with the Prince.

"Prinny's just a man," she told herself, "and not a particularly wonderful man, at that." Raymond Jeffries, however, *was* a wonderful man. Not only was he witty, well bred, and intelligent, he was extraordinarily kind and generous too. How else to explain why he had given up his whole day for her?

For it was becoming clear that was exactly what he had done. When he had proposed taking her driving, Caroline had supposed it would be for an hour or two at most. In truth, she had been so distraught at the thought of seeing Robert Cullen again, and so amazed that Raymond had personally come to warn her of his presence—and to offer her a way of escape—there was no room in her thoughts for such trifling considerations as the duration of their drive.

But it had quickly become evident that Raymond had no intention of returning to Shelton-on-Sea within an hour or two. He had followed the coast road that ran along the cliffs, where they could see the sands on the shore below and the whitecaps dancing on the bay. When the horses had begun to tire, he had stopped at a posting house, and while his cattle were watered and baited, ordered sandwiches and lemonade for him and Caroline. They had taken this simple repast out to the inn yard and eaten it in the shade of a spreading oak, where they could watch the ostlers going about their business and the traffic rattling by on the road.

It had been a delightful interlude, and Caroline had been sorry when it ended. She had resumed her seat in the curricle with a heavy heart, supposing the time had come to return to Shelton-on-Sea. Instead of turning back the way they had come, however, Raymond had continued down the coast road. They had been traveling southward ever since, and Caroline felt certain they could not reach Shelton-on-Sea before early evening even if they turned back immediately.

Once or twice she had been on the verge of saying something. In the end, however, she held her tongue. The fact was, she did not want to turn back. She was enjoying herself more than she would have believed possible under the circumstances. It was as though she had left her difficulties behind her in Shelton-on-Sea. And though she felt sure they would be waiting for her on her return, she was enjoying the respite too much to wish to hasten its end.

With gratitude, she reflected on how much she owed Raymond. It would have been a horrible ordeal to come unexpectedly face-to-face with Robert Cullen in the streets of Shelton-on-Sea, as she surely would have if Raymond had not come to warn her. Indeed, when she reflected on this circumstance, she felt such a rush of feeling for him that it half alarmed her. She told herself she was taking the whole matter too seriously. Raymond had admitted he did not care for her ex-fiancé, and nine tenths of the trouble he had taken had probably been motivated by dislike for Robert rather than by regard for her. Still, she was very grateful to him. She was so grateful that when he had merrily described how he had maneuvered Robert into drinking seawater that morning, she had been unable to resist the urge to lean over and kiss him.

The memory made Caroline blush now to recall. She could not imagine how she had come to do such a thing. It was not the sort of behavior a well-bred young lady ought to indulge in. Of course she was not what most people would consider a well-bred young lady, but even her worst critics had never called her fast or forward. It was definitely fast to kiss a gentleman one barely knew, even when it was a simple kiss on the cheek. Still, as Caroline assured herself, she had not meant to be fast. The kiss had been a spur-of-the-moment impulse motivated solely by gratitude. Fortunately, Raymond had seemed to understand. He had behaved as though being kissed by a young lady he barely knew was a perfectly ordinary occurrence.

"Perhaps it is," Caroline told herself ruefully. She knew how sought after he was in London and the stratagems ladies used there to attract his notice. *I would never go to such lengths as that,* she assured herself. But she could not help recalling uneasily how her aunt Emilia had maneuvered him into being introduced to her two Seasons back. Perhaps he remembered it, too, and regarded her kiss as all of a piece with her other behavior.

This was a thought to make Caroline burn with shame. It did no good to remind herself that she had come driving with Raymond today only under compulsion, and that he had been the one to seek *her* out. She still could not help remembering that they had met in the first place because of a vulgar stratagem on the part of her aunt. That being the case, it behooved her to behave with even more than ordinary dignity, not to kiss him like a gazetted flirt right out in the open for anyone to see.

Thank heaven nobody did see, Caroline reflected with dry humor. *All I need is for Mrs. Cullen to hear I have been kissing Mr. Jeffries. No doubt it would cause her to conclude I am twice as bad as she already believes me to be.*

Once again, she could only bless heaven that Raymond had not been inclined to draw similar conclusions. It was extraordinary how well he seemed to understand her. But even with this reflection to comfort her, the recollection of her behavior had destroyed some of her pleasure in the day, and that, in turn, was enough to nerve her to say something about returning to Shelton-on-Sea. "Don't you think we had better be turning back?" she asked diffidently. "It must be at least three o'clock, and we have come a long way."

"A very long way," agreed Raymond. Reining in his horses, he carefully backed and turned them, then urged them into motion once more. Soon they were traveling back along the road that led to Shelton-on-Sea.

Caroline, studying Raymond's profile once again, was filled with a desperate desire to know his thoughts. He had appeared not at all perturbed by her suggesting they return to Shelton-on-Sea. Yet it did not look as though he would have turned back if she had not spoken. How far would he have gone if left to himself? What did he mean by driving and driving as though he meant to take her right away to Portsmouth and beyond?

In the end, her curiosity grew so great she had to ask the question aloud. "I hope I have not spoiled your plans by suggesting we turn back," she said carefully. "Was there anywhere in particular you were wishing to go?"

He turned calm gray eyes upon her. "Nowhere in particular," he said. "As long as you were content to drive, so was I."

"But we have been driving a very long time," said Caroline. "I imagine your horses must be growing tired."

"Yes, I had thought to stop and change them if we kept going much longer," he replied. "As it is, though, I think they'll make it home if I don't push them too hard."

"I am glad to hear it," said Caroline. After a pause, she added, "Do you really mean to say you would have kept driving if I had said nothing?"

Raymond considered the question for a moment, then nodded. "I suppose so. As I said, I was quite content to keep going as long as you wanted to."

Caroline laughed incredulously. "But what if I had wanted to keep going and had never mentioned turning back?" she said. "You would have been in a pretty fix then!"

Raymond smiled. "True," he said, "but fortunately you did mention it."

"Yes, but what if I hadn't?" insisted Caroline.

Raymond shrugged and gave her another smile. "I suppose I had sufficient faith to trust you would suggest it sometime or other," he said. "I was content to leave the matter in your hands."

"But that's ridiculous!" said Caroline. "You mean to say you weren't going to say anything about our going back *ever?* You were just leaving it up to me?"

"Yes, I suppose I was," said Raymond.

"Well, that's ridiculous," repeated Caroline, her voice disapproving. "You can't go around trusting people like that. Sooner or later you will find yourself most dreadfully taken in!"

Raymond smiled. "No doubt you are right," he said. "You certainly can't go putting unreserved trust in people in the aggregate. But now and then you run across an individual whom you *can* trust. Don't you agree, Miss Sedgewick?"

"Yes—at least, I suppose I do," said Caroline doubtfully. "But still I do not like to think you would place such trust in *me.* I have such a strong incentive to avoid going back to Shelton-on-Sea that I might well have said nothing and let you drive all the way to John o'Groat's!"

Raymond threw back his head and laughed. "I have never been to John o'Groat's," he said. "I wouldn't mind seeing it someday. But it's probably as well we didn't undertake to drive there today. Another time, perhaps." He threw Caroline a sideways smile.

"Yes," said Caroline. Inwardly she was marveling at his words. Did he really mean what he was saying? Not that they should drive to John o'Groat's—clearly that was a joke—but that he might ask her to go driving another time? Caroline found her heart soared at the prospect. Immediately she undertook to drag it down to earth again. It was all very well to enjoy driving with Raymond this once, but she must not take it for granted he would ask her a second time. Still, her heart continued to soar just the same. Caroline began to feel alarmed. She had the sense that events were moving too fast for her. In another effort to ground herself, she reminded herself that Raymond was a gentleman of exalted position and exclusive reputation who inhabited social circles far above her. That only increased her sense of unbalance, however. He was so different from his reputation, so much warmer, more human, and more approachable, it was enough to make her question her assumptions about everything.

In this unsettled mood, she rode back to Shelton-on-Sea beside Raymond. It took several hours to retrace their steps, in part because it was necessary to stop to rest the horses midway. This would not have been necessary if she had allowed Raymond to change the horses for a fresh pair, but Caroline would not hear of his doing so. She told him she did not wish him to incur more expense on her behalf than he had already done. What she did not say, or even admit to herself, was the fact that stopping and resting the horses kept her away from Shelton-on-Sea another hour. And it also allowed her to spend another hour in his company.

It was no longer afternoon but early evening when they finally arrived at Lady Katherine's door. At Caroline's suggestion, it was the back door they went to, for she had no wish to encounter Robert if he was still about. It turned out this precaution was needless, but only by a small margin.

"My dear, he left less than ten minutes ago," Lady Katherine told Caroline, her expression divided between amusement and horror. "And he has been here *the whole afternoon!* Indeed, you had not been gone an hour before he appeared on the doorstep. I told him you were out, but he refused to believe it, and he has been sitting in the parlor ever since, wearing out my carpet with his pacing and ringing the bell every ten minutes to ask if you were back. You can't think what a nuisance he has been."

"I should think so," said Caroline. She had thought very little of Robert during the afternoon—amazingly little, it now seemed to her. The shift in perception that had caught her off guard in regard to Raymond seemed to have affected her vision of Robert too. For the last eight hours, he had somehow been transformed into an abstract problem that engaged her thoughts without troubling her heart. Now, however, that vision had shifted back with a sickening jolt, and she was once more faced with Robert as a real and immediate problem. For a moment it seemed almost more than she could bear. Only for a moment, however, for suddenly Raymond cleared his throat.

"I rather thought he might prove persistent," he said. "It's as well we didn't hurry back, isn't it, Miss Sedgewick?"

"Yes," agreed Caroline. Looking at him, she felt the turmoil in her heart subside a little. He looked so calm and unperturbed, an oasis in the midst of a howling desert. He smiled when he encountered her eye, and she found herself smiling back with an involuntary lifting of spirits.

Lady Katherine was studying them both curiously. "You were certainly gone a very long time," she said. "I was beginning to wonder if you would be home in time for dinner! But it's as well you did not hurry, as you say. You would have only encountered Robert in the parlor, and then there would have been a scene."

"There is bound to be one sooner or later," said Caroline. Her spirits sank once more at the thought of such an encounter. But again Raymond spoke, and once again his calm, well-bred voice had the effect of elevating her mood.

"If you stay here at Shelton-on-Sea, it's certain you must meet him sooner or later," he said. "You can hardly remain mewed up in the house for the rest of the summer."

"But what else can I do?" said Caroline. "If I leave here, he would only follow me. There is nothing to stop him from following me wherever I go. And I don't want to leave Shelton-on-Sea. Kate had planned to spend all summer here, and I would not spoil her plans for anything."

"Darling, you know I would cheerfully change my plans for your sake," said Lady Katherine affectionately. "But I don't think Mr. Jeffries meant you should leave Shelton-on-Sea. Did you?" she asked Raymond.

"No, I didn't," said Raymond. "I meant only that when you do meet Mr. Cullen, it should be on your terms and not his. I would suggest a public meeting rather than a private one—in the pump room, for instance. If you are in public and surrounded by your friends, it stands to reason he cannot be as offensive as if you met him privately."

"That's true," said Lady Katherine, nodding vigorously. "If I were you, Caro, I would do what Mr. Jeffries says and get it over as soon as possible. In my experience, it's always best to get uncomfortable things over with quickly, and then you can be comfortable again."

These words made Caroline smile and sigh at the same time. It did not seem to her that she would ever be comfortable as long as she was afflicted by Robert's presence. Still, she had to own there was sense in what her friend was saying. "I suppose so," she said. "Perhaps I'll go to the pump room tomorrow morning."

"An excellent plan," approved Lady Katherine. "Mrs. Cullen always goes there of a morning, and Robert will likely be there too. I will accompany you, of course, and perhaps Mr. Baddington will go along with us. It's always better to have a man about in these situations."

Raymond cleared his throat. "As to that, you needn't trouble Mr. Baddington," he said. "I was going to the pump room tomorrow anyway. There's no need to make Mr. Baddington go along too, unless he wants to, of course."

Both Caroline and Lady Katherine were staring at him, the one with amazement and the other with speculation. He flushed under their regard, but addressed Caroline in an earnest voice. "I would be glad to support you, Miss Sedgewick, if my presence would be of any use. Perhaps I am being presumptuous, but I hope I may be counted among your friends after today."

It was Caroline's turn to flush. "Of course," she said. "I would be *honored* to call you my friend, Mr. Jeffries. But I really couldn't ask any more of you than you have already done."

"I beg you won't regard that," he said soberly. "Today was a pleasure, and I would be happy to do as much again tomorrow if you had need of me."

"Well, I hope it won't be necessary for you to drive me halfway to John o'Groat's again," said Caroline with a nervous laugh. "That would be outside of enough!"

"Even if it is, I will gladly do it," Raymond assured her. "Merely let me know what time you will arrive at the pump room, and I will take care to get there before you."

They settled on eleven o'clock as the hour, Caroline repeating nervously that she hoped she was not putting him to any trouble. Raymond waved aside this idea, however. "It's no trouble. Likely my aunt and I would have gone to the pump room anyway. Speaking of my aunt, I suppose I had better be getting back to her house," he added with a glance at the longcase clock in the corner. "She will be expecting me for dinner this evening, as I gave her no word I would be dining out."

Lady Katherine immediately suggested he send word to Miss Jeffries and stay to dine at her house. Raymond refused, but Caroline thought he looked a little regretful as he did so. "I must be going," he said. "But I will see you both tomorrow. Thank you for a delightful day, Miss Sedgewick," he added, smiling at her. "And remember, I wouldn't mind doing the same thing tomorrow. Not in the least." With these words, he took leave of them both.

Nine

As the sound of Raymond's curricle faded into the distance, Lady Katherine spoke. "Well, Caro," she said, "if I were to judge by appearances, I would say you have made a conquest of that man."

Caroline flushed. "It's no such thing," she said. "Mr. Jeffries was only being kind."

"I see," said Lady Katherine.

Her voice held undisguised amusement. Caroline eyed her resentfully. "Kate, I beg you won't say another word," she said. "It's nonsense, utter nonsense. You know what Raymond Jeffries is, and you know what I am. Can you seriously believe I should make a conquest of him?"

"Easily, darling," said Lady Katherine, smiling at her with affection. "But I can as easily believe you would refuse to credit it, even when confronted with the most overwhelming proofs!"

Caroline made an exasperated noise. "I'm going to change for dinner," she said, and walked out of the drawing room to the accompaniment of Lady Katherine's laughter.

Meanwhile, at his aunt's house, Raymond was also changing for dinner.

He had gone straight to his room on entering the house, wishing to avoid his aunt and her servants. He had a curious disinclination to talk to anyone. Although Miss Jeffries had asked no questions when he had taken leave of her that morning, she must by now have a strong curiosity to know what had kept him away for nearly the whole day, and her servants would likely be curious too. As Raymond tied his neckcloth and shrugged his way into a topcoat, he tried to make up his mind how much he would tell of his activities that day. On one hand, he disliked lying, but then, he did not particularly care to tell the truth either. To admit that he had spent the day driving with Caroline would lead to other questions more difficult to answer. And that would lead to the most difficult question of all, a question Raymond could hardly answer himself.

"Why Caroline Sedgewick?" he demanded of himself. "Why her, of all women?"

Raymond had already asked himself this question a hundred times without getting any very cogent answer. He knew only that Caroline had suddenly become very important to him. He felt a powerful interest in her welfare, so much so that he would have driven twice as far, under conditions twice as onerous, and counted it a privilege rather than a chore.

Still pondering this paradox, he went downstairs to dinner in a very thoughtful mood.

He had been correct in supposing his aunt would ask questions. "Where did you go, Raymond?" she demanded as soon as the soup had been served. "When you said you had an errand, I did not expect you would be gone all day."

"Neither did I," said Raymond. "As it happened, there were complications." He threw a warning look toward the servant standing behind his chair.

His aunt apparently understood, for she said

nothing more until dessert was placed on the table and the servants left the room. Then, having helped herself largely to apricot tart, she began to question him once more.

"If your purpose is to intrigue me, then I freely confess you have succeeded," she said. "Clearly there is some mystery behind your absence today. May I know what it is, or would it be better not to ask?"

Although the words were jovial, there was an underlying note of hurt in her voice that made Raymond decide to tell her the truth. She was, as he knew, an intelligent woman whose discretion might be depended on. Besides, if he did not tell her, she was likely to assume his business was more illicit than it really was. She might suspect him of carrying on an affair with a serving girl, for instance, or some other low intrigue. Raymond was eager to avoid such a suspicion. In the first place, low intrigues were the kind of thing Robert Cullen indulged in, and he had no wish to be associated with that gentleman in any way. But he had another and better reason for allaying his aunt's suspicions. It seemed important that his relations with Caroline should not be tainted by such a base suspicion, even for a moment.

So he nodded to his aunt and answered affably enough, "Certainly you may know if you like. I ask only that you not spread the story abroad, Aunt. It might cause trouble for Miss Sedgewick, and she has quite enough of that as it is."

He went on to relate his conversation with Robert Cullen in the pump room that morning. His account was fairly complete, omitting only the mention of La Bella Verlucci and the part she had played in the breaking of Caroline's engagement.

It had been Caroline's wish that her ex-fiancé's infidelities not be noised abroad, and Raymond felt obliged to respect her wish. He was not obliged to be equally discreet in regard to Robert's remarks about the dark-haired maidservant, however. Those he repeated along with the Robert's statement to the effect that he expected to talk Caroline over without any real difficulty.

He reckoned he would be more likely to enlist his aunt's sympathies if she knew all this, and he was right. By the time he was finished with his account, his aunt was making remarks like "Disgraceful! Of all the conceited puppies" and "I begin to think Miss Sedgewick was quite justified in jilting him."

"I think so too," said Raymond. "At any rate, that's why I left the pump room in such a hurry this morning. I thought Miss Sedgewick ought to be warned that Cullen was in town and planning to see her."

"And did you succeed in reaching her in time? I suppose you must have, for Mr. Cullen did not leave the pump room until some time after you did."

"Yes, I got there in time." Encouraged by his aunt's approval, Raymond described how he had taken Caroline for a drive, that she might escape Cullen's persecution.

His aunt approved this action also, though she looked a little odd when he mentioned the duration of the drive. "It was certainly generous of you to go to such lengths to assist Miss Sedgewick, Raymond," she said, "but it seems also a little imprudent. You might easily have compromised yourself, going out for the best part of a day with an unmarried lady and not even a groom along for chaperon."

Raymond's first instinct was to dispute this

speech. He bit back his objection in time, however, and answered quite mildly, "Do you think so? I don't see it myself, Aunt. We were riding in an open carriage and kept entirely to the main roads. Under the circumstances, there could have been no imprudence, let alone impropriety."

His aunt gave him a disbelieving look. "Raymond, I always thought you were a tolerably wide-awake man, but now I begin to wonder," she said. "You must know that men have been landed with breach of promise suits for less than you have done today. What if you and Miss Sedgewick had suffered a breakdown while you were miles from home? Or what if she were to claim you made improper advances toward her?"

"She won't," said Raymond sharply. "Miss Sedgewick will do nothing of the kind. I would stake my reputation on it."

"Well, you may have to if she is less scrupulous than you think," said his aunt with equal sharpness. "I don't see how you can be so certain about her integrity, Raymond. Perhaps she had reason to jilt Robert Cullen, but what of her first two engagements? Surely she cannot have been justified in jilting three men in a row."

Raymond was silent out of necessity. As before, he felt sure his aunt was wrong about Caroline's character. But he had no means of proving it, and so he sat gazing at the uneaten dessert on his plate and saying nothing. His face must have expressed the unhappiness he felt, however, for after glancing at him several times, his aunt spoke in a relenting voice.

"At any rate, I am glad you put a spoke in Robert Cullen's wheel," she said. "He seems to have richly deserved it."

"Yes," said Raymond heavily. "It was a pleasure to thwart him. I wish only that I could keep him from seeing Miss Sedgewick at all."

His aunt regarded him quizzically. "Indeed! That sounds as though you think he might yet do so."

"Well, it's bound to happen sooner or later," said Raymond. "Likely it will be sooner if Miss Sedgewick doesn't leave Shelton-on-Sea. And of course she doesn't want to do that."

"Of course not," agreed his aunt. There was a hint of amusement in her voice that made Raymond look up sharply.

"What do you find so funny?" he asked. "For my part, I think Mr. Cullen's pursuit more unfortunate than humorous."

"So should I if I were sure it was unwanted pursuit. But it wouldn't surprise me if Miss Sedgewick were less reluctant to meet him than you think."

Raymond stared. "You don't know what you are talking about," he said after a pause. "There is nothing Caroline—Miss Sedgewick—wants more than to avoid Robert Cullen completely."

"That's as may be," said his aunt good-humoredly. "But I can't tell you how many times I've seen a woman break with a good-for-nothing man only to take him back in the end. There's an old saying that women love a rake better than a milksop, and unfortunately it seems to be the truth. I've never understood the attraction myself. It stands to reason that if a man behaves badly before marriage, he ain't going to be a model husband afterward."

This speech caused Raymond so much consternation, he could not speak for a full minute. "I am sure Miss Sedgewick has no intention of taking

Cullen back," he said when at last he could speak again. "She spoke against him quite strongly today."

"She may well have done so. But that won't stop her from taking him back," predicted Miss Jeffries cynically. "I've seen it happen too many times to doubt it."

"Well, *I* doubt it," retorted Raymond. "Miss Sedgewick has more intelligence than that."

His aunt gave him a pitying smile. "Intelligence has nothing to do with it," she said. "I've seen lots of intelligent women make fools of themselves over men—aye, and vice versa too. But it's an ill wind that blows nobody good. If Miss Sedgewick becomes engaged to Cullen again, we can be sure she won't come bothering you with breach of promise suits!"

This speech did not bring Raymond any comfort. He had never believed for a minute that Caroline would bring a breach of promise suit against him. But he was by no means so certain she would remain impervious to Robert Cullen's blandishments. Like his aunt, he knew many otherwise intelligent men and women who had made disastrous choices in selecting a life partner. The thought that Caroline might be one of them was enough to turn him sick to his stomach.

Later, as he lay in bed that night, the thought was still troubling him. Nor was this the only thought to trouble him. Indeed, when he reflected on all that had happened that day, he felt quite unsettled. It seemed as though he had lived a whole lifetime in the last fifteen or sixteen hours.

He had arisen that morning heart-whole, or almost heart-whole, for on looking back he could see he had been cherishing a partiality for Caroline since dancing with her the night before. He had been thinking about her and wishing he might see her again. But it had not been until they had gone driving that the real damage was done. At the moment she had leaned over and kissed him on the cheek, the ownership of his heart had passed formally from his own keeping into hers. It was a very odd feeling. All his life he had prided himself on his self-possession, his ability to think and reason without reference to emotion. Now when he thought of Caroline, all thought and rationality went out the window, and emotion came rushing in.

His conversation with his aunt just then was a good example. She had said nothing that was not reasonable, adduced no opinion that his own intelligence did not endorse. Yet he had disputed with her on every point with a passion that must have struck her as highly suspicious under the circumstances. Raymond smiled wryly in the dark. Did she already suspect he had fallen victim to Cupid's arrows? He thought she must, and he was quite sure that Lady Katherine suspected it as well. But what about Caroline herself? Did she realize she had captured his heart?

Offhand, Raymond would have been prepared to swear she did not. Even in the matter of that kiss on the cheek he was sure she was guileless. But with a sense of dismay, he realized his certainty meant nothing given his present disordered state of mind. His instincts where Caroline was concerned were not rational, and therefore not to be relied on.

But I'll eat Aunt's best bonnet if Caroline brings a breach of promise suit against me, he told himself grimly. *I wish only I felt as sure she would not listen to Cullen when he comes begging her to take him back.*

It was some comfort to reflect that Lady Katherine felt as he did on the subject of Robert Cullen. She was an ally worth having, living actually in the same house as Caroline and thus being in a much better position to prevent her from weakening toward Robert Cullen. Still, he wished he might forcibly eject Cullen from Shelton-on-Sea and prevent his ever coming back.

The world's grown too damned civilized when you can't prevent a lady from being annoyed, he told himself irascibly. *It's all wrong that Caroline should have to see him. By God, I wish I might make sure she never does.*

In any case, he was in a position to make sure she saw him no more than absolutely necessary. They had made plans to meet in the pump room the following day. If Robert Cullen was there, and if he made a nuisance of himself—two ifs that seemed more than probable to Raymond—he resolved he would do something about it, civilization or no civilization.

Ten

There was a flutter of nerves in the pit of Caroline's stomach as she entered the pump room the next morning.

That in itself was nothing unusual. She had felt a similar flutter of nerves every time she had gone out in public the last few weeks. Ever since she had broken her third engagement, people had had a way of staring and exchanging knowing nods and winks that was highly disconcerting. Sometimes, too, there were more outspoken expressions of disapproval. Caroline still remembered that whispered "Hussy!" she and Raymond had overheard on the night of the assembly.

Likely it was one of Mrs. Cullen's friends, she told herself gloomily. "Or maybe Mrs. Cullen herself." She had endured many demonstrations of Mrs. Cullen's resentment since coming to Shelton-on-Sea. Now she was purposely putting herself in the way of more. The pump room of a morning was a stronghold of the local dowagers, and Mrs. Cullen was certain to be there. It was not this, however, that made Caroline's insides feel as though they were being put through a clothes mangle. It was the idea that Robert Cullen might be there along with her.

Caroline did not want to see Robert Cullen—not

today, not tomorrow, not ever. She had loved him once, but her love had died a painful death on finding he had been unfaithful to her. Now she was faced with the prospect of seeing him again in spite of her wishes. To Caroline's resentful fancy, he was like a corpse that refused to stay decently buried but went walking abroad with ghastly form and tattered cerements for all the world to see.

It was all very well to say Robert was nothing to her now. The unhappy fact was that he *was* something. He was the man she had once loved and thought to marry, and that made him something very particular indeed. *Something particularly humiliating,* reflected Caroline ruefully. She could not help writhing when she recalled how completely Robert had betrayed her. But it was not so much the thought of his betrayal as her own blindness that made her writhe. There had been plenty of clues if she had had the wit to look for them. She had behaved like a fool, and now she was being punished for it.

Caroline could acknowledge that punishment in these circumstances was no more than just. But it seemed a little hard that her punishment must be such a public one. Assuming Robert was in the pump room that morning—as she felt in her bones he would be—he was bound to speak to her. Even if he contented himself with the briefest of greetings, people were sure to stare and whisper. And quite likely he would not be content with a brief greeting. His spending hours at Lady Katherine's house the previous day looked as though he had something to say—as though, in fact, he were intent on trying to patch things up with her. The thought was like a twisting of a knife in Caroline's midsection. She could not avoid seeing him, but she was one hundred percent resolved against taking him back.

Never again, she vowed. *I've behaved foolishly, but I've learned my lesson. I won't make such a mistake again anytime soon.*

In the meantime, she was stuck with the consequences of her folly. The hour immediately before her was likely to be a hard one. She had spoken of the pillory that evening she had danced with Raymond, but this morning was likely to be more like a session on the rack. Robert had, as she well knew, an instinct to self-dramatization coupled with a complete disregard for anyone's feelings but his own. If she refused to hear his entreaties, he might well cause a scene that would be discussed over the tea tables of Shelton-on-Sea for months to come. The little reputation she still possessed would be swept away, and likely Raymond would want nothing more to do with her.

Oddly enough, this second prospect was even more upsetting to Caroline than the first. She was more or less resigned to being the subject of tea-table gossip. It was not pleasant, but she had borne it for some weeks now and felt she could bear it for some weeks longer. The thought of losing Raymond's friendship, however, struck her in a peculiarly tender spot. She had not known him long, but she had admired him for years, and to have him seek her out and take her driving was an honor she had never expected. That his attentions were motivated by simple kindness made no difference. The great thing was that he had seemed to understand.

But it was one thing to understand a person and another to associate with her. Raymond had shown no scruples about associating with her thus far, but perhaps he simply did not realize what a controversial person she was. Caroline reflected gloomily that this morning's ordeal was likely to enlighten him in a hurry.

What was I thinking of? she demanded of herself. *I ought to have refused to let him come today. I might be obliged to meet Robert, but there's certainly no need to drag poor Mr. Jeffries into it.*

Her qualms on this score were not wholly on Raymond's account. Bad as it was to have to meet her former fiancé, the idea of meeting him under Raymond's eye made it somehow worse. She was sure that she would behave like a fool with the elegant Mr. Jeffries as audience. Not only that, but there was a certain quality about Raymond—an indefinable distinction—that was sure to throw all Robert's shortcomings into high relief. Caroline felt anyone of ordinary penetration ought to have been able to see through a charm so shallow. She could see through it now, at any rate, and the thought that she had been so easily gulled made her feel very low and foolish.

To counteract this sensation, she had chosen to wear her favorite hat, a French bonnet of white satin faced with tulle. At first she had thought of wearing a plain gown and severe bonnet so as to look as unapproachable as possible, but at the last minute she had changed to the other. *And why?* Caroline demanded of herself. She knew why, and the answer was all of a piece with her other folly. Important though it was to look unapproachable to Robert, it had seemed still more important to look pretty for Raymond. And that in spite of the fact that he was certain to wash his hands of her before the day was over!

Caroline, as she went up the steps of the pump room, felt it would be best for all concerned if Raymond were not present at all.

Still, she could not help being glad when, on passing through the doors, the first person she saw was Raymond. He smiled and bowed, and began making his way in her direction. Caroline felt an involuntary lifting of her spirits. He was such a handsome gentleman, but it was not merely his looks that distinguished him. From the top of his dark head to the soles of his polished boots, he was the picture of masculine elegance and refinement. She stood quite still, watching him as he came toward her through the crowd. And at that moment she was accosted by a familiar voice at her elbow.

"Caroline!" it said. "My dear Caroline, I have found you at last."

With the utmost unwillingness, Caroline turned to face the speaker. For a moment she had actually forgotten Robert might be in the pump room that day. It struck her with passing wonder that she could have forgotten such a circumstance, even for a moment. But she had no time for wonderment, for Robert had grasped her by the hand and was addressing her in an impassioned voice.

"Thank God you're here," he said. "I waited all day for you yesterday at Lady Katherine's, but she said you were out. It's good to see you again, Caroline. You're just the same as ever—pretty as a picture."

Caroline was dreadfully aware of elderly ladies around her straining to hear every word. She was equally aware of the pressure of Robert's hand on hers. Hastily she drew it away from him and made a frigid bow. "Mr. Cullen," she said.

Robert gave her a smile that was half amused and half reproachful. "'Mr. Cullen,'" he repeated. "And only a bow for greeting! You would think we were strangers, Caroline. I had thought you were more generous than that."

Caroline merely gave him a cool smile in return. She was feeling anything but cool, however. Her face felt aflame with shame and her body awash in a bath of perspiration. It was, beyond doubt, the most dreadful moment of her life. Here was Robert, grinning down at her, dozens of people gawking, Mrs. Cullen glaring, and somewhere out there Raymond was witnessing the whole thing.

Strangely, it was this last thought that galvanized Caroline into action. She had been staring at Robert as if she had been turned to stone, but now it occurred to her she had the power to cut the interview short. "Good day, Mr. Cullen," she said, and turned away with finality.

"Wait," he said, grasping her arm.

Caroline gave him such a look that he quickly let go of her arm. He continued addressing her, however, in a coaxing voice. "I must speak to you," he said. "If you will only listen to me, I am sure you will see that you have made a mistake. My phaeton is outside, and it's a beautiful day. Come with me, Caroline. We'll take a little drive along the coast, and I will explain everything."

"That's quite impossible," said Caroline

He smiled down at her, the easy, confident smile she had once found so irresistible. "Impossible for us to take a drive, or impossible for me to explain?" he said. "Come, Caroline, I think you owe me at least a chance to explain myself. It's not right I should be condemned without an opportunity to speak."

Put like that, his proposal sounded quite reasonable. But all Caroline's instincts rose against it. She spoke with desperate calmness. "I must go," she said. "I have another engagement."

Robert looked more amused than ever. "Surely not," he said. "You just got here." As Caroline was searching for a reply, he went on, his voice even more coaxing than before. "Come with me, just for a little while," he said. "Only give me a chance to explain, Caroline. This whole thing has been a misunderstanding from start to finish."

As before, he sounded eminently reasonable, while her own objections seemed both childish and irrational. Caroline had the horrible sense of her defenses crumbling away one by one. In desperation, she looked around for an ally. Lady Katherine had been detained coming in by Mr. Lindensmyth, who was holding her in lively conversation, and clearly there was no help to be expected from that quarter. But Raymond was near at hand now, barely ten feet away. Caroline recalled the words he had spoken to her at parting yesterday. They suggested a course of action, and before Caroline knew it, she spoke aloud.

"I'm afraid I cannot go driving with you, Mr. Cullen," she said. "I am already engaged to drive with Mr. Jeffries."

Robert's amusement changed to incredulity at these words. "I beg your pardon?" he said. "Did I understand you to say you are going driving with *Raymond Jeffries?*"

"Yes," said Caroline firmly. "I am."

As she spoke, Raymond came up to where they

stood. "Good day, Miss Sedgewick," he said pleasantly, and greeted Robert with a civil bow. Caroline hoped desperately Robert would go away at this point and say nothing more about their going driving, but these hopes were destined to disappointment. Instead, Robert turned toward Raymond and addressed him with an easy smile.

"Hullo, Jeffries," he said. "Caroline tells me you're taking her driving this morning."

There was challenge in his words, and an even bigger challenge in the look he threw Caroline. *See, I am calling your bluff,* his eyes said as plainly as possible. *Let us see if Mr. Jeffries will confirm your so-called engagement.*

His expression changed, however, when Raymond merely nodded imperturbably. "Yes, to be sure," he said. "I am fortunate enough to have that privilege." Smiling at Caroline, he added, "I am ready to leave whenever you are, Miss Sedgewick."

Ever since the previous afternoon, Caroline had been wondering how she could have been bold enough to kiss him. Now she understood, for she had an impulse to kiss him right then and there. Somehow she choked back the impulse, but there was a smile on her lips and a glow in her eyes as she looked up at him. "I am ready now, Mr. Jeffries," she said. "Just let me speak to Lady Katherine, and then we can be off."

Robert was looking at them both, his eyes narrow and his jaw set. Caroline gave him an offhand nod by way of farewell, accepted the arm Raymond gave her, and together they walked away.

As soon as they were out of earshot, she addressed him in an urgent voice. "Do forgive me, Mr. Jeffries," she said. "I don't really expect you to take me driving. It was only that Robert was being persistent, and I spoke the first excuse that came to mind."

"I understand," said Raymond. "But believe me, I am glad to be of service, Miss Sedgewick. I told you yesterday I would be happy to take you driving again, and I am pleased you took me at my word."

"But I cannot impose on you to that extent," said Caroline. "I should feel so ashamed! Indeed, I feel ashamed already when I think of yesterday."

"Do you?" said Raymond. "And here I had been fancying it was an enjoyable outing for us both."

He spoke so mournfully that Caroline could not keep from laughing. "You know I don't mean it that way, Mr. Jeffries!" she said. "It *was* a very enjoyable outing. But if I had not been so stupid, I could have turned Robert off today without bringing your name into it. As it is, I have embroiled you as well as myself."

Raymond shook his head. "It's of no consequence," he said. "I tell you again I'm happy to be of service. Can't you take me at my word, Miss Sedgewick? I'm as capable of hypocrisy as the next man, but on this occasion I happen to be speaking the truth."

There was that in his face and voice that made Caroline give way with a shy smile. "Very well," she said, "but I don't see how I am to ever thank you enough for your kindness."

He gave her a quick sideways look, seemed about to say something, then thought better of it. Caroline felt her cheeks go crimson. There was no reason to imagine he had been thinking about the kiss she had given him the day before, but that was what she had been thinking about, and she felt a strange inner certainty that their thoughts were coursing along the same path. When Raymond spoke, however, it was merely to beg her once again not to thank him, for he was happy to be of service. He then suggested she wait for him by the door while he went to explain their intentions to his aunt and Lady Katherine. Caroline hovered near the door, watching anxiously as he confronted first one lady and then the other. Lady Katherine said little but looked a great deal, and Miss Jeffries's face was similarly expressive, but neither lady apparently made any objection. In a matter of minutes Raymond had rejoined her beside the door, and they left the pump room together.

Eleven

Caroline drew a deep sigh as soon as she was seated in the curricle. Raymond said nothing but glanced at her as he whipped up his horses. In a few minutes, they had reached the outskirts of Shelton-on-Sea. After a minute's hesitation at the crossroads, he once again took the coast road that ran along the shore.

"I hope you don't mind," he told Caroline. "It was such an enjoyable drive yesterday that I wouldn't mind repeating it."

Caroline merely nodded. Raymond then observed the weather was a bit cooler than on the previous day, a remark that won him a similarly inaudible response. He was just about to essay a third remark about the hay looking nearly ready to harvest, when his ears caught a faint sniffle. Looking sharply at Caroline, he was dismayed to see tears running down her cheeks. "My dear Miss Sedgewick!" he said. "Is something wrong?"

Caroline sniffed again and shook her head. "Nothing," she said, "except that I am an idiot."

Raymond was too startled by this speech to immediately reply to it. Caroline dabbed at her face with a handkerchief, then made a weak effort to smile at him. "I am an idiot," she repeated. "It all comes home to me now. Why, oh, why did I not keep my wits about me in the pump room this morning?"

"What do you mean?" asked Raymond.

"I mean that when I was talking to Robert, I behaved like an unmitigated idiot. There were a hundred things I might have said, or I might have simply cut him altogether. But instead, I stood like a tailor's dummy when he invited me to go driving, and the only way I could find to escape was to drag you into it."

"I've already told you I don't mind being dragged into it," said Raymond. "After all, I did give you permission to use my name. And I would protest most strongly against your statement that you are an idiot. It seems to me you behaved with great presence of mind."

Caroline laughed harshly. "Hardly," she said. "If I had behaved with great presence of mind, I would have told Robert to go to the devil!"

She threw Raymond a defiant look as she spoke, evidently expecting him to be shocked by this strong language. But he merely nodded understandingly. "That would certainly have been one course of action," he said. "Still, I am not surprised you did not take it, Miss Sedgewick. I don't feel, myself, that there is anything inherently wrong in answering impertinence for impertinence, but in the heat of the moment I can quite understand it would not come naturally to a lady like you."

Caroline's response was to burst into tears once more.

Raymond was so concerned, he immediately drew his horses to a halt regardless of the fact that there was a post chaise with four horses approaching rapidly from the rear. The driver went around him with a shouted imprecation and only inches to spare, and Caroline laughed shakily. Raymond regarded her with approval. "That's better," he said. "I hope I did not say anything to upset you, Miss Sedgewick. Nothing could have been further from my intentions."

Caroline ceased laughing and turned on him a pair of tear-drenched green eyes. "No, you did not upset me," she said. "It is only that you do me too much credit, Mr. Jeffries. It was not ladylike reticence but simple idiocy that prevented me from speaking to Robert as he deserved."

"Well, we won't argue about that," said Raymond. "It's my opinion that if a lady isn't in the habit of telling people to go to the devil, the words aren't likely to be on the tip of her tongue even when they're justified. But whatever you might or might not have said to Mr. Cullen, you cannot argue that the matter is not settled nicely just as it is. You have met him and withstood his advances, and if he chooses to persevere, I have no doubt you will find it far easier to refuse him next time around."

Caroline gave him an unhappy look. "But what if I don't find it easier?" she said in a low voice. "I can hardly call on you every time I find myself at a loss, Mr. Jeffries. It's that which makes me feel worst of all. I knew I would likely meet Robert today, and yet when he spoke to me, it was as though all my presence of mind evaporated."

These words made Raymond feel a little odd. Against his will, he was reminded of his aunt's assertion that Caroline might still care for Robert and be willing to take him back. He did not want to believe this, but the fact that Cullen's presence unnerved her so seemed to argue that she still harbored feelings for him. "Indeed," he said in a voice he strove to make matter-of-fact. "Well, I don't know that that is so out of the ordinary. It's customary to feel a little awkward when one encounters someone whom—well, someone whom one once cared for."

He glanced at Caroline as he spoke, hoping she might contradict this statement. But she only said dully, "I suppose so. Only it is so awkward and unpleasant. Why did Robert have to come to Shelton-on-Sea? I was doing well enough before he arrived."

"Perhaps he won't stay long," suggested Raymond. He watched like a hawk to see if this idea appeared welcome to Caroline. But she just shook her head.

"I don't know that it matters," she said. "The damage is done now, and there's nothing I can do about it."

Raymond wondered whether this meant she was contemplating taking Robert back. The idea made him feel so savage that he sent the horses forward with a jerk that came near to unseating both Caroline and himself. When they were both in their seats again, and the horses cantering smoothly along, he turned to look at her again. She returned his look briefly, then looked away. "Please don't," she said.

Raymond thought she was referring to his driving. "I beg your pardon," he said penitently. "My cattle are rather fresh, and I was a bit abrupt just now in whipping them up. I'll try not to let it happen again."

Caroline gave him a look of surprise. "Oh, but I didn't mean—" she began, then bit her lip.

Raymond saw she had not been referring to his

driving after all. He looked at her curiously. Under his regard she flushed and turned her face away. "Please don't," she said again. "Please don't look at me. I look such a fright when I've been crying!"

Raymond felt an abrupt lifting of his spirits. If Caroline could be concerned about her appearance at such a time, it seemed to argue that her feelings for Robert Cullen were not so overpowering as he had feared. In fact, it seemed to argue a number of things favorable to his cause. Raymond did not analyze the matter in any great depth, but he immediately felt more cheerful, and he could not help throwing a glance at Caroline despite her injunction not to look at her. The injunction was needless in any case, for he could see nothing wrong with her appearance. Her nose and cheeks were a trifle red, and so were her eyes, but the eyes themselves were so deep and green that this was hardly a disfigurement in his book. The face was still Caroline's, red nose or no.

"You do *not* look a fright," he said firmly.

Caroline laughed weakly and said he must be experiencing a touch of sunstroke. Her tone was gratified all the same, however. Raymond promptly pursued his advantage, saying he admired her toilette and congratulating her upon her taste in bonnets. This led into a discussion of bonnets in general, with a digression into caps and hats. Soon they were chatting away as companionably as on the previous day. Caroline insisted on their turning back after they had driven only an hour, however. "It will take us at least another hour to return, and that is quite long enough to impose upon your good nature, Mr. Jeffries. I cannot accept any more favor from you than that today."

Raymond accepted this edict without demur, although he was secretly disappointed. When they had retraced their steps, however, and were standing in front of Lady Katherine's house, Caroline electrified him by leaning over and kissing him on the cheek once more. "Thank you, Mr. Jeffries," she said, and hurried into the house.

Neither of them observed the elderly lady standing goggle-eyed across the street.

It was Miss Emily Renquist, the lady whose balcony had so often served as a vantage point for surveillance of the bathing machines and esplanade. It was sheer luck that had taken her by Lady Katherine's house that afternoon—luck, together with a faint hope she might find one of Lady Katherine's servants about and pick up some scrap of news about Caroline. Being a friend of Mrs. Cullen's as well as an inveterate gossip, she considered it her duty to keep abreast of all Caroline's activities insofar as possible. Naturally this particular activity was too exciting to be kept to herself. She flew down the hill in spite of her game leg, and before many minutes had passed, she was seated in Mrs. Cullen's drawing room, pouring her story into that lady's affronted ears.

Raymond, meanwhile, was serenely unaware of what was going on a few blocks away. He had returned to his aunt's home practically floating on air. Miss Jeffries had looked him up and down grimly as he came into the parlor but said nothing beyond, "What, back so soon? When you said you were going driving again with Miss Sedgewick, I expected you'd be as late as you were yesterday."

"No, we drove for only a couple of hours," said Raymond cheerfully. "I wouldn't have minded going farther, but Miss Sedgewick felt it was time we were getting back."

His aunt looked skeptical but let his words pass without comment. Instead, she observed that it had been a pleasant day for a drive.

"Very pleasant," agreed Raymond. "Quite perfect, in fact." It occurred to him belatedly that his aunt might enjoy some share of the day's perfection, and he immediately suggested he take the curricle out again with her as a passenger. "My horses will soon be rested, and I should very much enjoy showing you the view from the cliffs," he told her.

His aunt refused this invitation, but her voice was somewhat mollified as she did so. "Personally, I prefer walking to driving," she said. "Perhaps we can walk down to the esplanade after dinner if you have no other engagement."

Raymond hurriedly disclaimed any other engagement. Still, he found himself wondering whether Caroline, too, might be on the esplanade that evening. He could not help hoping she might be. *I would like to introduce her to Aunt Bel,* he told himself. *It's clear Auntie still thinks Caroline an adventuress. If only she would meet her and talk to her, she would soon see she's nothing of the kind.*

Accordingly, he set out for the esplanade that evening in a mood of high hope. It was a lovely evening, and there were a number of people on the esplanade strolling about or gathered in groups to talk. Raymond noticed a number of them looking at him very hard but attributed this to his status as a newcomer. Caroline, to his disappointment, was not there, but he took his disappointment philosophically, telling himself he could hardly hope to have the luck of seeing her twice in one day. All in all, he was quite content to stroll arm in arm with his aunt, thinking of the day just past and looking forward to the morrow.

He looked forward to it even more when, on returning home, he found a note from Lady Katherine, inviting him to a picnic party.

"She includes me in the invitation too, I see," said his aunt, reading the note over his shoulder. "Mighty civil of Lady Katherine when we scarcely know each other to nod to. Of course I won't go, but it was a kind thought."

Raymond looked up quickly. "You won't go?" he repeated. "But why not, Aunt? You haven't anything else planned for tomorrow, have you?"

"No, but I abominate picnic parties," said his aunt. She surveyed him quizzically. "And I rather thought you abominated them too, Raymond. So you told me, at least, when you attended Mrs. Henry's house party last year."

Raymond flushed. "Oh, that! But that was totally different. Mrs. Henry's picnic involved a twelve-mile ride on a blazing August day, and there wasn't a breath of air stirring the whole time. But Lady Katherine's party is to take place on the shore only a few miles away, and we are taking carriages to get there. It's sure to be pleasantly breezy this close to the sea."

"Aye, and pleasantly dirty too," said his aunt dryly. "I'd as lief take my meals in the dining room, thank you. The last time I went to a shore picnic, the patties had more of sand than salmon about them."

"So you don't intend to come?" said Raymond. He could not keep the disappointment out of his voice, and his aunt looked at him in surprise.

"Don't tell me you really want me to come, Raymond?" she said. "I can't see how my going would affect your plans one way or another. Just because I stop at home doesn't mean you must do so."

"I know that, Aunt. And of course you are free to choose your own engagements. But I had hoped that if you went, I might introduce Miss Sedgewick to you. I would like you to know each other."

His aunt regarded him for a moment in silence. "Indeed," she said.

"She is a very nice girl," continued Raymond, trying not to look as self-conscious as he felt. "You must not believe all the gossip you hear about her, Aunt. The more I come to know her, the more clear it becomes that she has been slandered by people who have not understood her or her situation."

"And you do?" queried his aunt as he paused.

"No, not completely," admitted Raymond. "She has not spoken at all of her first two—er—attachments. But she has told me enough about her dealings with Robert Cullen to convince me she was quite blameless in that affair."

Miss Jeffries nodded slowly. "It sounds as though she was justified in jilting him," she said. "But I should like to know the circumstances of her other engagements before I absolved her of all blame."

Raymond said firmly that he was sure there must have been extenuating circumstances. "Miss Sedgewick is not the sort of girl to make a commitment of that kind, then break it for no reason. I am sure of it."

"I can see you are," said Miss Jeffries dryly. "But it wouldn't hurt to find out for certain. Why don't you ask Miss Sedgewick what her reasons were? That would be the sensible way to go about it, rather than relying upon what appears to me nothing more than wishful thinking."

Raymond flushed. "We are hardly on such terms as that," he said. "I would not feel comfortable asking Miss Sedgewick such a personal question."

"Well, when you are upon such terms, ask her. Then, if the answer is favorable, I'll be glad to be introduced to her."

With this concession Raymond had to be content. He was glad to see his aunt willing to relent even slightly toward Caroline, even if she were not willing to take her on faith as he was. He sent a note to Lady Katherine accepting her invitation, and settled down to wait as patiently as he could for the morrow to arrive.

Twelve

Caroline, upon learning of Lady Katherine's picnic party, was both pleased and dismayed.

"You invited Raymond Jeffries?" she said. "To a *picnic* party?"

"Yes, I did, darling. I don't see why you need sound so dismayed. It will be a very exclusive party—just a dozen of us, and all done in the first style."

"I don't doubt it," said Caroline. "But I'll bet my best bonnet Mr. Jeffries won't come."

Lady Katherine smiled. "If I were a less principled woman, I'd take your bet, Caro darling," she said. "And I'd win too. For he has already accepted, though he writes his aunt cannot come."

Caroline was silent, digesting this information. She could not help being happy that Raymond was to be of the party. There was no longer any point in denying she was attracted to him, and improbable as it seemed, the attraction appeared to be mutual. But the fact that his aunt refused to attend the party gave her pause. She knew how she was regarded among the elderly ladies of Shelton-on-Sea. It was too much to hope that Miss Jeffries did not partake of the general opinion.

The idea that Raymond's family disapproved of her sobered Caroline and tended to mitigate against the happiness she felt at the prospect of his attending the party.

"So Miss Jeffries is not going," she said. "I don't know that I ought to go myself."

Lady Katherine looked at her sternly. "You'll come if I have to carry you," she said. "Show a little sense, Caro dear. I am quite certain Mr. Jeffries is coming only because he thinks you will be there. If you aren't, he will feel most dreadfully taken in."

Caroline could not help laughing at this, though she shook her head. "I am sure you exaggerate, Kate," she said. "He has probably had enough of me, after the way I have abused his good nature this week."

Lady Katherine advised her not to talk nonsense. "Just hurry up and get dressed, there's a good girl. I've had Hannah lay out your new flowered muslin and green spencer. You look a dream in that, and it's a perfect costume for a picnic."

By ten o'clock the picnic party was assembled. Raymond had been among the first guests to arrive, and by adroit management Lady Katherine had seen to it that he and Caroline were placed in the same carriage. This circumstance both pleased and embarrassed Caroline. She feared he and everyone else might think the arrangement had been her own scheme rather than Lady Katherine's. Yet she would have felt dreadfully disappointed if he had been seated in another carriage. Why should it be so wrong to follow one's inclinations? Caroline found herself musing on this question as she rode to the picnic site with Raymond and the other two occupants of the carriage, a stout colonel of the army and his middle-aged wife.

There were, as Lady Katherine had promised,

only a dozen in the party in all. The colonel and his lady, Caroline, Raymond, Lady Katherine, and Mr. Baddington comprised half of the party; the other half included a pair of maiden ladies no longer in their first youth, Miss Vivian Tallbridge and Miss Rachel Tallbridge; Mrs. Westmoreland, a vivacious matron of elegant appearance and her equally elegant but less talkative husband; and a couple of bachelor gentlemen, Mr. Phipps and Mr. Blondin.

Upon reaching the picnic spot, the servants began spreading the cloth and laying the table, while the party walked about, inspected the view from the cliffs, and conversed among themselves. Caroline perceived almost at once that the Misses Tallbridge were hostile to her. Previous to then they had always been civil enough—Lady Katherine would hardly have invited them to the party if they had been otherwise—but today they showed definite signs of spite. Miss Rachel, especially, made a point of addressing small remarks to her that were evidently meant to sting.

"Oh, Miss Sedgewick, I beg you won't monopolize Mr. Jeffries like that," she called as Caroline and Raymond paused to inspect some small flowers sprinkled among the rocks. "It's not fair you should keep *all* the men to yourself."

Caroline merely smiled, but she felt the barb of Miss Rachel's words quite as much as that lady meant her to. And when the meal was laid, and the party sat down to eat, Miss Rachel continued to address to her a series of needling remarks disguised as teasing.

"Miss Sedgewick, I beg you will try some of this pullet. See that Mr. Jeffries gets some too. He seems content to feast upon your *beaux yeux* at present, but I am sure he will feel hungry later on if he does not partake of some more *substantial* nourishment."

Caroline flushed at these words, and Raymond threw Miss Rachel a surprised look. "I beg your pardon?" he said. "I didn't quite hear what you said, Miss Rachel."

The words were an unmistakable set-down, and it was now Miss Rachel's turn to flush. She was not silenced for long, however. "I was only saying that you must eat something and not let Miss Sedgewick distract too much of your attention," she told him. "I am sure it is no wonder if you are distracted, for she looks charming today, but it would be a shame to let the delicious luncheon Lady Katherine has provided go to waste."

She smiled fawningly at Lady Katherine as she spoke—a smile that was clearly wasted, for Lady Katherine was regarding her with disapproval. This depressed her no more than Raymond's snub, however, for presently she burst forth in a different vein.

"You have a most elegant carriage, Mr. Jeffries," she said. "I saw it the day before yesterday, when you were driving down the High Street."

Raymond thanked her politely for the compliment. Caroline, for her part, felt sure it was only the prelude to some further impertinence, and she was right, for Miss Rachel's next statement was of a more pointed nature. "There was a lady with you—it looked to me like Miss Sedgewick here. Was it? Ah, indeed!" She turned a false bright smile on Caroline. "You are very much privileged, Miss Sedgewick. All our belles have been endeavoring by hook and by crook to get a ride in Mr. Jeffries's curricle, but it seems you have triumphed over them all."

"The triumph was rather mine in having secured

Miss Sedgewick's company," put in Raymond swiftly. "And I assure you that I am fully cognizant of my good fortune."

Miss Rachel's smile took on a spiteful tinge. "Are you indeed? Then it's a triumph you have enjoyed at least twice, by all accounts. For a little bird told me you took Miss Sedgewick driving yesterday also, and that you appeared to be on most excellent terms."

"Well, and what if they were?" broke in Lady Katherine, who had been listening to this speech with growing disfavor. "What a fuss you are making about nothing, Rachel. What does it matter how many times Mr. Jeffries and Miss Sedgewick go driving?"

Miss Rachel did not exactly toss her head, but there was a suggestion of bridling in her manner as she responded to this question. "My dear Lady Katherine, I am sure it does not matter in the least. I only thought it was *interesting*. Mr. Jeffries is so lately come to town that naturally we all take note of his actions."

For a time after this she behaved herself, but when the dessert was laid on the cloth, she broke into a fresh access of impertinence. Mr. Blondin had offered to help Caroline to an almond tart, and this circumstance was evidently more than Miss Rachel could bear. "Only see how chivalrous he is! I do believe Miss Sedgewick has made *another* conquest. I wish you would tell me your secret, Miss Sedgewick. I am sure I would enjoy receiving as much *masculine attention* as you do."

A dreadful pause followed this speech. "Thank you, but I have no secret," said Caroline at last. "You had much better ask Lady Katherine her secret.

She has made such a conquest of Mr. Lindensmyth that he consented to have a cotillion at the last assembly, when he has allowed nothing but country dances for years. And I notice when Dr. Lodge's curate is in the pulpit, he preaches directly at our pew in the most passionate manner."

"And a right demmed nuisance it is too," added Mr. Baddington, putting in his laconic two pence. "Makes it dev'lish hard for a fellow to sleep through the sermon, what?"

This evoked a general laugh, and the tension was relieved for a time. Caroline, however, was still furious at Miss Rachel's remarks. Making the excuse that her legs were cramped with sitting, she got up and made her way down the cliffs to the shore. She had not gone a hundred feet before she heard footsteps behind her. Turning, she saw Raymond following along the path behind her.

"My legs were growing cramped too," he explained. "I hope you don't mind if I join you?"

"I wouldn't under other circumstances," said Caroline. "But on this occasion, I think it would be better if you took your walk in another direction, Mr. Jeffries. Otherwise, Miss Rachel will have but one more reason to accuse me of monopolizing your company."

With eloquence and concision, Raymond consigned Miss Rachel to perdition. "That's all very well," said Caroline. "But until she finally arrives there, we must suffer her here. And I tell you frankly, I can't endure any more of her jibes today. I wonder what I did to offend her? She has always been perfectly civil before today."

There was a plaintive note in her voice that made Raymond long to take her in his arms. "Jealousy accounts for it, no doubt," he said. "That speech about wishing she enjoyed as much masculine attention as you shows it plainly enough."

"But that's nonsense," said Caroline. "Why should she be jealous? If I looked like Lady Katherine, there might be some reason for it, but she has no reason to envy me as it is. It's true you have taken me riding a couple of times, but that was mere kindness on your part."

Raymond was just getting ready to refute this statement, when they rounded a cluster of rocks on the shore and found themselves face-to-face with Robert Cullen.

Robert did not appear as surprised by this encounter as they were. Frowning, he looked from one to the other of them. "So," he said, and laughed harshly.

"So," agreed Raymond with a bland smile. "Taking some exercise, Cullen?"

Robert returned his smile with a look of hostility. "No," he said. "I was looking for Caroline." Addressing Caroline directly, he added, "Caroline, I must talk to you. Come away with me a moment, won't you?"

"No," said Caroline.

Raymond observed with gratification that she had tightened her grip on his arm as she spoke. "I am engaged at present, as you see," she went on. "I trust you will excuse me."

Unfortunately, Robert misunderstood these words. "Engaged!" he exclaimed, and took a hasty step forward. "The devil you are! You don't mean to say you're engaged to Jeffries?"

Caroline's face was crimson, but she managed to speak calmly. "No, you misunderstand me, Mr.

Cullen. I merely meant I am engaged to *walk* with Mr. Jeffries."

Robert's face lightened somewhat at these words. "Thank heaven for that!" he said. "It gave me quite a turn when you said—but never mind."

Caroline spoke quickly to avoid further embarrassment. "I think it is time we were returning to the picnic," she said. "Mr. Cullen, I give you a good day."

She gave him a slight bow. Raymond, quick to follow her cue, bowed in turn and wished Robert a good day. Robert, however, was having none of it.

"Don't be ridiculous, Caroline," he said. "I've walked all the way from Shelton-on-Sea just to see you. Surely you can spare me a quarter of an hour."

"No," said Caroline. "I can't."

This uncompromising reply seemed to take Robert aback. He went on after a moment, however, with a coaxing smile. "Come, Caroline, don't be unkind," he said. "Fifteen minutes is all I ask. Mr. Jeffries will surely excuse you that long. Won't you, Jeffries?" he said, turning to address Raymond with a hint of steel in his voice.

Raymond met his gaze with an equable smile. "I will gladly excuse myself, Cullen," he said. "But only if Miss Sedgewick wants me to. And if you will forgive me for saying so, I don't think she does want me to."

"I don't!" said Caroline quickly. "I don't at all. Please take me back to the picnic, Mr. Jeffries."

Before Raymond could act on these instructions, however, Robert had placed himself squarely in their path. He spoke with barely restrained temper.

"This has gone far enough," he said. "I'm a patient man, but I'm demmed if I can take any more of this nonsense. Caroline, you can't refuse to hear me forever. I know you still care about me, and I care about you too. As far as I'm concerned, you're still my betrothed wife. I'm not about to let you slip away just because of a silly misunderstanding about an opera dancer."

Caroline took a deep breath. "Robert," she said, "the only misunderstanding between you and me is your refusal to believe I mean what I say. I'll admit you had reason to think me a credulous fool up till three weeks ago, but since then I have come to my senses. I'm not planning to leave them again any time soon."

Robert gazed at her open mouthed, clearly unable to believe his ears. Caroline went on with a hint of acerbity. "Whether you accept it or not, I am *not* your betrothed wife," she said. "And I never will be again. I'll thank you to go away now and let me alone."

"You don't mean it—" began Robert.

"I do mean it!" said Caroline.

He shook his head. "Caroline, you can't," he said. "You can't throw me over so easily, and on no better evidence than hearsay."

"It wasn't hearsay," said Caroline. "I saw you kissing Signorina Verlucci with my own eyes."

This had the effect of silencing Robert once again. Raymond took advantage of the moment to seize Caroline's arm and start leading her back toward the picnic party. But they had not gone far when Robert caught up to them. He addressed Caroline in a contrite voice. "Perhaps I did kiss her," he said. "But if I did, I assure you it meant nothing, Caroline. A man must sow his wild oats, y'know. Once we're married, it will all be different, I promise. I won't even so much as look at another woman."

"That's a promise you may safely make," retorted Caroline. "Because we never will be married, Robert. Can't you understand I mean what I say?"

"I understand that someone's been poisoning your mind against me. And I'll wager I know who it is too." Robert looked unpleasantly at Raymond. "Profiting by my misfortune, are you, Jeffries? I heard rumors, but I didn't choose to credit them until now."

"Robert," said Caroline in ringing tones, "you are a fool. The only person who has poisoned me against you is you yourself."

Robert disregarded this speech. "Don't think I'll stand for trespassing," he told Raymond. "You heard what I said before. As far as I am concerned, Caroline—Miss Sedgewick—is still my betrothed wife. I'll thank you not to forget it."

"Yet you expect her to forget about your kissing Signorina Verlucci," returned Raymond equably. "Seems to me you're a trifle unreasonable in your expectations, Cullen."

At this, Robert took a wild swing at him. Raymond ducked, then countered with a punch that struck Robert squarely in the jaw. The force sent him reeling, and in the course of his backward egress he tripped on a piece of driftwood and went down heavily into the surf. He scrambled up quickly, however, and stood for a moment with his clothes dripping and chest heaving. Then he made for Raymond with murder in his eye.

Raymond, however, spoke in peremptory tones. "That's enough, Cullen," he said. "I know better than to brawl in front of a lady, if you don't. If you insist on having satisfaction, I will be glad to give it to you, whenever and wherever you like."

"No!" cried Caroline.

Robert ignored her. "You're damned right I want satisfaction," he said, breathing heavily through his nose. "And I'll have it too. Name your friends, Jeffries. I'll meet you as soon as you please."

Raymond was at least as angry as he was, but not so angry as to forget all discretion. Dueling inevitably meant scandal, and it was vital such a scandal not be allowed to touch Caroline. Undoubtedly the picnic party on the cliffs above must have witnessed Robert and him exchanging blows. This was unfortunate, but Raymond reckoned the best might be made of a bad situation by keeping the whole business within the party. Therefore, he suggested that Mr. Phipps might stand for him, and Mr. Blondin for Robert. Since Mr. Blondin was a friend of Robert's, he readily assented to this suggestion, and so the matter was arranged. Caroline, meanwhile, was regarding them both with disbelief.

"You cannot mean to fight a duel over such a silly thing!" she said. "It's ridiculous—nonsensical."

Neither man made any reply, being still intent on discussing the dueling arrangements. When it had been finally agreed that the seconds would meet on the following day to settle the details of the arrangements, Robert gave Caroline a low bow and headed back down the beach, squelching audibly at every step.

As soon as he was gone, Caroline turned to Raymond.

"Mr. Jeffries, you cannot meet him," she said. "You must not!"

"I'm afraid I must," said Raymond gently. Striving for a light tone, he added, "But I can give you good odds if he chooses pistols. I'm accounted a fair shot, while he is middling at best."

Caroline managed a faint smile, but she was very pale beneath the frills of her bonnet. "You must not," she repeated. "If you were to get hurt, it would be all my fault!"

Her words gave Raymond an unpleasant twinge. The idea that he might be injured was not an agreeable one, but it was a consolation to see Caroline was concerned with his safety. "I don't see that it's your fault at all," he said. "It's Cullen's fault: Cullen's and mine. For I did provoke him, though he undoubtedly asked for it."

"Yes, he was very obnoxious. But still it's not worth getting injured for. Or, God forbid, killed." There was a quaver in Caroline's voice as she went on speaking. "Mr. Jeffries, there must be some other way. Cannot you call the duel off?"

As gently as possible, Raymond tried to explain why this was impossible. "My dear, I cannot refuse to give satisfaction when it is demanded of me," he said. "Surely you can understand that?"

Caroline did seem to understand, for she said no more about calling off the duel. But her voice was vexed as she began to speak once more of Robert's behavior.

"I don't see why he should demand satisfaction of you. He should be angry with me if he's angry with anyone."

"I think it's as much a matter of embarrassment as anger," said Raymond. "Initially he was embarrassed to have me witness your rejection. And then I went on to embarrass him further by making him fall down. I expect that was as big a grievance as your refusing him."

Caroline meditated on this for a moment or two. "Well, but he tried to hit you first," she said. "And though you hit him back, you did not really knock him down. It was an accident that he slipped and fell in the water."

"Yes, but I'll wager he still considers it my fault. And I would imagine my previous behavior still rankles as well. I whisked you away under his nose yesterday, if you remember, and compelled him to drink the waters the day before that. Indeed, if you count today, that's the second dose of waters he's taken at my behest!"

Caroline laughed hysterically. "True," she said. "Oh, dear! I can't help laughing, but how I wish this had never happened. It's my fault—my fault—all my fault."

Raymond wished to contradict this statement, but by this time they were within earshot of the picnic party, and he judged it best to say nothing more on the subject. He did, however, pat her arm in a comforting way.

Caroline appeared to be comforted. At any rate, her face was composed as she went over and resumed her place beside Lady Katherine. Lady Katherine greeted her and Raymond in her usual friendly manner, but her face was frankly curious as she surveyed them both. There was curiosity in the faces of the others as well, and a certain amount of constraint in the atmosphere. Raymond was sure all of them had witnessed the scene on the beach. Nobody was crass enough to allude to it, however, not even Miss Rachel, and after a while the atmosphere relaxed again, with Lady Katherine pressing another round of food and drink on her guests and a gay flirtation taking place between Mrs. Westmoreland and Mr. Blondin.

Although the other guests soon recovered their spirits, Caroline was noticeably quiet for the rest of the afternoon. Raymond, too, found himself disinclined to talk. He did find pretext, later on, to draw Mr. Phipps aside and explain what had arisen. He found Mr. Phipps very understanding and quite willing to act as his second.

"Couldn't hear what all went on, but I saw it plain enough," he explained. "So did all of us, unfortunately. The Tallbridge harpy's eyes looked like they were ready to burst out of the sockets. Still, she won't be able to make much of it by itself, and we'll take care to keep the whole business of the duel under wraps. I'll be happy to stand your second, and I'm sure Blondin will do the same by Cullen. Between us, we ought to be able to keep Miss Sedgewick's name out of it. A nice gel, Miss Sedgewick. Pity she has to be involved in this business."

Raymond agreed it was a pity and found himself quite in charity with his second. By the time they parted, they were on their way to becoming fast friends, and it had been settled that Mr. Phipps would call on Mr. Blondin the next day and make arrangements for a meeting between the two principals.

Thirteen

Raymond did not sleep particularly well that night.

He had a great many things on his mind. One of them was Robert Cullen. Over and over, he assured himself that he had been justified in hitting Cullen that afternoon. He also assured himself he was bound to offer satisfaction for the blow if Cullen insisted on it. Yet strangely enough, he could not seem to satisfy himself on either of these scores. Doubts kept creeping in, tormenting him with the question of whether he could or should have acted differently.

Perhaps he should have refrained from speaking to Cullen, contenting himself with removing Caroline from the vicinity as soon as he could. Or if he could not do that, he might at least have refrained from making that last jeer about Cullen's relations with Signorina Verlucci. That had seemed to be the jab that goaded him into violence. Yet it was nothing like as offensive as some of the things Cullen had said to him. In any case, as Raymond assured himself, the words had been spoken now, and it was impossible to unsay them.

Still, the idea that he ought to have managed the business differently continued to haunt Raymond. So did the idea that he was engaged to fight a duel. He had never been involved in an affair of honor before, as it happened. Dueling was going out of fashion, and although one still heard of gentlemen meeting on Doctor's Commons or Hampstead Heath to settle their differences, such meetings were growing increasingly rare. It was no wonder, either, for the law dealt severely with duelists. Only the previous year, a gentleman Raymond knew had to flee the country because he had wounded his opponent in an affair of honor. He had been forced to remain abroad for several months, until it became certain that his victim would eventually recover.

Raymond did not like to think of having to leave the country because he had killed or wounded Cullen. Still less did he like the idea of being killed or wounded himself. And yet it was entirely possible—far more possible, indeed, than the likelihood of his wounding Cullen. He had already made up his mind that if pistols were the weapon, he would fire into the air and harmlessly discharge his debt that way. But there was no assurance Cullen would do the same. He might, on the contrary, try to do all the damage he could. And though Raymond knew him to be an average marksman, even an average marksman might hit the bull's-eye on occasion.

This reflection would have been enough to trouble Raymond's sleep even by itself. But there were other reflections that troubled him more. Those reflections had to do with Caroline. She had scarcely spoken to him following the incident on the beach. It was true she had given him her hand at parting and even attempted to smile, but he felt gloomily certain she was angry with him.

With contrition, Raymond acknowledged she

had reason to be angry. By following her to the beach and exchanging words with Cullen, he had plunged her into what might be a very ugly scandal. Certainly if he or Cullen were injured or killed, Caroline would be blamed for it. Her past connection to Cullen was well known, and enough people knew of his own recent attentions toward her to piece the story together.

"Besides, that cat of a Rachel Tallbridge saw Cullen and me brawling on the sands," Raymond told himself gloomily. "She'd see the word got around, even if nobody else did."

This brought him back around to his starting point, the idea that he had been remiss in his actions. Somehow or other, he ought to have found a way to protect Caroline while also protecting her good name. He ought to have been as wise as a serpent and as gentle as a dove instead of plunging in like a hotheaded fool and making a mess of the situation. Now here he was, alienated from Caroline, embroiled in an affair of honor, and dreading the morrow, when he would learn what form his fate would take.

Mr. Phipps brought word of that fate bright and early, while Raymond was still at breakfast. He happily accepted Raymond's offer of coffee, ham, and eggs, and consumed such a quantity of them that Raymond found himself resenting this display of insensible cheer. He was cheerful, too, as he described the agreement he and Mr. Blondin had hammered out regarding the duel.

"It's all arranged. We're to meet at dawn tomorrow on the sands beyond the men's bathing beach," he told Raymond. "There shouldn't be anybody about at that hour, and if there's a little fog hanging over the water, as there often is, it will help screen us from view of the town."

Raymond, thinking of Emily Renquist and her spyglass, agreed that a little fog would be no bad thing. With as much cheer as he could manage, he thanked Mr. Phipps for his efforts. Mr. Phipps disclaimed his thanks and bowed himself off, having agreed to pick up Raymond shortly before dawn the next morning so they might travel together to the meeting spot. The door closed behind him, and Raymond was left to his own thoughts.

He was not left to them for long, however. Mr. Phipps had scarcely been gone five minutes when Miss Jeffries entered the breakfast parlor.

"Good morning, Raymond," she said cheerily.

Raymond, as he returned her greeting, wondered why everyone insisted on calling it a good morning. To him, it was as disagreeable a morning as he had ever lived through, and tomorrow looked even worse. But he did his best to appear in his usual spirits while his aunt ate her breakfast. He even agreed when she proposed a visit to the pump room. He had no wish to go to the pump room, or anywhere else for that matter, but the hours between that morning and the next had to be gotten through somehow, and he reckoned the pump room was as good a place to pass them as any. Besides, he reflected this might be the last day he ever spent with his aunt. It was only right he should indulge her wishes so she would have some pleasant memories to console her when he was gone.

In this humor, he escorted his aunt to the pump room, where he succeeded in finding a certain amount of diversion. Not all of it was strictly enjoyable diversion, to be sure. Mrs. Cullen was there, and so was her son, but Raymond had been prepared for this eventuality. He nodded coldly to Cullen, and Cullen nodded coldly back, after which greeting they took care to keep as much distance between them as possible. Raymond observed that Cullen appeared much as usual, although rather pale. Mrs. Cullen, who came over to talk to him later, while he was securing a cup of tea for his aunt at the counter, reinforced this impression.

"I'm worried about Robert," she told him. "This last day or two, I had fancied I had seen an improvement in his health, but this morning he could eat no breakfast at all, and he looks very sickly. I'm going to get him a glass of seawater. If anything can save him, seawater can, I am firmly convinced."

"I have no doubt you are right, ma'am," said Raymond with perfect solemnity. "If I were you, I would certainly see that Mr. Cullen took seawater on a regular basis. He ought not be allowed to neglect his health at any price."

Miss Jeffries, who was standing nearby, also gave assent to this proposition, albeit with a quizzical look at Raymond. After Mrs. Cullen had gone, she addressed him directly.

"It appears to me Robert Cullen's not the only one who's looking sickly this morning," she said. "You don't look as though you slept at all last night, Raymond. Is my guest chamber uncomfortable, or did you take cold at the picnic yesterday?"

Raymond protested against both these ideas, saying her guest chamber was exquisitely comfortable and he was sure he had taken no cold at the picnic. "That may be, but you look hangdog enough this morning," retorted his aunt. "I'm beginning to think a dose of seawater might not do you any harm either!"

Raymond, forcing a laugh, said he would take the waters later on at the bathing beach. He did go bathing later that day, but it was not so pleasant an experience as it had been before. The sky was overcast, for one thing, and the wind rather chill, and the attendant in a surly humor. Altogether, the rapture of his first experience was lacking. Raymond, as he made his way back to his aunt's house afterward, felt it had been a dismal way to spend what might be his last day on earth.

He must have looked as gloomy as he felt, for upon entering the drawing room his aunt took one look at him and shook her head.

"You still look down in the mouth, Raymond. Are you certain you're not taking cold?"

Raymond reassured her as best he could. He felt guilty in so doing, for it was possible she would be mourning over his lifeless body in less than twenty-four hours. It seemed unfair she should have no warning of it. "Perhaps I feel a little seedy," he said cautiously. "But nothing to signify."

"So you say, Raymond. But I've never known you to be so silent and stupid before. It seems to me you must be sickening for something. Perhaps you ought to stay home tonight rather than go with me to Fanny Mueller's. She would excuse you, I'm sure, and it doesn't look the nicest evening to venture out, especially for a person who is already feeling seedy. The barometer is falling, and it looks like rain."

Raymond was thankful to close with this offer. He had never felt less like attending a party. Besides, there was no chance that Caroline would be at Fanny Mueller's. He had already casually inquired of his aunt who would be present, and the other guests appeared to be mostly elderly people like herself. He longed with all his heart to see Caroline and explain his actions the day before. He wanted badly to justify himself in her eyes. In fact, when he thought about it, most of the agonizing he had been doing since the previous day was an attempt to justify himself in her eyes. He had qualms on his own account as well, but they were nothing compared to the idea that his actions might have injured Caroline. And tomorrow he would meet Cullen and might be shot—might be killed—might never see her again on this earth. He had worked himself into the darkest possible depression when his aunt's butler appeared and announced that Mrs. Cullen wished to see him.

"Did you say *Mrs.* Cullen?" inquired Raymond. He thought it more likely that Robert had called, perhaps to discuss some detail of the dueling arrangements. Unconventional though this would have been, it seemed more likely than that Mrs. Cullen should come to see him. But the butler nodded firmly.

"Yes, sir, it is Mrs. Cullen," he said. "She said to tell you it was a matter of some urgency. I have put her in the small parlor."

Raymond, as he followed the butler, wondered what on earth could be urgent enough to make Mrs. Cullen call on him at such an unconventional hour. The only thing he could think of was that she had gotten wind of the duel somehow. This supposition proved perfectly correct, for Mrs. Cullen's first words on entering the room were "Oh, Mr. Jeffries, how could you? To think of you and Robert fighting a duel! I was never so shocked in all my life."

Since this statement did not seem to require a response, Raymond contented himself with merely bowing. After a reproachful pause, Mrs. Cullen went on in a passionate voice. "I had not thought you capable of such a thing. When Robert told me what had happened, I could scarcely believe my ears. What possible excuse could you have for your behavior?"

"If your son has told you what happened, then you know my excuse," said Raymond coldly. "It was he who struck the first blow. I was only defending myself."

It was evident that Robert had not divulged this detail. Mrs. Cullen appeared taken aback for a moment, but she made a quick recovery. "Perhaps, but you must make allowances for Robert's temperament," she said. "He has a quick temper, I know, but his essential character is very gentle. If you had not given him provocation, I am sure he would never have struck you."

"Struck *at* me, you mean," said Raymond. "He did not succeed in striking me, though he certainly tried. As for my giving him provocation, the boot is quite upon the other foot, Mrs. Cullen. He forced the quarrel upon me, first by means of insults, and then by the use of his fists. As a result, I was forced to hit him in return. And if I am meeting him tomorrow, it is only because he demanded satisfaction of me."

It appeared that this, too, was news to Mrs. Cullen. She digested it in silence for a moment, then decided to take a different tack. "Well, regardless of who provoked the quarrel, it's certain that dueling is no way to settle it," she said severely. "I was extremely shocked when I heard such a thing was being contemplated. You cannot be cruel enough to go through with it, Mr. Jeffries. Robert is my only son—my only child—my sole prop and mainstay. If you kill him, it would kill me as well. Can you strike such a blow to a mother's heart?"

"I would rather *not* strike such a blow to a mother's heart," said Raymond. "For that matter, I would liefer not strike a blow to anyone. But when a man forces a quarrel on me, he can hardly expect I will not defend myself. And if he demands satisfaction in return, what can I do but give it to him?"

"But I am sure Robert regrets his behavior very much, Mr. Jeffries. He is of such a gentle disposition—impulsive, but gentle. If you were to beg his pardon, I am sure he would forgive you."

Raymond surveyed her with incredulity. "Don't you have that backward?" he said. "If Mr. Cullen regrets his behavior, then it should be for him to beg *my* pardon."

"Yes, but Robert is very proud, Mr. Jeffries. Even as a child, he hated to admit he was wrong. If you would only apologize to him first—"

"No," said Raymond with finality. "I am sorry, ma'am, but really, you are asking too much. Mr. Cullen knows the etiquette of these situations as well as I do. It was he who made the challenge, and so he must be the one to withdraw it."

"He did say something of the sort," admitted Mrs. Cullen. With the air of one driven to the last ditch, she opened her reticule. "He wrote you a note—but he said not to give it to you unless I failed to appeal to your better nature."

With a sense of mingled amusement and irritation, Raymond took the note. It was short and to the point.

Jeffries:

I daresay I shouldn't have spoken as I did yesterday. The fact is, I've got a quick temper and acted like a fool. Now Mother's got wind of our meeting tomorrow, and the devil himself is to pay. Someone told her you were a crack shot, and she's certain you're going to kill me. I wouldn't put it past her to notify the authorities if she thought there wasn't any other way to prevent it. That being the case, I don't have any choice but to ask if you'd mind calling the whole thing off. As I said, I probably shouldn't have spoken as I did, but seeing you and Caroline together put me in a state, and one thing led to another. Blame it on Caroline if you will. You know I'm still crazy about her, and until I can get her to hear my apology, I'm hardly responsible for my own conduct.

Yours, etc.,
Robert Cullen

Raymond's feelings on reading this missive were mixed. On the one hand, he was relieved, for though the tone of the note was not strictly apologetic, it was apology enough to free him of the obligation of meeting Cullen on the morrow. On the other hand, Cullen's mention of Caroline stirred his resentment anew. He resented the casual use of her first name and Cullen's blaming her for his own bad behavior. Still more did he resent the words "Until I can get her to hear my apology." It was evident that Cullen still felt convinced Caroline would forgive him. The thought of his continuing to harass her with his attentions was enough to make Raymond forget his qualms of the last twenty-four hours and long to meet Cullen with pistols then and there.

Still, he had to acknowledge that Mrs. Cullen was right in one sense. Dueling was no way to settle a disagreement. There were other ways to clip Cullen's claws, and he realized suddenly he had the means to do so right in front of him, in the form of Mrs. Cullen. Gathering his wits about him, Raymond settled down to put her to use.

"Mr. Cullen has written me an apology of sorts," he said. "But though I am willing to overlook his behavior this once, it must be with the understanding that he will refrain from harassing Miss Sedgewick in the future. That is the only condition under which I can accept his apology."

Mrs. Cullen, who had relaxed at his first words, stiffened at the mention of Caroline. "Miss Sedgewick!" she said. "Don't speak to me of that woman! Of all the unprincipled, abandoned creatures—"

"Pardon me, but I cannot permit you to abuse Miss Sedgewick," said Raymond sternly. "In all this dispute, she is the only really innocent party. She has been dragged into it quite against her will."

Mrs. Cullen regarded him with pity. "No doubt she told you so, Mr. Jeffries," she said. "But I beg you will not believe a word of it. She has been at the bottom of all this trouble from the start, beginning with the fickle way she threw Robert over without a shred of justification. It was all caprice and ill nature."

Raymond hesitated before replying. He did not want to betray Caroline's confidences, but at the same time he thought it would be very much to her advantage if Mrs. Cullen were aware of her son's misconduct. He reasoned that Caroline's desire to keep that misconduct quiet was motivated chiefly by a dread of publicity. There was no fear Mrs. Cullen would publicize it, for she would scarcely wish to air a matter that reflected so badly on her own son. More important, knowing the truth might make her less vocal in her criticism of Caroline, even if it did not silence her altogether.

So Raymond spoke again, deliberately. "It's clear you haven't been informed of all the facts, ma'am," he said. "I take it you never saw the letter by which Miss Sedgewick broke the engagement between her and your son."

Mrs. Cullen started to make an affirmative, then stopped. "No," she said after a minute. "I don't believe I did see the letter. But Robert told me what she said. It was all caprice and ill nature, as I said before."

"On the contrary. Miss Sedgewick had concrete reasons for breaking the engagement." Raymond looked steadily at Mrs. Cullen. "If I were you, I would ask Mr. Cullen what was in that letter. It might make you realize you have wronged Miss Sedgewick in this affair."

"Wronged her! No, I think not, Mr. Jeffries. I don't doubt that is what Miss Sedgewick would like to have us believe, but for my part, I believe Robert. He said she gave no real reason for her decision, only some nonsense about their not suiting, which means exactly nothing."

"That's probably because he was embarrassed to tell you the truth," said Raymond. As he spoke, it occurred to him he might as well get all the mileage he could out of the matter. He had promised Caroline he would not publicize her ex-fiancé's misdeeds, but Mrs. Cullen need not know that. The threat of disclosure would be a tool more powerful than any other against such a woman. "The fact is that during his engagement to Miss Sedgewick, your son was conducting an—er—amorous affair with an opera dancer. It was that circumstance that made Miss Sedgewick decide to break with him."

"I don't believe it!" Mrs. Cullen's face had gone white with fury. "How dare you make such an accusation, Mr. Jeffries! If Miss Sedgewick told you that, it was a lie."

"She did tell me that, but it happens I already knew of it. Quite a few people about town have seen him with the lady in question, Mrs. Cullen. And even if I had not witnessed his behavior with my own eyes, I would know it was true, for he himself confessed to it in the pump room the other day."

"I don't believe it," said Mrs. Cullen. Her voice was a little less certain than before, however, and there was a note almost of pleading in her voice as she went on. "If you imagine Robert said any such thing, then you must have misunderstood him, Mr. Jeffries. Of course he has had his affairs. Young men must sow their wild oats, we all know that. But to imagine he would conduct himself in such a manner—I simply cannot believe it. I will ask him about it when I get home, but I am sure there must be some mistake."

"I'm afraid not, ma'am," said Raymond. "As I said, he told me of it himself."

Repeating that she was sure there was some mistake, Mrs. Cullen turned to go. "When I have spoken to Robert, I will know better what to believe," she said over her shoulder. "I can trust him to tell me the truth, no matter what."

Raymond felt cynically disposed to doubt this

statement. His cynicism must have shown, for Mrs. Cullen drew herself up a trifle. "You doubt me, Mr. Jeffries, but it is the simple truth," she said with dignity. "A mother always knows. Robert will tell me if there is any truth in the allegations you have made. Take this business of the duel. When he came home yesterday dripping wet, I knew right away something was amiss. In the end, I made him tell me about it. And if there is any truth in what you say regarding this—this woman in London, then I will not rest until I get to the bottom of it."

This statement Raymond *could* believe, and said so. "Very well, ma'am," he said. "But understand it is not my word alone upon which my accusation rests, nor Miss Sedgewick's either. I can bring other witnesses to attest to his behavior if necessary. And not only will I do so, I'll make the whole matter public if you and Mr. Cullen continue to harass Miss Sedgewick. I have held my peace so far, but it's all wrong that she should bear the brunt of blame in an affair that is none of her fault. I intend to see she doesn't have to bear any more of it."

To this statement, Mrs. Cullen merely accorded a sniff. It was a rather subdued sniff, however, and Raymond was inclined to think his words had made an impression. He therefore wished her a good day and bowed her out of the house with a feeling of strong relief.

Fourteen

From relief, Raymond's mood passed quickly to exultation.

It was a comfort to know he would not be obliged to face Cullen on the morrow with pistols for two. He hoped he was not a coward, but he had the usual attachments to life, home, and happiness, and he was glad to think he would not be obliged to risk all of them over an affair of honor. The world, which had seemed as wrong as possible only a short time before, now seemed as right as possible, except for one thing. That one thing was Caroline. Undoubtedly she was still angry with him, and nothing could be altogether right while that state of affairs existed.

Yet, even this thought did not depress him overmuch. His spirits, formerly sunk in gloom, were so buoyed up by relief that he felt in a mood to conquer all obstacles. He would see Caroline and apologize for his actions. He would make her understand he cared for her. In the rush of feeling consequent upon his release from anxiety, he realized just how much he did care for her—that he loved her, in fact. He had been skirting the truth for the past few days, but now he looked it boldly in the face. He loved Caroline Sedgewick as he had never loved any woman before, and he wanted nothing so much as the privilege of loving and caring for her all his life.

But there were difficulties in the way. Even in his present hopeful mood, he did not underestimate them. Caroline's own attitude was undoubtedly the biggest difficulty. She had been ambivalent before about accepting his attentions, and since the incidents of the previous day, she was no doubt more ambivalent than ever. He wondered if he dared write her a note telling her how he felt. He had already written a note to Mr. Phipps notifying him the duel was off, and now he sat at his writing desk with a pen in hand and a blank sheet of foolscap before him, debating the merits of declaring himself on paper. He was still debating, when his aunt's butler once more appeared in the parlor doorway.

"I beg your pardon, sir," he said. "But you have another caller, a young female person. Do you wish to see her?"

The tone of the butler's voice showed clearly he did not approve of young female persons calling on single gentlemen at ten o'clock in the evening. Raymond, however, said he would see the woman. As he rose from his desk, he wondered who she could be. His best guess was that she was a servant attached to Mrs. Cullen's household. Possibly she had come with some message from that lady, bringing him word, perhaps, of the outcome of her interview with Cullen. He only hoped it was not a message from Cullen himself rejecting his conditions and saying he wished to resume their quarrel. That would really be too much, after having had his fears set to rest.

With a mounting sense of anxiety, Raymond crossed to the parlor, where a woman, heavily veiled, stood fidgeting beside the fireplace. "The butler said you wished to see me, ma'am," he said. "How may I be of assistance?"

The woman said nothing but threw back her veil, revealing a pale face with a pair of tragic green eyes, surmounted by a mass of tawny hair. "Caroline!" said Raymond. Without pausing for greeting or even to think of the consequences, he took her in his arms and kissed her.

Caroline let out a little gasp but did not shrink from his embrace. In fact, she returned his kiss with an ardor that fully equaled his own. It was only when he released her that he saw there were tears in her eyes.

"Caroline!" he said again, this time with concern. "My dear, whatever is wrong?"

She gave him a weak and disbelieving smile. "Can you ask?" she whispered. "Oh, Raymond—Mr. Jeffries—I cannot bear it. This business of your fighting a duel with Robert is all wrong. I feel so dreadful when I think of your risking your life because of me! There must be some other way to settle the matter."

Raymond laughed joyously. "But there is," he said. "In fact, the matter is all settled." His heart was singing because he felt that Caroline's coming to him in such a way was proof she did not hate him. In fact, it seemed clear that she cared quite a bit, for she would hardly have risked calling on him so unconventionally otherwise, let alone having kissed him with such passion. "There will be no duel," he told her happily. "Mr. Cullen has apologized, and everything is as right as rain."

Caroline stared at him, then sat down abruptly on the nearest chair.

Her face had been pale before, but now it was so

white that Raymond took up the brandy decanter, splashed some liquor in a glass, and handed it to her. "Here," he said forcefully, "drink this. Quickly!"

Caroline took a sip, choked, and shook her head. Raymond stood over her, however, and alternately coaxed and bullied her until the glass was empty. She smiled wanly as she handed him the empty glass.

"Truly I'm all right, Mr. Jeffries," she said. "It was only the shock. I did not know the matter had been already settled."

"Yes," said Raymond. Remorsefully he added, "I suppose I should have broken the news to you more gently instead of simply blurting it out. I did not realize it would be such a shock to you."

Caroline gave him another wan smile. "It *is* a shock," she said. "A pleasant shock, of course. Only it makes one feel such a fool."

There was a catch in her voice that made Raymond look at her closely. "A fool?" he repeated.

"Yes, a fool," she said, looking back at him with unhappy green eyes. "To get here, I had to borrow a veil from Kate's Hannah and steal out the back door. I did not dare walk all the way in the dark, so I took a hackney coach from the square. And the driver looked at me in such a way—and so did your butler when he let me in—and I know they both thought the worst of me. And then to find I did it all for nothing! But I am glad, at least, there will be no duel." She smiled a little, then quickly got to her feet. "I had better go."

"Please don't," said Raymond. He took a step toward her.

"But I must," she said, avoiding his eye as she drew down her veil with nervous fingers. "Indeed, I should not have come in the first place. I can see it all very clearly now. Aunt Emilia was always saying I am prone to act without thinking, and it seems she was right."

"Not at all," said Raymond. "You did nothing that was not natural and even admirable, from my point of view at least. I am *glad* you came, even if it proved not to be necessary. Just between you and me, I've spent the last twenty-four hours envisioning myself in exile or lying on my deathbed. I'd probably still be doing it if Mrs. Cullen had not called on me and delivered Robert's apology."

He went on to describe Mrs. Cullen's call. Caroline left off adjusting her veil to listen to his account. She even smiled a little when he described how Mrs. Cullen had attempted to extort an apology from him before relenting and delivering her son's instead. As soon as Raymond was done speaking, however, she began tugging at her veil once more. "I had better go," she repeated. "I am glad everything has turned out so well, Mr. Jeffries. But since there is nothing more for me to do here, I had better go."

"But there *is* something you can do," said Raymond. "I want to talk to you, Caroline. In fact, I was just sitting down to write you, when the butler announced you were here."

Caroline looked at him doubtfully. He suspected she had been taken aback by his use of her Christian name, but he could see no harm in it. Had not she used *his* Christian name earlier that evening, even if she had quickly corrected herself? "Please, Caroline," he said in a supplicating voice. "I wish you would stay and hear me. I think my conduct requires some explanation, particularly my conduct when I first saw you this evening."

At these words, Caroline flushed pink as a peony.

"No, it doesn't," she said. "I understand completely, Mr. Jeffries. You were relieved and happy about the duel being called off, and that's why you kissed me."

"My dear, I do not go around indiscriminately kissing young women whenever I am relieved and happy!" said Raymond. "It's necessary that you distinctly understand that. Otherwise I can understand why you might be reluctant to hear me!"

Once more Caroline was betrayed into a smile, but when she spoke, her voice was agitated. "Please don't," she said. "I am perfectly sure no explanation is necessary."

She had fixed her eyes on the floor as she spoke. Raymond put a hand under her chin and raised it so she was forced to meet his eyes. "Truly?" he said. "Because I want there to be no misunderstanding between us, Caroline. It's possible you don't return my feelings, in which case I will say no more. But I thought you ought to know that—well, that I care for you most sincerely. In fact, not to put too fine a point on it, I've fallen in love with you."

"Oh!" said Caroline, drawing in her breath sharply. "Oh, Raymond, I wish you wouldn't! I wish you hadn't told me."

"Why not?" said Raymond. He studied her reflectively. "If you don't return my feelings, you need only say so. I won't harass you, I promise."

"But I *do* return them," she said, and burst into tears once more.

It must be confessed that Raymond did not take these tears too seriously. He gave her his handkerchief, to be sure, and patted her on the shoulder while she wiped her eyes, but all the while he was murmuring little endearments such as "My dear, don't cry!" and "My own dear Caroline." As soon as she had control of herself once more, Caroline shook her head and drew away.

"Raymond, you mustn't," she said. "It's too much. I don't deserve it."

"Well, I should like to know who deserves it more!" said Raymond warmly. "As far as I am concerned, you are the most wonderful woman in the world. I intend to see you are treated as you deserve, insofar as I am able."

"Oh, but that's nonsense. I am not wonderful at all. I don't deserve such a tribute." Through her tears, Caroline gave him a searching look. "Don't tell me your aunt hasn't talked about me and my broken engagements? You must know that nearly everyone in Shelton-on-Sea considers me a jilt and a hussy, if not a wholly abandoned woman."

"I know that is the popular opinion," acknowledged Raymond. "But I am in a position to know popular opinion is wrong. I know, at least, that you were justified in jilting Cullen, and it's only your own scruples that keep you from making public your reasons for doing so." He smiled at her. "And such is my faith in your character that I am equally sure you were justified in jilting your other two fiancés."

Caroline smiled a rather watery smile. "As it happens, I *didn't* jilt them," she said. "Certainly I couldn't have jilted Lord Scroggins, for I hadn't accepted him in the first place! But people think I did, and that's all that matters. As far as they're concerned, I'm a common jilt, and nothing I do or say will make the slightest difference."

"Possibly," acknowledged Raymond. "It's much harder to stop gossip than to start it. But who cares about the opinion of people in general? Most of the populace wouldn't recognize the truth if it stared them in the face."

Caroline nodded dejectedly. "But I don't know that the truth is any better than what's said about me," she said. "I may not have been fickle, but I have certainly behaved like a fool."

Raymond assured her warmly that she could not possibly behave like a fool. Caroline only shook her head, however. "If you knew the story, you would say otherwise," she said. "It's ten to one you would want nothing more to do with me."

"Well, there's only one way to find out," said Raymond. Sitting down beside her, he drew her hand into his own. "Tell me all about it."

Drawing a deep breath, Caroline proceeded to do just that.

Raymond heard her story with no great surprise but with plenty of indignation. He knew enough about Emilia Hurston to be unsurprised by her stratagem in regard to Lord Scroggins, but it made him furious to think she would have attempted such a trick at Caroline's expense. Likewise, he was furious to think her youthful engagement with Lieutenant de Very had been subject to such misinterpretation. The facts must have been readily available if anyone had bothered to investigate. She and de Very had parted on good terms, and that gentleman would undoubtedly have borne out her story if anyone had asked him about it. But in fact, no one had asked. It made a better story simply to say that Miss Caroline Sedgewick had jilted three men in succession and was fickle and unprincipled.

Neither could Raymond agree with Caroline's assertion that she had acted like a fool. She had done nothing but what was natural under the circumstances and, he thought, inevitable for one of her temperament. Possessing a warm and generous heart and endowed with powers of attraction of which she was unaware, it was no wonder if she had been taken advantage of. That it had not damaged the sweetness of her character was the wonder. Her past experiences had clearly eroded her confidence, however, both in herself and others, and Raymond could see why she had recoiled so violently when he had declared his feelings for her a few minutes before. The very word "love" must seem hateful to her, considering how it had been used to manipulate her in the past.

Caroline, having finished her narrative, was looking at him timidly. Raymond took her hand and raised it to his lips. "My dear, I am glad you told me," he said. He would have liked to kiss her lips as well, but if her story had taught him anything, it was that he must go slowly in his efforts to woo her. Undoubtedly she would need time to assure herself of the sincerity of his feelings and her own as well. So he contented himself with kissing her hand once more, then rose to his feet. "Let me fetch my hat and coat," he said. "I'll walk you home so you needn't take another hackney."

Caroline protested at this, saying he ought not to go to such trouble, but Raymond insisted, and they left the house together, using the side door to avoid meeting any of the servants. Caroline was largely silent on the walk home, but she gave him her hand at parting. Raymond kissed it, told her he would wait on her the following day, and returned home feeling tolerably satisfied they had reached an understanding.

Fifteen

Raymond would have been dismayed to know how differently Caroline had perceived their interview.

She had found it a great relief to tell someone the full story of her past. Up till then, she had told no one but Lady Katherine, and not even Lady Katherine was privy to all the details of her first engagement. Caroline had never cared to talk much about that long-ago affair, being unable even to think of it without sensations of pain and regret. But having summoned up the courage to tell Raymond, she now felt a sense of relief, as though a painful chapter in her life were finally closed. That was very odd, for Lieutenant de Very had married a few years before, an event that should surely have closed the chapter if anything could. But telling Raymond had in some way made its closure more real and final than even Lieutenant de Very's marriage.

Caroline, as she lay that night in Lady Katherine's guest bedchamber, rejoiced that it was so. She rejoiced also that she had had courage enough to tell Raymond the whole story. She owed him that much, considering how kind he had been to her. But overall her mood was very far from one of rejoicing.

What must he think of me? Caroline asked herself. *He can't possibly care for me now. Now he knows what a mud-*

dle I've made of my life, he must be thoroughly disgusted with me.

With pain, Caroline contemplated the separate incidents of her past. She had deceived herself in her relations with her first suitor, been deceived by her aunt in her second, and been deceived by the man himself in her third. Considered individually, each separate incident might have been forgiven, but taken together they made a damning whole. No man could wish to involve himself with a woman whose past was such an overwhelming record of folly. And when Caroline considered that she had not only behaved like a fool but now bore the stigma of public condemnation as a result, she felt it put the matter beyond question as far as Raymond Jeffries was concerned. She knew his reputation for elegance, discretion, and good taste. It had seemed unlikely that he could care for her in the first place. Now she knew it to be impossible.

It appeared he realized it too. For had he not contented himself with merely kissing her hand when they had parted that evening? He had kissed her lips at meeting—a passionate kiss, accompanied by an equally passionate embrace. Caroline shut her eyes, remembering, and two tears squeezed between her lids. She wished with all her heart the affair might have ended differently. How dreadful to have the man of one's dreams declare himself and be forced to speak the words that must drive him away! For a wild moment, Caroline found herself wishing she had not spoken those words. But soon she was able to acknowledge she had done the right thing. It was fair that Raymond know about her past before he was in any way committed to her. If the recounting of that past was enough to change his mind about wishing to marry her, then that was right too.

Only it did not feel right. On the contrary, it felt like a tragedy.

Caroline, as she lay tossing and turning through a long, sleepless night, had full opportunity to consider that tragedy in all its elements. It had taken this blow to make her realize how superficial were her previous disappointments. Even when she had learned of Robert's betrayal, she had not felt the heartbreak she felt now. Robert's betrayal, in a sense, had been its own cure. Once she had known the truth about him, she had no longer wanted to marry him. But in this case, the situation was reversed. It was she who had had a shameful truth to reveal, and upon its revelation Raymond had drawn away from her—politely but unmistakably. The contrast between his first passionate kiss on the lips and the cool salute he had given her at farewell was too marked to be doubted.

"In any case, I don't doubt it," said Caroline aloud. "It's exactly what I was expecting. Still, that doesn't make it any easier to bear."

In spite of her efforts, two more tears squeezed from between her eyelids. She blinked them away, however, and shook her head resolutely. It seemed to her she had done more than enough crying already. If there was one thing that jarred her more than the remembrance of her past folly, it was the memory of her weeping on Raymond's shoulder, not once but nearly every time they had met during the past week. He must think her a perfect wet-goose, and no doubt that had done its part to disgust him too. Everyone knew there was nothing men hated more than a woman who was eternally dissolving into tears.

I won't cry anymore, Caroline vowed. *I will make the best of things.* And accordingly she tried to do just that, telling herself the loss of Raymond's love was only the natural outcome of events that had taken place weeks, months, and even years before. But the memory of his words and his kiss continued to haunt her like a beautiful thing that had died a-borning, and it was long before she could fall asleep.

She awoke the next morning weighted by sorrow but with her sense of determination intact. With the dawn's light had come a clarity of outlook that had evaded her the night before. After all, it was not so much her past that was a bar between her and Raymond, she reminded herself. She might be the most notorious jilt in England, but that was only because she possessed bad judgment and folly to an extraordinary degree. Those were the qualities that defined her, and they were qualities that must necessarily separate her from a man like Raymond Jeffries. Besides, there were plenty of other ways in which she was separated from him. He was universally acknowledged to be an exceptionally handsome man, while she had never been spoken of as more than passably good-looking. He belonged to one of the most exclusive families in England, while her own background was merely genteel. He was wealthy and well educated and heir to a lofty title, all things she was not, and his tastes were known throughout London society as being both refined and discerning.

What could such a man want with Caroline Sedgewick? Even if he had been able to overlook her shortcomings, she was sure they would disgust him over time. It was as well his eyes had been opened sooner rather than later. So Caroline told herself, but she could not convince herself it was so, and she prepared to face the new day in a mood of sorrowful resignation.

As she got out of bed and began to wash and dress, she kept thinking about Raymond. Most especially she thought about his parting words the night before. He had told her he would call on her that day. There might be men who would say such a thing without meaning it, but she was sure he was not one of them. No doubt it would merely be a formal call, a gesture to show he was willing to remain her friend even if he no longer wished to be anything more. But the thought of seeing him kindled in her heart a faint spark of hope—a hope she had thought extinguished. It did no good to tell herself his call would merely be the necessary prelude to a permanent parting of ways. Her heart hoped otherwise, and it continued to hope in spite of all the arguments she could bring against it.

Finally, exasperated by her own folly, Caroline threw on a morning dress, twisted her hair into a knot, and set out for the ladies' beach. It was earlier than her usual hour for bathing, but she hoped fresh air and exercise might bring her to a more sensible state of mind. She had another reason for going as well. If Raymond intended to break with her and this was to be his final call, there was no need for her to be there; the mere fact of his calling would suffice. She would rather not be present at an interview that must necessarily be painful for them both, she told herself. If, on the other hand, her hopes were justified and he intended to keep pursuing her in spite of his better judgment, then it was plainly her duty to discourage him. The news that she had gone bathing on a morning when he was expected ought to convey a message to him of sorts. It was a message that Caroline felt she would rather convey with actions than words.

I don't know that I could refuse him, if it came to the point of his proposing to me, she thought as she went along the esplanade, now deserted except for a few children and nursemaids. *Thank heaven it isn't likely to come to that. I am sure he must be disgusted with me now, or at least with my situation. He cannot have forgotten how Rachel Tallbridge needled me the other day. A Jeffries would never take to wife a woman whose conduct left her open to such impertinence.*

This was so obviously true that Caroline's hopes dwindled once again, leaving her sober and silent. She located her favorite bathing machine, greeted the attendant, changed into a bathing dress, and sat silent and absent as they went through the ritual of putting out to sea.

She got her allowance of exercise and fresh air that day, but virtually no enjoyment. All the while she kept thinking about Raymond. She wondered if he had called while she was gone, and what he had thought when he found her absent. She was eager to get back home and question Lady Katherine, but reluctant too—so reluctant that she stayed in the water until the bathing woman told her sternly she had had enough and ordered her back into the machine.

Back onshore and dressed in her own clothing once more, Caroline walked along the esplanade, her eyes fixed on the ground. Her thoughts were still occupied with the subject of Raymond. So deep in cogitation was she that she never saw Robert Cullen until he fell into step beside her.

"Caroline?" he said.

Caroline looked up in dismay. Seeing him there,

she had no choice but to give him a bow of recognition. "Mr. Cullen," she said.

Robert returned the bow, but with a diffident air, as though he were uncertain of his welcome. Caroline, looking at him more closely, thought he appeared not merely diffident but chastened. She wondered what accounted for it. Had it been his quarrel with Raymond? Certainly Raymond had forced him to swallow not only the insult of being knocked into the water but the indignity of having later to apologize for his words. Considering how very few apologies he had been called on to make in his life, Caroline thought it was no wonder if he looked a trifle chastened.

She had supposed Robert would insist on accompanying her home when he saw her walking by herself. He looked as though he wanted to, but in the end he merely bowed again, wished her a good morning, and continued along the esplanade at a quickened pace. Caroline was much surprised. She looked after him speculatively as she went along the graveled walk. Was this the same Robert Cullen who had pursued her so relentlessly for the past few days? She could hardly believe he would cease his campaign of harassment just like that. She was even more surprised when, a few minutes later, she met Mrs. Cullen walking with Emily Renquist, and Mrs. Cullen nodded to her—a frosty nod, to be sure, but a nod nevertheless. Quite staggered with surprise, Caroline returned the nod and hurried on, her mind buzzing with speculation.

She tried to think what could account for such a change. When Raymond had spoken of his interview with Mrs. Cullen the day before, she could dimly remember his saying something about having threatened Mrs. Cullen if she and Robert did not cease harassing her. Undoubtedly it was this threat that was operating on the two of them now. But what exactly had the threat been? Caroline could not recall any specific mention of it. She had been too taken up with other feelings at the time—feelings of love and relief mingled with remorse and humiliation.

"It must have been an uncommonly powerful threat, whatever it was," she said aloud. Although relieved by the issue, she was filled with a faint uneasiness. It was a relief to have the Cullens no longer plaguing her, but at what cost had this miracle been achieved? What had Raymond said to them that had induced them to let her alone?

I must know, Caroline told herself. She began to hasten her steps, eager to reach home, where Raymond might be waiting for her. She flew along the High Street and almost ran up the hill, but when she entered Lady Katherine's house it was to encounter Raymond's card lying on the silver tray in the hall and no other sign of him about.

Entering the drawing room, she found Lady Katherine serenely working at a tambour frame. Lady Katherine looked up with a smile as she came in. "He has been here, Caro dear, but he is gone," she said. "You missed him by only a minute or two. What possessed you to go bathing at this hour? Normally you go later in the day."

Caroline sat down abruptly on the sofa. The exertion of running up the hill, together with the hour she had spent in the water and the disappointment of missing Raymond, combined to leave her suddenly exhausted. "I don't know," she said. "I thought I could use some exercise."

"Well, it is a pity you did not wait. You might have taken your exercise in the form of a drive with Mr. Jeffries. He came on purpose to invite you."

Caroline sat motionless, her thoughts busy. She had not expected this turn of events, though she had hoped for it. Evidently Raymond did not mean to give her up after all. The record of her folly, staggering as it was, had done nothing to dissuade him. This ought to have been a joyous thought, but somehow Caroline found it wasn't. She still had the sense of being beneath him, of being tied like a millstone around his neck. Added to this was the sense of obligation she felt in the Cullen affair. Whatever he had said to Mrs. Cullen had compelled Robert to give over pursuing her and caused his mother to accord her at least a grudging recognition. That made her wonder again what exactly he had said to Mrs. Cullen. Before she knew it, she was pouring out her doubts and fears to Lady Katherine.

"It's such a mess, Kate," she said at the conclusion of her recital. "I can't imagine what he said to her, and I'm not sure I want to know. It's all so sordid and ugly. I can't bear to think he has had to soil his hands with it."

Lady Katherine looked amused. "You *are* an idealist, aren't you, darling?" she said. "The man must be thirty if he's a day. No doubt he has had to deal with unpleasant situations before now."

"Yes, but this is *my* situation. It's wrong he should be embroiled in it."

"I don't think he minded being embroiled," said Lady Katherine, setting a stitch with precision. "In fact I think he would like to be embroiled with all your affairs, and on a permanent basis too."

Caroline twisted her hands. "Please don't, Kate!" she said. "I can't bear to think of it. You must see it would be all wrong for me to accept him, even assuming he has serious intentions. And I am not at all sure that is the case."

Lady Katherine looked roguish. "I will give you ten to one, in guineas, that he does," she said. "Caro, you are an idiot. The man's clearly head over heels in love with you. You've told him the worst about yourself, and he's seen for himself how bad it is, and it still hasn't frightened him off. What more do you want?"

Put like this, Caroline could not say. "I don't know," she said, twisting her hands once more. "I know only that something isn't right, Kate. Perhaps it's because all this happened so quickly. If he came to know me better, he might change his mind and decide he doesn't care for me after all."

"He might," agreed Lady Katherine. "And then again, he might find he loves you more than ever. Then what would you do?"

"He couldn't," said Caroline with a catch in her voice. "Kate, we're such different people. You know what his reputation is in London."

"Yes, I know," agreed Lady Katherine. She smiled at Caroline. "Like all the Jeffrieses, he refuses to be satisfied with anything but the best. And he is said to have an uncommonly critical eye in discerning wherever it is to be found."

"Well, then!" said Caroline. "That should show you how impossible it is that he should love me, Kate. I am anything but the best, judged by any criteria you like."

"But don't you see, in this case the only criteria that matter are Mr. Jeffries's," said Lady Katherine in a voice one might use to soothe a small child. "It seems to me he ought to be allowed to decide what's best for him."

Caroline set her jaw mulishly. "No, he shouldn't," she said. "I am thinking about what is best for him too. I won't let him be dragged down with me even if he wants to be. This matter of the duel has made it all clear to me. Good God, Kate, he might have been killed! And it would have been all my fault."

Lady Katherine said dismissively that Caroline was being ridiculous. "The duel never came off, and so nobody was killed or even injured. What's more, it seems to have encouraged Robert to behave himself if all you say is true. Does not that show the worst is over?"

"The worst, perhaps, but what's left is plenty bad enough. I would as soon not marry as be a source of shame and embarrassment to my husband. Especially to a man like Raymond Jeffries."

"That's pride," said Lady Katherine with a disapproving expression. "It's Mr. Jeffries's own lookout whom he marries. If he asks you to marry him, it's because he has decided he would rather marry you, even with all these drawbacks you are fretting about, than any other woman."

"Well, I won't let him do it!" said Caroline. "Don't you see, Kate, if I refuse him, it's not pride for myself that motivates me but pride for him. He has something to be proud of, after all—his name, his reputation, the title he will bear someday. I won't have him sacrifice it all for my sake."

Lady Katherine shook her head. "That sounds good, Caro darling," she said. "But I think the point you make is a meaningless distinction. Pride is pride, whether it's on your account or his. And I say it's wrong if it keeps you from marrying a man who loves you and whom you love back."

Caroline lifted her chin. "We see things differently, then," she said. "Honestly, Kate, I cannot believe you would have married Mr. Baddington if you had known doing so would bring him shame and notoriety."

Lady Katherine gave her a quizzical smile. "Caro, I did bring him notoriety, if you'll recall," she said.

"But not shame," insisted Caroline.

"No, not shame," agreed Lady Katherine. "It was he who was convinced he would be shaming *me* if we married."

This point had not previously occurred to Caroline. She was silent, and Lady Katherine took advantage of her silence to go on in a persuasive voice. "He was full of the most ridiculous scruples—quite as many as you are, darling. But I talked him over in the end. We married, and we are very happy, as you have no doubt observed."

"Yes, but Mr. Baddington had nothing personally of which to be ashamed," argued Caroline. "He was not so wellborn as you, perhaps, but in other respects he was quite respectable. I think our situations are different."

"Not so different as all that, darling. Indeed, I believe you ought to talk to Mr. Baddington. He might be able to set your mind at ease."

Caroline was convinced Kate was wrong. She was in any case reluctant to talk to Mr. Baddington, who was a very pleasant gentleman, but with whom she was hardly on close enough terms to feel comfortable discussing such a personal subject. "In any event, Kate, I think likely I am only borrowing trouble," she said, striving for a light tone. "Whatever Mr. Jeffries may or may not feel for me, he has said nothing about marriage. It's quite possible he never will, and then all this fretting will prove needless."

Caroline spoke these words, little knowing that in less than twenty-four hours she would be receiving the proposal she was both dreading and hoping for.

Sixteen

Having no idea the extent of Caroline's scruples, Raymond had likewise no idea of the difficulty he would have in overcoming them.

Even in his ignorance, he was hardly sanguine. He had told Caroline he loved her, and she had admitted to loving him, but even so she had seemed to find the situation more upsetting than exhilarating. Knowing her reservations, he could not be surprised that this was so, but he regretted it. For him, the discovery that their love was mutual had been the most wonderful thing in the world. It hurt him to recall how Caroline had said "I wish you hadn't!" when he had told her of his feelings.

It was some help to remind himself that they had known each other in a real sense only a very short time. The idea that their love had sprung to life practically overnight still struck him as slightly unreal. He had always laughed at the notion of love at first sight, but now it appeared the laugh was on him. "Though strictly speaking, it wasn't at first sight we fell in love, but third," he told himself whimsically.

Still, when he recalled what Caroline had told him concerning her previous engagements, he could see why she might hesitate to enter into another one.

Hesitation was entirely natural under the circumstances. He had gone to call on her that morning with no greater hope than that he might advance his suit in some small measure. He knew it would be a work of time, and he was prepared to take as much time as was necessary to overcome his lady's reservations, but he had a lover's natural impatience with delays and hindrances. To find her away was a delay and hindrance of the most exasperating kind. Raymond did not let it cast him down overmuch, however. He reasoned that he would see her again before long, and when he did, it would be soon enough to start overcoming her scruples.

In the meantime, there was at least one difficulty he could set his hand to. Among other things, Caroline had expressed fear that his family would not approve of his marrying her. As things now stood, she was undoubtedly correct, but his relatives' opinions must change when they knew as much about her as he did. So he sat down and wrote a letter to his parents, describing his intentions toward Caroline and giving enough details of her past to surmount any objection they were likely to make. He did not anticipate too many objections, for his father was an easygoing man for a Jeffries, and his mother so eager for him to marry that she would have embraced any daughter-in-law who was likely to provide her with the grandchildren she longed for.

His aunt was a different story. Not only was she as jealous of his consequence as if it had been her own, she had already shown she disapproved of Caroline. And while his parents were in Sussex and could express their reservations only via letter, his aunt was right there in Shelton-on-Sea, where she could make her reservations very plain indeed.

Even if she said nothing directly to Caroline, she would show by her attitude she disapproved of her. He knew Caroline well enough to know that such an attitude on his aunt's part might have everything to do with her decision to accept him. Indeed, he doubted his ability to win her in the teeth of his relatives' disapproval.

So, since he was balked of seeing Caroline that morning, he decided he would have a serious talk with his aunt. Miss Jeffries had cut him short before when he had tried to talk about Caroline, saying he had better find out first why Caroline had broken her first two engagements, but he was in a position now to know Caroline's reasons had been very cogent indeed. He would see his aunt as soon as possible and describe those reasons and get her consent to have Caroline formally introduced to her as soon as it might be arranged.

He knew his aunt had gone to the pump room that morning, in accordance with her usual custom. To the pump room he went also, and found her there, talking amiably to Miss Timms. Miss Timms turned a beaming face to him as he approached. "Mr. Jeffries! I have not seen you in an age! Come sit with your aunt and me and tell us all the news."

Raymond politely disclaimed having any news worth the telling. "I thought perhaps my aunt was ready to leave, so I have come to walk her home," he explained. "Are you finished here, Aunt, or will you stay a little longer?"

"Oh, do stay!" urged Miss Timms before Miss Jeffries could speak. "And you must stay too, Mr. Jeffries. It's too cruel that you should desert us as soon as you arrive."

Raymond persevered in his cruelty, however,

having ascertained that his aunt was ready to leave. He would not even give a definite assent when Miss Timms begged to know if he was attending the assembly the following evening. Neither would he engage her for the opening dances as she was clearly hoping. She stood looking after him with palpable frustration as he gave an arm to his aunt and led her away.

"Well, you gave her short shrift," said Miss Jeffries, looking over her shoulder with sardonic amusement. "I never saw a girl drop so many hints and be so ill paid for the effort!"

Raymond merely gave an absent nod by way of reply. His aunt surveyed him quizzically. "I suppose you're used to having all the girls chase after you, but it's a new experience for me," she said. "Miss Timms never had two words to spare for me before you came to Shelton-on-Sea. Since you did, though, she's been so friendly, I can hardly get elbow space. T'other day when you were out riding with Miss Sedgewick she was bound and determined to know where you were and whom you were with. If it hadn't been for the fact that I didn't know myself, I believe I'd have ended up telling her just to get rid of her."

Raymond smiled at this, but it was a perfunctory smile. His nerves had snapped to attention at the mention of Caroline. "Indeed," he said. "I'm as glad you didn't know, then. It would have only caused gossip, and Miss Sedgewick has been subjected to enough of that as it is. Most unjustly too."

"Maybe," said Miss Jeffries with a sideways glance. "Or maybe not. I know you've appointed yourself her champion, but it still looks damned queer, her jilting three men in a row."

"Ah, but it happens she did not jilt the first two at all, Aunt. I know the whole story now, and I can say without hesitation, it's a case of her being more sinned against than sinning. Listen, and see if you do not agree with me that gossip has done her a great injustice."

He went on to recount all Caroline had told him concerning her first two engagements. He had no doubt of being on solid ground where her engagement with Lord Scroggins was concerned, and indeed his aunt expressed great indignation to learn how Emilia Hurston had maneuvered her niece into that situation. But to his surprise, she seemed even more affected by the story of Caroline's first engagement.

"I was engaged myself once," she said in an abrupt voice. "Years ago, when I was just a girl. He was the son of a neighbor and eligible in every way." She was silent a moment, musing. "He asked me to marry him, and I said I would. But later that night, I started having second thoughts. By the next morning, I knew I'd made a mistake. So I wrote him a note and called it off. It was cowardly of me, but I couldn't bring myself to face him. He was a nice boy, and his sister was one of my best friends. She never forgave me—and indeed, I had a hard time forgiving myself. I've always felt badly about the way it turned out." She cleared her throat. "I must say, I think Miss Sedgewick was foolish to stand by this soldier fellow even after she knew she'd made a mistake, but it shows a nice loyalty on her part. I don't know that I blame her, all things considered."

Raymond nodded. He was greatly surprised to find his prosaic aunt harboring such a romantic past. "I think myself Miss Sedgewick's conduct at the time was excusable enough, considering she was not even out of her teens," he said. "I'd hate to be judged by my own conduct when I was that age."

His aunt agreed that few people's conduct at the age of seventeen could endure much scrutiny. "There's nothing strange in a girl making a decision she later comes to regret. The wonder to me is how the story ever got about that she had jilted Lieutenant de Very. I suppose Miss Sedgewick couldn't have been lying to you?"

"I would stake my life she was not," said Raymond with some heat.

"Well, there's no need to go as far as that," said his aunt with a good-natured smile. "Obviously you're bound to take her part. But I must say I'm inclined to believe she was telling the truth. The story's just queer enough to be true. Besides, it would be silly for her to lie about something that could be so easily disproved. There must be dozens of people back in her home county that know the truth of the matter. Ophelia Albert, for one. She's from Lincolnshire, and she prides herself on knowing everything that goes on. I believe I'll write her and ask her what she knows about Miss Sedgewick's first engagement."

"No!" said Raymond involuntarily.

His aunt turned surprised eyes on him. "What's your objection, Raymond?" she asked. "I would think since you're such a champion of Miss Sedgewick, you'd want the truth about her to be known. Assuming it's what she says it is," she added cynically.

Raymond did not rise to this bait. He had regained his composure by then and even managed a smile as he responded to his aunt's speech. "I have no doubt as to that, Aunt. And certainly I would like Miss Sedgewick to be cleared of what is a false charge against her character. No, if I have an objection against your making such inquiries, it is because of the time they would take. Even if you write your friend today, you cannot hope to have an answer back from her much under a week."

"No," agreed his aunt, surveying him quizzically. "But I don't see what your hurry is. It's been rumored for years that Miss Sedgewick jilted Lieutenant de Very. What does it matter if people believe it for a few more days?"

"It doesn't matter at all as far as setting the public record straight. But if you insist on having confirmation from your friend before you are willing to receive Miss Sedgewick, then it will be another week before I can introduce her to you. And I was hoping I might do so at tomorrow night's assembly."

His aunt's face cleared at these words, and she even looked amused. "So that's your objection!" she said. "In a hurry, aren't you, Raymond? But since you make a point of it, I don't know that I need wait for confirmation from Ophelia. I'm already convinced Robert Cullen's a blackguard, and I can readily believe Emilia Hurston had everything to do with Miss Sedgewick's engagement to Lord Scroggins. You can go ahead and introduce her to me tomorrow night if you wish. Poor girl, she seems to have had a hard time of it by all accounts."

"Indeed she has," said Raymond. "I hope to make it up to her, however."

His aunt surveyed him with raised eyebrows. "So it's like that, is it?" she said. "I can't say I'm surprised. You've been smelling of April and May ever since meeting her the other night."

Raymond flushed, then grinned. "I suppose it's fairly obvious," he said. "But I wouldn't want you to get the wrong idea, Aunt. I hope Miss Sedgewick will do me the honor of becoming my wife eventually, but just at present there are difficulties. Whether I can overcome them or not remains to be seen."

His aunt stared at him. "Difficulties!" she said. "What difficulties would those be?" With a proud lift of her chin, she continued. "She surely can't find fault with your position. You're better born than any Scroggins that ever was, or any Cullen either. Better off for money too. Besides, Miss Sedgewick's dowry is nothing special from all I've heard. She couldn't hope to do better than marrying you."

Again Raymond flushed. "I don't think those things enter into it, Aunt," he said. "Or if they do, it's in a negative sense. Miss Sedgewick is a sensitive young lady as well as an intelligent one. She knows the kind of remark you have just made is the kind of thing that would be said by all our acquaintance if she were to accept my suit. Do you think that an agreeable prospect for a sensitive young lady?"

His aunt started to speak, then stopped. "No," she said after a minute. "I don't suppose it would be. Still, I would hope Miss Sedgewick wouldn't let that prevent her from marrying you if she really cares about you. What people say is nonsense, at least nine tenths of it. No sensible woman ought to order her conduct out of regard for what people say."

"All things being equal, I would agree with you, Aunt," said Raymond. "But in Miss Sedgewick's case, I think an exception might be made. You know for some years now she has heard herself criticized, often with a great deal of bitterness and with no justification whatever. Is it any wonder if she shrinks from making herself the subject of further gossip?"

"I suppose not," said Miss Jeffries after another pause. "Poor girl, I know Sophia Cullen's given her a bad enough character. From now on I'll have to speak up if Sophia starts criticizing her again. Seeing as we're likely to be connected by marriage one of these days!"

"I hope so," said Raymond gravely. "As I said before, however, the issue is far from certain. Indeed, I am afraid that Miss Sedgewick's past brushes with matrimony may have left her questioning whether she wants to marry at all."

"Well, I can't criticize her for that, seeing as I'm still a spinster," said Miss Jeffries, smiling. "But I hope between us we may overcome her scruples. I'll do what I can on my side, Raymond, and frankly, I don't see why we shouldn't carry the day. I can laud you to the skies with a clear conscience, for the worst fault I ever had to find with you was your being too particular when it came to choosing a wife, and obviously that doesn't apply now. Indeed, Raymond, I think the better of you for choosing the girl you have. Most men don't look beyond the surface when it comes to women. Beauty's well enough, but it wears pretty thin after a time if there's no mind and character behind it."

"Yes," agreed Raymond. "Although I think Miss Sedgewick's appearance as lovely as her mind and character."

His aunt gave him a quizzical look, as if recalling a certain conversation in which he had described Caroline as plain. She was tactful enough to keep the recollection to herself, however. "As a matter of fact,

I think so too," she said. "I've always thought so. But what I'm saying is she's evidently got a brain and a character as well as looks. On the whole I'd a deal rather you married her than a forward jade like that Timms chit, who hasn't a thought in her head besides beaux and balls. Lord, won't she look blue when she hears you're engaged!"

"Well, you may tell Miss Timms as soon as I can convince Miss Sedgewick to have me. I beg only you won't do it before, Aunt! That would be all I need to finish my chances with Miss Sedgewick, for she would certainly punish such presumption as it deserved."

Repeating that Caroline was evidently a girl of character, Miss Jeffries promised to say nothing until Raymond's suit might prove successful. "And I'll help all I can to make sure it is, Raymond," she added. "You may introduce us tomorrow night, and I'll do all I can to make her comfortable about joining the family."

Raymond was pleased with this pledge. He was equally pleased with his aunt's praise of Caroline, which struck him as both intelligent and discerning. With her help, he felt certain he could overcome at least some of Caroline's scruples. Indeed, he wondered whether the time might have come to declare his intentions. Although he had declared his feelings the night before, he had refrained from mentioning his intentions, for her mood had been so uncertain, he feared she would not give his proposal a favorable hearing. But she knew his feelings now as well as her own and had had time to think them over. This, added to the fact that he had his family's approval behind him—or at least the approval of one member of his family—made him feel she might be more willing to hear him. Raymond hoped so, at any rate. He made up his mind that if a suitable occasion offered the following evening, he would ask Caroline to become his wife.

Seventeen

In the event, Caroline came perilously close to not attending the assembly at all.

When Lady Katherine had suggested they go, she had agreed, albeit reluctantly. Raymond would probably be there, and the thought of seeing him was a lure that drew her even against her better judgment. She made a careful toilette, spent extra time on her hair, and even borrowed a little rice powder from Lady Katherine to touch up her complexion. But at the last moment, she experienced second thoughts.

"Kate, I shouldn't," she said. "I'm sure Raymond will be there, and what if Robert is there too? Only think what an awkward situation it would be!"

"I don't see that your being there would make it any more awkward," said Lady Katherine, adjusting a circlet of pearls atop her dark curls. "They must meet sometime, or else abandon society altogether."

"But my being there will make it more awkward, I'm sure of it. It's because of me they fought in the first place."

Lady Katherine gave Caroline an amused look. "That smacks of conceit, darling, if you will forgive my saying so. It's been my experience that men don't require much pretext to fight. They do so at the drop of a hat, and over the most trivial things. Not that I mean to imply you are trivial," she added generously.

Caroline could not help laughing in spite of her misery. "So you think I was only a pretext for their fighting?" she said. "If only I might think so too! If I am conceited, I assure you it is not a comfortable conceit, Kate."

"No, I'm sure it's not, darling. Your conceit is rather the kind that seeks to take the weight of the whole world onto its own shoulders."

"Is it?" said Caroline, much struck.

"Yes, it is, darling," said Lady Katherine firmly. "I've noticed it before, but you've gotten much worse since Mr. Jeffries arrived in Shelton-on-Sea."

Caroline looked down at the floor. "But that's because I care about him, Kate," she said in a small voice. "I would not have him injured or inconvenienced because of me. If I stay home tonight—"

"Then you will merely be dealing him a different kind of injury. He will be looking for you at the assembly, and if you are not there, he will be disappointed."

"But it would be for his own good," argued Caroline.

"How do you know it would be for his own good?" said Lady Katherine sternly. "He's a grown man, and presumably he knows his own mind. That's what I mean about taking the weight of the world on your shoulders, Caro. It's all very well to be conscientious, but at some point people must be responsible for their own actions."

"Perhaps," said Caroline doubtfully. "But I still think it would be better if I stayed home tonight."

"And I think you're wrong. And I'm so sure of it

that I'm willing to take full responsibility in the matter. So get your cloak, darling, and come along with me. I'll take the weight of the world on my own shoulders this once!"

So coaxing was her smile and so irresistible her manner that Caroline ended up giving way. Perhaps she gave way the easier because she really wanted to go in spite of her reservations. But when she entered the Assembly Rooms and she saw Raymond standing there, tall, handsome, and exquisitely turned out from the toes of his shining dancing pumps to the top of his dark head, she was seized with compunction once more. He seemed hardly human in his elegance, a veritable Olympian among the commonplace dowagers and valetudinarians of Shelton-on-Sea. How could such an Apollo ever lower himself to be with her?

As she was thinking these thoughts, he caught sight of her standing in the doorway. His face lit up, and he came toward her with an alacrity that made the people around them look after him curiously. "I am so glad you are here," he said as he bowed over her hand. "I called yesterday, hoping to see you, but the servant said you were out."

"Yes, I heard you had called," said Caroline. She had to force the words out, for she was feeling awkward in his presence. It seemed impossible that only two days before, this man had kissed her and told her he loved her. The whole episode seemed unreal in retrospect. Looking at him now only made it seem more unreal. The warmth of his manner could not ease her impression of him as an elegant and intimidating stranger.

There were plenty of other things to make Caroline feel awkward as well. She had an uneasy sense of being the center of attention, a sensation that was not wholly unjustified. A great many people were craning their necks to see what had engaged Raymond Jeffries's attention. When they realized it was Caroline, they craned their necks all the harder. Dowagers peered at them through quizzing glasses; matrons whispered behind fans; and Miss Timms, from a bench beside her mother, glared at Caroline as though she had robbed her of her best ball dress.

All this was bad enough, but it soon became worse when Caroline spied Robert Cullen threading his way through the crowd. There was a scowl on his face as he came up to where they stood. He saluted Caroline politely enough, but his greeting to Raymond was chilly. "I wondered if you'd do me the favor of standing up with me?" he asked Caroline. "The first set is just beginning."

If Caroline had felt awkward and tongue-tied before, it was nothing to what she felt now. She had hoped Robert would be content with a formal greeting such as had sufficed on the esplanade the day before. But now, by asking her to dance, he had put her in a spot. A lady could not refuse to dance with one gentleman, then turn around and dance with another. If she refused Robert, then she must refuse all her other would-be partners, including Raymond. Not for the first time Caroline wished she were as unprincipled as most people thought her. She had not known how much she was counting on dancing with Raymond until she saw it made impossible once and for all.

"No," she said coldly and evenly. "I thank you, Mr. Cullen, but I do not plan to dance this evening."

She could not help looking at Raymond as she

spoke. It was impossible to tell from his face whether he appreciated her quandary. He was looking at Robert, and his expression was politely inscrutable.

Robert's expression was anything but inscrutable, however. At her refusal, his scowl became even more pronounced. "Indeed," he said. "Well, if you will not dance, then perhaps you will do the honor of sitting with me."

Caroline was furious at his persistence. She had already given up all hope of dancing for the evening, and now he was bidding fair to keep her from having any enjoyment at all. "No," she said sharply. "I thank you, but it is quite impossible."

She saw immediately that he did not intend to take this refusal as final either. As she was racking her brain for an excuse that would keep her busy all evening, Raymond spoke.

"Miss Sedgewick is otherwise engaged," he said. "She has agreed to sit with my aunt this evening and keep her company."

Caroline could not help starting at these words. She turned an astonished look on Raymond, but he only gave her a reassuring smile in return. "Miss Jeffries is greatly looking forward to talking to her," he said. "If you will excuse us, Cullen?"

It was clear Robert did not want to excuse them. The chastening he had endured a few days previously evidently still held good, however, for he bowed and muttered something that might have been an acquiescence. "Perhaps later in the evening," he said.

"Unfortunately Miss Sedgewick will be engaged the whole evening," said Raymond. A warning note was noticeable in his voice as he added, "I hope you understand me, Mr. Cullen. I had thought you did, but perhaps I was mistaken."

Looking sullen, Robert said he understood. "I was only asking her to dance," he said in an aggrieved voice. Fixing his eyes on Caroline, he added, "Caroline knows I'd never do anything she didn't like. Don't you, Caro? What I mean to say is, you have only to say the word, and I'll never bother you again. But if you do say it, make sure you mean it. Because I won't stay around to have you tell me a second time."

Caroline felt like laughing and crying at the same time. She reflected that being humiliated in front of Raymond seemed to be her lot in life. Here was Robert, making her look a fool as usual. She could only hope he meant it when he said any refusal she gave him now would be taken as final. That was the best she could hope for under the circumstances: a lone spar saved from the wreck of the evening. "Very well," she said. "Then I will take you at your word, Mr. Cullen."

It was clear Robert did not comprehend her meaning. He leaned forward eagerly. "You understand?" he repeated.

"Yes, I understand that you will accept my word as final. That is as it should be, for I have no intention of changing my mind, Mr. Cullen."

It was evident he did understand these words. His color changed, and his jaw tightened. "Your decision is final, then?" he said. "Remember, once you say the word, there is no going back, Caroline."

"I already *have* said it," said Caroline crossly. "I hope only I will not have to say it again."

This refusal was plain enough even for Robert not to mistake. He bowed and turned to go. But the urge to have the last word was too much for him. He had gone only a few steps when he turned to address Caroline again. "I hope you'll be happy," he said. "You and Jeffries will make a match of it, I suppose. It stands to reason nothing I could offer you would measure up against a viscountess's coronet." With a half-muffled oath he added, "Fickle! People may call you fickle, but it seems to me you've done pretty well for yourself. God save me from all fickle women." With which pious wish, he turned and strode away.

Caroline found she was shaking with a mixture of laughter and tears. "I don't believe he spoke loudly enough," she said. "There must be at least a dozen people in the room who didn't hear him."

Raymond was smiling down at her. "Two dozen at least," he said, "not counting the people in the card room."

Caroline noticed with amazement that he seemed utterly unconcerned. At least half the heads in the assembly room were turned their way, and a buzz of conversation had erupted at Robert's parting words. Raymond, however, seemed unaware of it. He continued to smile down at her. "At least we may hope he meant what he said about letting you alone after this," he said. "On the whole, I think he did mean it."

"I hope so," said Caroline. She found her voice was shaking, and so were her hands. She could not imagine how Raymond could seem so unperturbed. Did he not mind being embroiled in a public scene? "I'm sorry," she said miserably. "It's infamous of Robert to behave so badly."

"Yes, it is," agreed Raymond. "I'd be tempted to call him out again merely for the principle of the thing. I can see he has upset you."

"It's nothing," said Caroline. Her voice was shaking again as she added, "I beg you won't think of calling him out, Mr. Jeffries. I could not stand to think of your meeting Robert, though he behaved ten times as badly."

Raymond smiled at her. "Well, let's hope it doesn't come to that," he said. "At least I can promise not to meet him unless he offers a great deal more provocation than he did today. And I don't think such provocation will be forthcoming. Perhaps I am over-sanguine, but I have a feeling you won't be bothered with Robert Cullen after this."

Caroline repeated that she hoped so. Her voice was still shaky, and this seemed to concern Raymond, whereas the forgoing scene had not. "This has been unpleasant for you, I know," he said sympathetically. "Before I introduce you to my aunt, would you like me to fetch you a glass of wine? It might help settle your nerves."

Caroline stared at him. "You meant that?" she said. "About introducing me to your aunt? I supposed it was only an excuse to fob off Robert."

"No, I did mean it. My aunt is eager to meet you."

"Then I believe I could use a glass of wine," said Caroline weakly. She felt she could use a little stimulant before making the acquaintance of the formidable Mehitabel Jeffries. But when at last Raymond took her over to where that lady sat, she found Miss Jeffries all that was cordial.

"Raymond's told me a deal about you, Miss Sedgewick," she said, looking Caroline up and down in a not unfriendly way. "Just sit down beside me, if you please. Raymond, Miss Sedgewick looks as though she could do with another glass of wine, and I could use one myself if it comes to that."

Raymond obediently went off to fetch the wine. Once more Miss Jeffries looked Caroline up and down. "I'm glad to make your acquaintance, Miss

Sedgewick," she said. "As I said, Raymond's told me a deal about you. If half what he says is true, you're a remarkable young lady."

Caroline flushed vividly. "I'm afraid not," she said. "If Mr. Jeffries implied any such thing, he has misled you."

Miss Jeffries regarded Caroline with interest. "You're blushing," she commented. "Didn't suppose gels knew how to blush nowadays. A lost art, I thought, along with wearing stays and petticoats!"

This made Caroline laugh as well as blush. "It's a most vexing habit," she confessed. "I wish I could stop blushing as easily as one might discard a pair of stays or a petticoat!"

"Well, I wouldn't worry about it. It's nice to see a gel with modesty—real modesty, that is, not the false kind. One sees that often enough, God knows. But yours is obviously the real thing. A pleasant quality, modesty, but mind you, don't carry it too far, Miss Sedgewick. Like most good qualities, it does best in moderation."

Caroline wondered if this statement was in reference to anything in particular. She felt sure Raymond had made his aunt his confidante in some degree, for the trend of her questions was consistent with a lady investigating a possible wife for a cherished male relative. Miss Jeffries asked Caroline about her family, upbringing, and situation; made a few elliptical references to Lord Scroggins that showed she was acquainted with that situation; and spoke frankly about her engagement to Robert Cullen. "You mustn't feel badly," she told Caroline. "There are mighty few of us who haven't been taken in by a handsome face at one time or another. The whole business will blow over soon enough, I have no doubt."

Caroline had taken a liking to Miss Jeffries, and she found herself responding with reciprocal frankness. "I hope so, ma'am," she said. "But in truth, I wonder if I will ever be done with it. It seems to me that the shadow of my folly must haunt me all my life." She hesitated, then went on in a rush. "And I am afraid it must also haunt those who choose to associate with me."

Miss Jeffries raised her brows. "Lady Katherine doesn't seem to be much bothered," she observed. "She's a bit of an eccentric, of course, but I don't suppose any woman of spirit would be put off by such a thing. Or any man either."

Caroline hoped yet feared she would go on to say something about Raymond's courtship. She was thus both relieved and disappointed when Raymond came up just then with the wine, and the conversation took a more general turn. But her previous talk with Miss Jeffries had done her good, for she was relaxed enough now to hold her own in the conversation that ensued. She felt Miss Jeffries had been favorably impressed by her, and that they understood each other to some degree. Her case of nerves returned when Raymond asked her to dance, however.

"I thank you, no, Mr. Jeffries," she said, twisting her hands as was her habit in times of stress. "You know I am not dancing this evening."

She hoped he understood why she was not dancing. She did not like to allude to the matter in front of Miss Jeffries, having been embarrassed enough by that lady's previous mention of Robert Cullen. Fortunately, Raymond took her rejection quietly and without question. "Of course. In that case, perhaps I may bring you another glass of wine?"

Caroline temporized by accepting a glass of punch instead. She was beginning to feel she had already had enough wine that evening. There was something so pleasant and comfortable about sitting with Raymond and Miss Jeffries that, together with the wine, it came near to making her forget who she was and why it was impossible for her to ever really be one of them. In fact, she did find herself forgetting this for minutes at a time. Now and then she was jolted back to earth by the sight of some matron staring at her or the sound of a whispered conversation in which the word "jilt" was audible. But when she finally rose to take leave of the assembly, she was in a happier and more hopeful mood than she had been in weeks.

Raymond's parting words were further cause for hope and happiness.

"Shall I see you tomorrow?" he asked. "At the pump room? My aunt and I make a regular habit of going there of a morning."

"Perhaps I will come too, then," said Caroline, and took leave of them both, with a sense that her spirits were on wings.

Eighteen

Caroline's happy mood lasted precisely as long as it took her to leave the Assembly Rooms and go down the stairs to the street. As she was stepping into Lady Katherine's carriage, she overheard the words that caused her happiness to collapse as though it had been a pricked balloon.

"Well, I think it would be a terrible comedown for a man like Mr. Jeffries to marry a woman like her," were the words she heard, spoken in Miss Timms's fluting soprano. "I can't imagine what he sees in her. Indeed, I have never seen what anyone sees in her! She's a commonplace enough creature to look at."

"Aye, that she is," agreed a second voice, identifiable as Miss Timms's mother. "As far as I can tell, the only thing that sets her apart is the fact she's jilted three men in a row. Indeed, my dear, I cannot believe Mr. Jeffries has serious intentions about her. All his family think a deal of their consequence, as you know."

"It would be very strange if he were to forget himself far enough to marry Miss Sedgewick," agreed Miss Timms.

"Yes, he is heir to the title and has his future position to think of," said Mrs. Timms pontifically. "Is this our carriage? I shall tell the coachman to hurry going home. Such a stupid party. Next year we shall have to try to go to Brighton instead. It seems to me the tone of this place has fallen off sadly in the last year or two."

The sound of the carriage door slamming shut cut off the rest of this conversation, but the damage was done as far as Caroline was concerned. She knew Miss Timms's words had been prompted in part by jealous spite, but there had been just enough truth in them to hurt. People were saying she was unworthy of Raymond. They thought he would be lowering himself to marry her. If she were to become his wife, they would see it as a disastrous blow to his consequence. How could she let him do such a thing? She loved him. She loved him more than she had ever supposed it possible to love a man. What she had felt for Robert Cullen was nothing in comparison.

Indeed, it was now clear to Caroline that her feelings for Robert Cullen had not been real love at all. Feelings for him she had certainly had, but their nature had been essentially selfish. It had never occurred to her to reject him because her past might hurt him. Any qualms she had felt had been tied to her own fears, her own doubts. But it was not her own fears and doubts that held her back in the present instance. Rather, it was fear and doubt on Raymond's account.

He was a different sort of man from Robert Cullen. She knew it instinctively, felt it with a certitude based on her whole acquaintance with him. There was an integrity about him that was part of his essential character. That integrity had caused him to stand by her thus far, even despite the trouble her acquaintance had cost him, and he would continue to stand by her if he were allowed to do so. But he should not be so allowed. She would save him the heartbreak of a disastrous and unequal union. He had been generous to her, generous to a fault; now it would be her turn to be generous. She, Caroline Sedgewick, would save him from himself.

Lady Katherine was watching her from the opposite banquette. "You're very quiet, Caro darling," she commented. "What are you thinking of?"

Caroline said evasively she was thinking of the assembly. She felt sure Lady Katherine would ridicule her qualms if she voiced them aloud. She would accuse Caroline once again of taking the world on her shoulders, and of being a foolish idealist.

But I am an idealist, Caroline told herself. *I am.* She had no longer any doubt that it was so. Idealism burned within her, a high white flame of selfless love. She could not make Raymond happy by being with him, so she would make him happy without her. She would then find happiness in seeing him happy, which was the only happiness she could enjoy under the circumstances.

This fire of idealism continued to burn within Caroline through the night. It was still burning within her when she arose the next morning. She had slept little, having spent most of the night making plans for her conduct in regard to Raymond. It would not do to meet him and his aunt in the pump room that morning as she had half promised. She must avoid him instead, and go on avoiding him as much as possible. If his attachment were genuine, it would take some time to fade, but she was sure it would fade eventually if given no encouragement. And she did not mean to give it any.

Soon enough he would forget her. She had no doubt he would, and Miss Timms, Miss Thompkins, and the other belles of Shelton-on-Sea would no doubt aid in the process in so far as they were able.

Instead of reassuring her, however, the thought of these young ladies gave Caroline her first sense of doubt. What if Raymond did successfully transfer his feelings to Miss Timms or Miss Thompkins? Would he be better off? Miss Timms and Miss Thompkins would almost certainly not appreciate his sense of humor, his intelligence, or his kindness and consideration. They would care only for his money and position. On the other hand, they would not bring him shame and notoriety as part of their dowry. Caroline tried to tell herself this was the more important concern, but somehow her inner flame of idealism had been damped by the thought of Raymond's marrying a young lady who did not really care for him. Try as she might to restore the flame to its former heat, it never burned quite so hot again.

This was unfortunate, for even with her idealism at full flame she would have found it difficult to get through the days that followed. In order to avoid Raymond, she was forced to become virtually a hermit. For more than a week she did not leave the house at all, refusing to set foot out-of-doors and declaring herself not at home to visitors. Raymond called several times during this period, but she declared herself not at home to him too. Still, each time she had a renewed struggle within herself before she could send him away unseen. In point of fact she did not send him away unseen, for she was unable to resist the urge to watch him through a crack in the curtains as he went away. The first couple of times he left the house, he had looked disappointed but not cast down; the third time, however, there had been a discouraged droop to his shoulders that had given Caroline a stab of compunction. She had moped for the rest of the day, feeling that a life of sacrifice and selfless love was even more difficult than she had imagined.

Although this episode had dampened her spirits, it did not shake her resolution. She was still determined that Raymond should be saved from himself. It was about this time that Lady Katherine realized what was going on. She had no hesitation in telling Caroline she was a fool. "You are the most vexing girl," she told Caroline. "Do you mean to say you have refused him out of some nonsensical notion he is too good for you?"

"It's not a nonsensical notion," said Caroline defiantly. "And in any case, I have not actually refused him, Kate. I could hardly do so since he has never made me an offer!"

"But he would have if you had let him. I can see it all, Caro, and I declare I could shake you for it. I *know* you care about him. I know it as well as I know my own name. If you have doubts, for heaven's sake, why do you not see Mr. Jeffries and tell him about them? I daresay he could settle them in a trice."

"No, he couldn't," said Caroline, setting her jaw mulishly. "No one can. I am doing what is best for him, Kate—best for both of us. It's no use talking, for I have made up my mind."

Lady Katherine, who had been looking irritated, suddenly smiled. "Well, just remember it's a woman's prerogative to change her mind, darling," she said. "I want you to promise me you will not be too proud to tell Mr. Jeffries if you *do* change it. So long as you do that, I will not tease you anymore."

Caroline had no hesitation about giving this promise. Indeed, she wished with all her heart that she *could* change her mind. A week without Raymond had been nearly intolerable, and here she had a whole lifetime to look forward to—a whole lifetime bereft of his company. Altogether it was a bleak prospect. She sighed, causing Lady Katherine to comment she sounded as though she were blowing up for a squall.

"I beg your pardon?" said Caroline, surveying her with astonishment.

"Blowing up for a squall," repeated Lady Katherine. "The way you're sighing, you sound like the wind when a storm is in the offing."

Caroline, trying to smile, said she was not used to her friend expressing herself in such nautical terms. Lady Katherine said cheerfully that living on the shore, one was bound to pick up a few such phrases. "But that's nothing to the point, darling," she added. "You really are sighing fit to break anyone's heart. I hate to see you so blue-deviled."

Caroline, with another attempted smile, said she was not really blue-deviled. "I'm only feeling rather tired," she said. "Which is very odd, for I haven't done anything this last week to get that way."

"That's why you're tired," said Lady Katherine with authority. "There is nothing so fatiguing as doing nothing. You ought to go for a walk or a drive."

Caroline said quickly she did not want to go for a walk or a drive. She knew the odds were good she would encounter Raymond if she went outside the house. Indeed, she would not have put it past Lady Katherine to arrange such an encounter if the thing were possible. "If you're afraid of meeting Mr. Jeffries, you can take the chaise and pull down the shades," said Lady Katherine, who seemed able to read her thoughts. "The chaise doesn't have our coat of arms on it like the town carriage, so he would never know you were in it."

Caroline said again she did not wish to go for a drive, but Lady Katherine's words had given her pause. There was something very attractive in the idea of getting a little fresh air after so many days cooped up inside. It struck her suddenly that what she would most like to do (setting aside the idea of seeing Raymond, which was out of the question) was to go sea bathing. And that was a thing she could do without any fear of breaking her resolution. She could take the chaise, have it deliver her directly to the ladies' bathing beach, and instruct the coachman to wait while she bathed. Afterward, he could take her directly home, and there would be absolutely no chance of encountering Raymond anywhere along the way.

"I think perhaps I will go sea bathing," she said aloud. "It's been such a warm day, I am longing for a bathe."

Lady Katherine looked pleased, then doubtful. "It's rather late in the day," she said. "Are you sure you would rather not go driving instead?"

Caroline said she was sure. It might be rather late in the day for sea bathing—a glance at the clock showed her it was almost the dinner hour—but she was sure she could find a bathing machine still operating. She said as much to Lady Katherine, causing that lady to declare once again that she was a vexing girl. But she made no further objection. "At least you're getting out of the house, which is something," she said. "I'll have Cook put dinner back, and send a message to the stables to bring round the chaise."

Caroline nodded absently. Now that she had decided to bathe, she found herself looking forward to the experience with an almost frenzied longing. To feel herself buoyed up by the waves with nothing but the sky above her and unlimited horizon before her seemed the nearest thing to ease she might find in her unhappy situation.

It was indeed rather late in the day for sea bathing, as she discovered when she set out for the shore. The sun was low over the western horizon; the gulls were crying a mournful vespers overhead; and a handful of fishing boats were making their way back to harbor as Lady Katherine's chaise wended its way along toward the ladies' bathing beach. On the esplanade, she could see a number of people strolling about, taking a constitutional before dinner. One of those people looked a great deal like Raymond. The gentleman in question possessed Raymond's tall figure, at any rate, and he was making his way along the esplanade with a quick and purposeful stride. Caroline half rose from her seat to get a better view, but the distance was too great, and she could not be certain it was he.

At the ladies' bathing beach, the chaise drew to a stop, and Caroline got out on the sands. Behind her, houses rose in serried ranks to the top of the hill. The light of sunset was reflected in their windows, setting them ablaze with fiery flashes of red and gold. If she had looked closely toward the hotel, she might have seen a smaller flash that was Emily Renquist's spyglass, but Caroline had no thought of spyglasses just then. It was Raymond she was looking for, and she was relieved not to see him, albeit disappointed too. With a sigh, she turned back toward the beach and crossed the sands toward the row of gaily painted bathing machines that were stationed along the shore.

At her usual machine, she suffered a check. The woman had evidently gone home for the day, for neither she nor her horse were present. The next machine was empty too, and the next. Caroline began to be afraid that she would not get her bathe after all. She hurried down the shore, encountering machine after empty machine with sinking spirit. She was just on the point of giving up, when, at the point the beach met the cliffs, she found a stout, red-faced dame in the act of unharnessing her horse from a shabby bathing machine.

"Could you take me out?" panted Caroline. "It's not too late, is it?"

The woman paused to survey her in a measuring fashion. "I dunno," she said. "The sun's near to setting, and I want my dinner. I'd have to charge you extra." She looked Caroline up and down again with a calculating air. "Say, six shillings?"

This was rank extortion, as Caroline knew. She was too eager to bathe to haggle over terms, however. Having paid the woman six shillings, she stepped into the machine. The woman reharnessed her horse, and with much creaking and squeaking the machine moved jerkily out to sea.

With brusque efficiency, the woman set about stripping off Caroline's clothes and attiring her in a voluminous bathing dress. She remarked as she did so that Caroline was a skinny one. "Red-haired too," she added as she bundled Caroline's hair into an oilskin cap. "I had a red-haired beau once. A fractious fellow, he was—always quarreling over the triflingest things. But there, most folks with red hair is fractious as far as I can tell."

Caroline thought this unfair, as she had withstood without complaint both the woman's far-from-gentle ministrations and her far-from-genteel conversation. She said nothing, however, for the sea was there, and it offered an escape from both impertinence and heartache. Stepping cautiously off the machine, she lowered herself into the water, shivering a little as its coolness enveloped her. Her dress bellied around her, eddying in the waves—rather larger waves than she was used to. Looking around, she realized that Lady Katherine's mention of squalls might have been prophetic. Not only was the surf higher than she had seen it before, but a brisk wind was blowing, and a dark edifice of cloud gathering in the north offset the brilliancy of the sun setting in the west.

The bathing woman, squinting at it, said it looked like rain. "No hurry though," she told Caroline, who was also casting anxious glances at the sky. "Them clouds is building slow. It won't rain before morning, mark my words. You paid your money fair enough; might as well take your time and have your bathe out." With these words, she drew an evil-looking brown pipe from her pocket, applied a flint, and settled down to smoke.

The pipe was evil smelling as well as evil looking, and Caroline was driven farther out to sea to escape its noisome fumes. Her usual bathing woman would have sternly interdicted such venturesome behavior, but Caroline did not suppose her present attendant would protest, nor did she. The woman merely sat smoking and gazing at the sunset.

Caroline looked at the sunset too, treading water with some difficulty. The surf seemed to be growing rougher, or perhaps it was merely that she was farther out than she had ever been before. The waves were a little alarming, but she was unwilling to go back so soon, seeing she had paid more than double for the privilege of coming out at all. Besides, the play of light and cloud reflected on the sea was spectacular enough to offset some of her discomfort. She was regarding it with pleasure, when a well-bred voice spoke in her ear.

"A pretty sight, isn't it?" it said. "I don't think I've ever seen a more magnificent sunset."

The shock of this sudden address made Caroline gasp. It also made her forget momentarily about treading water. As a wave was going by just then, she would have gone under had not a strong arm caught her and bore her up. Caroline sputtered, wiping water from her eyes and gazing with disbelief at the figure treading water beside her. "Mr. Jeffries!" she said. "Raymond! Whatever are you doing here?"

"I should think that was self-evident," he said gravely. "I am sea bathing, of course."

Although his voice was grave, there was laughter in his eyes. His dark hair was plastered to his head like a seal's, and a shred of seaweed hung rakishly over one ear. He was wearing an ordinary shirt and—as far as she could ascertain—ordinary trousers as well. "I hope you will forgive my unceremonious arrival," he explained with a bob that was evidently meant for a bow. "It's not the usual time of day for calling, and my attire leaves something to be desired as well, but I thought it more appropriate than my usual bathing attire!"

Caroline let this remark go by, being still too stunned to attend to anything else. "But what are you doing here?" she repeated. "Do you mean to say you *swam* here?"

"Yes," he said, pushing a lock of wet hair out of his eyes. "All the way from the esplanade. Not quite such a feat as swimming the Hellespont," he added modestly. "I daresay I make a poor showing beside Leander's achievement. Still, the motivation was the same, and that must count for something."

It took a moment for this remark to register. When it did, Caroline's color rose. "Oh," she said inadequately.

By this time the bathing attendant had discovered Raymond's presence. She leaned forward with a scowl on her red face. "Here, now, what's this?" she called belligerently. "This is a ladies' machine, sir. No gentlemen allowed!"

"I beg your pardon," Raymond told her politely, treading water. "I won't be a moment, ma'am. I merely wanted a word with the young lady."

"A word, is it? *I'll* give you a word. This is a respectable machine, sir, and I'm a respectable woman. There'll be no goings-on of that sort while I'm on duty."

"I'll only be a moment," repeated Raymond with a winsome smile. The woman repeated sternly that she would tolerate no goings-on, but his smile seemed to have had an effect, for she subsided into silence, though continuing to keep a sharp eye on him and Caroline.

Caroline, meanwhile, was becoming aware that even with the woman as chaperone there was a good deal of impropriety in the situation. Raymond was clothed more or less, and so was she, but it was hardly usual to make small talk with a man while you were both chin deep in water. Besides, she was aware that her voluminous dress and encompassing cap were not very becoming. "Please, you had better go," she said with embarrassment. "I don't think this is a good place for conversation."

"No, but desperate situations call for desperate measures," returned Raymond, treading water. "And since I failed to get your ear by ordinary means, I was reduced to this expedient, which is, I think you will agree, sufficiently desperate!"

Again Caroline colored. "I'm sorry," she said. "I know you called several times this week—"

"Yes, and found you 'not at home' every time," interrupted Raymond, finishing the statement for her. "It's plain you don't want to talk to me. I can take a hint as well as the next man, and I would have given up and gone away, except I could not resist the urge to ask you why."

"Why?" repeated Caroline weakly.

"Yes, why," repeated Raymond. He gave her a searching look. "Was it not true, what you said before? Do you not care about me after all?"

The proper response to this was, of course, a lie. Caroline had determined on a policy of renunciation, and it clearly behooved her to destroy his feelings by any and all means necessary. But her lips refused to participate in such a heartless policy. She could only shake her head helplessly. "Yes or no?" he demanded, looking into her eyes. "Caroline, cannot you tell me the truth? You know that's the thing I've admired most in you since our acquaintance began. You are honest at any cost, both with yourself and others. Do you *want* me to go away?

This question put Caroline in a horrible dilemma.

If she followed her policy of renunciation, she ought to say yes, but if she did, it would be a lie. And he had just praised honesty as the thing he admired most in her. Could any woman face the man she loved and say the words that would destroy both his love and admiration for her forever? Caroline did not know about any other woman, but she found she could not do it. "No!" she answered with a wail. "I don't want you to go away. But you should, Raymond. It would be better if you did."

He nodded, as though this speech came as no surprise to him. "That's honest enough, at any rate," he said. "I knew you must feel that way, else why should you avoid me?"

"I didn't want to hurt you," said Caroline unhappily.

"Well, you *have* hurt me, my girl—hurt me damnably. But I can believe you didn't want to. Indeed, that thought is all that's kept me sane this past week. I daresay there's some people who have doubts as to my sanity even so." Raymond's teeth flashed in a grin. "The ones who saw me tear off my coat and jump off the esplanade just now, for instance!"

Caroline stared at him. "'Jump off the esplanade?'" she repeated. "Don't tell me you did that, Raymond? I know you said you came from there, but you don't mean you jumped in the water in front of all those people, fully clothed?"

"Not *fully* clothed. As I said, I jettisoned my coat first, and also my boots. But apart from that, I was as you see me now, only drier."

"But what must they have thought?" exclaimed Caroline. She could not imagine the elegant and well-bred Raymond Jeffries leaping off the esplanade in all his clothes to the amazement of the people around him.

"I wasn't worrying about what they thought," said Raymond. "I was only wanting to see you. Having been thwarted all week, I wasn't going to lose a chance, no matter what it cost me."

Caroline's mind was working slowly. "But how did you know I was there?" she said. "Did you recognize Kate's carriage in spite of its having no coat of arms?"

"Er—no," said Raymond with a sidelong glance. "As a matter of fact, I received a note from Lady Katherine saying you were going bathing. I had hoped to intercept you before you went in the water, but I arrived a little too late for that, so I had to take the—er—next best route."

Color flooded Caroline's face once more, but this time it was a flush of indignation. "I knew it!" she said. "I knew Kate was plotting something. That's why she wanted me to go driving instead of bathing."

"That would have been a drier rendezvous," acknowledged Raymond, looking down at his sodden clothing in a detached way. "But I must admit that this, at least, has the charm of novelty."

Caroline gave an involuntary gurgle of laughter, which was abruptly quenched as a wave broke over both their heads, submerging them inches deep in salty water. They rose to the surface an instant later, coughing and sputtering. As soon as she was able to speak, Caroline resumed her inquisition.

"So Lady Katherine told you I was here," she said. "I should have guessed. Oh, I could murder Kate for this! She is always so sure she knows what is best for other people."

"It seems to me she's not the only one," said Raymond with a sidelong look. "Caroline, you seem convinced I ought not to care for you. But I do care for you—I *love* you, in fact. You are the woman of all others I love and want to marry. It will be a source of misery all my life if you refuse me."

Caroline would have wrung her hands if they had not been busy treading water. "You can't know that," she said. "People change, Raymond. Feelings change. I am sure you would end up regretting it if I agreed to become your wife. Only the other day I heard Miss Timms saying you would be lowering yourself to marry me."

Raymond frowned. "What a hateful thing to say," he said. "I wish Miss Timms might say it within my hearing so I could set her straight."

"But don't you see, Raymond, what she said might have been hateful, but it was *true*. To most of society, I'm Caroline Sedgewick, the most celebrated jilt in England. Why would you want to tie yourself with such a woman?"

"Because I know she is not the most celebrated jilt in England but, rather, a most misunderstood young woman," said Raymond. "Because she is honest, and witty, and altogether delightful company. Because I never fail to enjoy myself when I am with her, even when she is making me work like the deuce to keep my head above water. And because I love her with all my heart. Is that not sufficient reason?"

Put like that, it seemed to be. Caroline could find no answer, at any rate. Raymond went on in a coaxing voice. "Caroline, I know you mean well by me. That's one of the things I love about you—that there isn't a selfish or mercenary bone in your body. Indeed, I am afraid your good qualities rather outnumber mine if the truth were told. You say I would be sorry if I married you, but I believe the opposite might be true. I freely admit I am not your equal, my dear, but I intend to be, God willing."

"Nonsense," said Caroline hotly. "How can you say so, Raymond? You have never done anything to cause gossip or make your name a byword on people's lips."

Raymond smiled. "Except for jumping off the esplanade just now," he said. "And do you know, I rather enjoyed that. I begin to think it's time I turned over a new leaf. Conventionality is all very well, but past a certain point it's like a strait-waistcoat. It keeps you from following your instincts—and your fancy."

"But—" Caroline was finding it harder and harder to argue. Not only was Raymond making a convincing case for his point of view, but the waves seemed to be getting higher. When she opened her mouth to speak again, a wave came by that made her gulp down a mouthful of water. "Seawater," she said, half laughing and half crying. "Oh, Raymond, this is absurd. *You* are absurd. I don't know what I should do. But I do know I can't stay afloat much longer in this surf!"

"Nor I," said Raymond. Leaning forward, he kissed her on the lips. A shout came from the direction of the bathing machine, but he ignored it. "My dear, I'll come and talk to you tonight," he said. "Will you see me?"

"Yes," said Caroline softly. He kissed her again, then struck out for shore while Caroline returned to the machine to receive both a vigorous rubdown and a thorough scolding from the bathing attendant.

Nineteen

Caroline returned home to be greeted by another scolding. "Darling, you have been gone an age! Don't tell me you have been bathing all this time?"

With a faint blush, Caroline said that she had. But this proved only cause for fresh grievance. "Your lips are blue, actually blue! And your hands are like ice. You ought not to stay in the water so long. I am sure you will be ill if you are not ill already. Here, take some tea, and I'll ring for Hannah. You must warm yourself before you eat, or you will be ill of a certainty."

With unbending authority, Lady Katherine saw that these instructions were carried out. Caroline was plied with tea, bathed, dried, and dressed in warm clothing before she was allowed to sit down at the table.

By this time, it had occurred to Caroline she had a grievance. Lady Katherine had, after all, alerted Raymond to the fact she was going bathing, and though that had not turned out to be such a bad thing—Caroline was beginning to think it had been quite a good one, in fact—she still had a few things she wanted to say to her friend on the subject of well-meant interference. But when they sat down at the table, Mr. Baddington was there, and his presence kept Caroline from saying everything she wanted to say on the subject of Raymond. In any case, when she thought about it, she realized it was a subject she was not quite ready to bring up. She wanted to think a little more about some of the things he had said that afternoon.

It was evident that Lady Katherine's thoughts were running on the same subject. She inquired casually if Caroline had seen anyone she knew on the way to the beach and seemed disappointed when she said she had not. As Caroline reflected wryly, it did not seem to have occurred to Lady Katherine that Raymond might jump off the esplanade and swim out to meet her in the water. Indeed, as Caroline consumed soup, fried sole, and mutton cutlets, she began to find it difficult to believe he had really done so.

Meanwhile, at a house just across the square, other people were finding it equally difficult to believe.

"You say he met her in the water?" said Admiral Humphrey in a voice of high skepticism. "Not on the beach, but actually in the water?"

"I saw it with my own eyes." Emily Renquist was enjoying the sensation she was making. Her discovery of Caroline's misbehavior could not have come at a better time, for she had been invited to dine that evening with a party of guests at the home of Admiral and Mrs. Humphrey in King's Square. Thus she was able to serve the news piping hot without fear anyone might have been helped to the same dish beforehand. "I could not believe that she was actually brazen enough to make an assignation in her bathing dress with a man," she continued in a hushed voice. "Such a shocking indelicacy! I would not have thought it even of Caroline Sedgewick."

"Aye, but look here." The admiral was still evidently struggling to make sense of her news. "You mean to say she met him while in her bathing dress? In the water?"

"That's exactly what I do mean to say. I saw it with my own eyes, I tell you!"

"Good Lord! But if they were both in the water, and she was in her bathing dress—what was *he* wearing? You don't mean to say the fellow was in a state of nature, do you?"

His wife gasped at these words, and the others at the table leaned forward with bated breath. Miss Renquist was forced to disappoint them, however. "No, he appeared to be wearing clothing," she said regretfully. "Still, it's shocking enough she should meet him there at all. And they were together an inordinate time—really an inordinate time, together in the water. I don't pretend to know what they were doing all the while."

The admiral, still in a voice of skepticism, said that he didn't suppose they were doing anything very shocking. "Likely they only wanted a bit of privacy," he said. "You can't exchange two words in this place without someone kicking up a fuss about it. Or staring at you through a spyglass," he added with a pointed look at Miss Renquist.

Miss Renquist said primly that if people were behaving themselves, they had no need to fear spyglasses. "Besides, I know they were not behaving themselves," she added. "I saw Mr. Jeffries kiss Miss Sedgewick! Not once but several times."

The admiral laughed. "That means nothing except he thinks she's worth kissing," he said. "And I don't think any the less of him for that. Or of her either, come to think of it. Nice little thing, Caroline Sedgewick. I can't think why all you women are so hard on her."

"Can you ask, Admiral? She has thrown over three men without so much as a by-your-leave. Indeed, I would think that you, as a man, would be bound to resent such an insult!"

The admiral shook his head. "That don't follow," he said. "Mean to say, I'm all for my own sex as far as it goes, but there's some fellows who deserve throwing over and no mistake. That fellow Scroggins, for instance. A mean fellow, Scroggins, and cross-grained to boot. I wouldn't blame any girl for giving him the heave-to. As for Robert Cullen, he's a rotter if there ever was one. Oh, he's all smiles and bows and scrapes when you ladies are around, but if you saw how he goes on in men's society, you wouldn't be so quick to defend him. I tell you, I wouldn't want to see any daughter of mine marry him."

Miss Renquist was silenced, but not for long. "Yes, but Miss Sedgewick was engaged to a Lieutenant de Very back in Lincolnshire before she ever came to London," she shot back. "And apparently she jilted him too. How do you explain that, Admiral?"

"I don't explain it," said the admiral firmly. "Don't know anything about it. Might be any of a hundred reasons why she broke with the fellow. Do *you* know why she did it?"

Miss Renquist was forced to admit she did not. It went against the grain to make any such admission, and she eyed the admiral with resentment. "You seem bound to defend Miss Sedgewick," she said. "But I can tell you this business today has given me a very poor idea of her character. Even if I knew nothing of her past, I should be shocked by what I saw today. A clandestine assignation, and in the water! I don't know how you can possibly excuse such a thing, Admiral."

The admiral smiled. "I daresay we'll see an excuse soon enough in the form of a betrothal," he said. "I've been expecting it anytime this week. It's plain to see she and Jeffries are crazy about each other."

Miss Renquist received this in unenthusiastic silence. So did the other ladies. They felt a betrothal would be a disappointingly tame outcome to what had promised to be a delightful scandal. "Do you really think he will marry her?" said one of the other ladies doubtfully. "He is a Jeffries, after all."

"What's that got to do with it?" demanded the admiral. "Last I heard, the Jeffrieses marry and are given in marriage like other folks."

"Yes, but not people like Miss Sedgewick. She is only passably pretty, Admiral, and not at all well-to-do. In fact, there is nothing special about her except the fact she's jilted her last three suitors. I would think that alone would keep Mr. Jeffries from proposing to her, for if he does she will likely jilt him too!"

The admiral laughed. "Maybe," he said. "But I take leave to doubt it. Raymond Jeffries strikes me as a fellow capable of carrying his point. I'll wager you five pounds that if they do become engaged, Miss Sedgewick don't throw *him* over."

The ladies felt one and all the sad probability of this idea. No woman lucky enough to become engaged to Raymond Jeffries would be mad enough to throw him over. There were no takers on the admiral's wager, and a dismal silence reigned over the table for fully a minute and a half. It was broken at last by Mrs. Timms, grandmother to the Miss

Timms who had sought to engage Raymond at the assembly. "Well, it's certainly better luck than Miss Sedgewick could have hoped for, considering her past," she said with the resentment of one who has seen her own granddaughter passed over in favor of an inferior candidate. "It doesn't seem fair, when there are so many more deserving girls he might have chosen."

The ladies agreed it was very odd. "I suppose soon we shall be obliged to give her the precedence at all our parties," said another disconsolately. "She will be a viscountess, after all."

"Well, viscountess or not, I do not intend to recognize her," said Mrs. Mackerly, a black-browed dowager in purple plush. "She has put herself outside the pale as far as I am concerned. I certainly shall not send her an invitation to one of *my* parties."

A brief silence followed this statement. Mrs. Mackerly's twice-yearly dinner parties were renowned both for the badness of the food and the dullness of the company. "Almost makes me wish I was in Miss Sedgewick's shoes, by Jove," said the admiral sotto voce, and signaled to his wife to ring for the next course.

Meanwhile, the lady who was actually in Miss Sedgewick's shoes—Miss Sedgewick herself, that is—was growing increasingly nervous. Raymond had asked if he might call on her that evening, and she felt tolerably certain that when he came, he would ask her to marry him. She had a strong feeling she would not be able to refuse him if he were as convincing as he had been that afternoon. But was it right she should accept him? Raymond had seemed positive he would be happier with her than without her, but she still cringed to think such happiness as she could bring him would be inevitably tainted by scandal.

Dinner was over by then. She and Lady Katherine were seated in the drawing room. Caroline moved restlessly about, picking up a book here or a cushion there and setting it down again at random. Lady Katherine eyed her curiously. "Whatever is wrong with you, Caro?" she said. "You're as nervous as a cat on hot bricks. Come, tell me the truth: *Did* something happen this afternoon?"

"Yes," said Caroline. She bent a stern eye on her friend. "You ought to know what it was too, Kate, for I understand it was you who told Raymond I would be at the bathing beach!"

Lady Katherine received this accusation with an unblushing smile. "Yes, I did," she agreed. "It seemed to me you were behaving absurdly, when you obviously care for the man. So I sent him a note by one of the servants while you were upstairs putting on your bonnet." With curiosity, she added, "I thought my note must have gotten there too late, as you did not mention meeting him on the way."

"I did *not* meet him on the way," said Caroline. "Neither on the way there nor on the way back. He jumped off the esplanade and swam out to meet me while I was actually in the water!"

Lady Katherine gave a crow of laughter. "You don't mean it! Raymond Jeffries did that? Oh, Caro, how delightful. Don't tell me he was in all his clothes too?"

"All except his boots and topcoat," said Caroline, smiling grimly. "So he told me, at any rate, and I have no reason to disbelieve him."

"Well, that will give the old cats something to talk

about in the pump room tomorrow!" said Lady Katherine, still shaking with laughter. "Jumping off the esplanade in all his clothes! I would not have thought Raymond Jeffries could be so romantic. Caro, you must believe he loves you now. He could not have proved it more completely if he had swum the Channel for you."

Caroline gave a brief strained smile. This caused Lady Katherine to stop laughing and survey her with a hint of concern. "You will accept him now, won't you, Caroline?" she asked. "I don't know what more you would want from him."

Caroline shook her head. No more than Lady Katherine did she know what more she could want. Yet she wanted something more—some assurance, perhaps, that Raymond fully understood the drawbacks of marrying Miss Caroline Sedgewick and was willing to endure them. She was seeking to put these thoughts into words, when a strange, discordant noise rose from the street outside.

"What's *that?*" said Lady Katherine. Rising from her chair, she hurried to the window that gave upon the balcony. Caroline followed suit. Unlatching the window, Lady Katherine stepped out, with Caroline right behind her.

Outside, the discordant noise was much louder. It was also recognizable as music, but music like nothing Caroline had heard before. She peered over the balcony. In the street below, she could dimly distinguish two figures. One was tall and dressed in gentlemen's evening clothes; the other was shorter, skirted, and oddly distorted. Indeed, this last figure did not even appear to be human, and Caroline was trying to make up her mind on this point, when the music came to an abrupt halt.

A voice with laughter in depths quoted, "'But, soft! what light through yonder window breaks?'"

"Raymond?" said Caroline incredulously. She leaned out over the balcony. The taller figure stepped forward until it was illuminated in a pool of light cast by a nearby streetlamp. It was indeed Raymond, and he smiled as he looked up at her. "I am credibly informed the tune you just heard was "Blue-Eyed Mary," though between us we may pretend it to be "Green-Eyed Caroline," he said. "Would you like to hear another tune, or shall I try my hand at singing?"

"Raymond!" said Caroline again in a voice of stupefaction. "Whatever are you doing down there?"

Beside her, Lady Katherine was laughing hysterically. "Can't you see, Caro?" she said. "He's serenading you. I never heard a serenade quite like that one, however." She, too, peered over the balcony. "What in heaven's name have you got there, Mr. Jeffries? It sounds like twenty tomcats tied up in a sack."

"Not at all," said Raymond reprovingly. "Lady Katherine, I am distressed to find you so lacking in musical appreciation. What you hear is the bagpipe, an instrument native to Scotland." He gestured for the figure beside him to step forward. In the light of the streetlamp it proved to be a human figure after all, a sturdy Scotsman clad in a sweeping plaid. Tucked beneath one arm was a loose bag from which protruded a cluster of pipes. "Private McNeill," continued Raymond—the Scotsman bowed gravely at the words—"piper to His Majesty's Royal Highland Regiment, is staying at the Blue Bull on the High Street. He very kindly consented to lend his aid when I told him I was wishing to serenade the lady of my heart this evening. I will admit a bagpipe was not my first choice of instrument for such a purpose, but since I found all the guitarists and violinists in town to be otherwise engaged, it appeared to be the best thing going. Besides, I am credibly informed that ladies appreciate spirit and originality in a suitor. Surely nothing could be more spirited and original than a bagpipe serenade!"

Taking these words as a cue, the piper began to play again, a tune Caroline recognized as "Nancy Dawson." Lady Katherine put her hands over her ears, but Caroline stood listening, smiling tremulously at Raymond, who smiled back at her from beneath the balcony.

Before the song was quite over, however, an interruption occurred. A burly man carrying a staff and lantern strode up to the piper and seized him by the arm, causing him to break off in mid-measure. "Here, what's this?" he demanded in a rough voice. "What are you doing here, you? Oh, and there's another one, is there?" he added, discerning Raymond's figure. "Well, you'd best be moving on, gentlemen. You're disturbing the peace, and I'll have to take you in charge if you don't quit the neighborhood at once."

"Good Lord, it's the Watch!" said Lady Katherine, and dissolved into hysterical laughter once more.

Raymond, with more address, began to explain to the Watchman the nature of his business in the neighborhood. He was somewhat hampered in these efforts by the piper, who had reacted furiously to the interruption of his music and was brandishing his fists, signifying his readiness to take on the Watchman in single combat. "It's all right," called Lady Katherine over the balcony as soon as she had recovered enough to speak. "Watchman, it's all right. We know these men."

"You know 'em?" said the Watchman dubiously. "This fellow here too?" He indicated the piper with a wave of his staff.

"Yes, I know them both. They are friends of mine," said Lady Katherine. With her sweetest smile, she added, "Please don't take them in charge."

The Watchman, being no more than human, was not proof against Lady Katherine's smile. "Well, I won't, my lady, if they're friends of yours," he said. "But begging your pardon, they can't go on making such a racket."

"They won't," Lady Katherine assured him. "They are finished now. I'll see there is no more disturbance."

The Watchman accepted this with a nod and strolled away, not deigning to look toward the piper, who clearly felt his had been the victory and was making gestures of derision toward him. A brief silence followed. Around the square, lights were blazing, and people had come out of their houses, curious to see what the disturbance was. Lady Katherine waved gaily toward the party on Admiral Humphrey's balcony and blew them a kiss. Her eyes were on Caroline, however, and so were Raymond's. So indeed were the piper's. Caroline felt the unspoken question in all their eyes. "I suppose you'd better come in," she said, avoiding Lady Katherine's eye. Addressing the piper specifically, she added, "Private McNeill, you must be thirsty after your—er—musical efforts. If you will go to the kitchen, I will tell Cook to give you some beer."

Private McNeill bowed gravely. "Much obliged to ye, ma'am," he said. Hoisting his bagpipe beneath his arm, he strode around the house in the direction of the servants' entrance.

Raymond, too, bowed. "I will see you presently," he told Caroline, and disappeared from view beneath the balcony. A moment later they heard a knock on the front door. Caroline looked at Lady Katherine appealingly. "You're coming down too, aren't you, Kate?" she asked.

Smiling, Lady Katherine shook her head. "Not for worlds, darling," she said. "I should only be playing gooseberry, and that, as you know, is a role I particularly dislike. I think I would rather go to the kitchen and talk to Private McNeill. I have an idea of asking him to perform at my next musicale. Think what a delightful change it would be from the usual pianoforte and harp sonatas!"

In the end, Caroline went down to the drawing room alone. She had no more than entered the room when Raymond entered it too, ushered in by the butler. They stood and looked at each other as the butler withdrew and discreetly shut the doors behind him. After a minute, Caroline spoke. "Raymond, how could you?" she asked with a catch in her voice.

Raymond was smiling, but his eyes held a faint anxiety. "I hope you did not dislike it very much," he said. "It was meant as a heartfelt tribute, Caroline, however it may have sounded. Unfortunately the bagpipe is not the most romantic instrument in the world, but I had hoped—"

"Oh, I don't care for that," broke in Caroline. "As a matter of fact, I rather liked it. But I don't understand what you meant by it."

"Don't you?" said Raymond. He came a step closer. "I should think that was clear by now. In an effort to overcome your qualms, I was courting you in the old style—the old Scottish style, that is—"

Caroline laughed, but at the same time she was shaking her head in bewilderment. "But why?" she said. "Everyone will think you have run mad, Raymond! Especially when people hear also about your jumping off the esplanade earlier today."

Raymond smiled. "I don't mind being thought mad," he said. "It's nothing to me what people think. All that matters is that *you* know why I did it. Don't you agree?"

"Yes," said Caroline uncertainly. "At least, I think I agree."

"Then wouldn't you agree the converse is true? Caroline, look at me." Raymond took another step toward her. "Don't you see, Caroline, it's the same thing you are fretting about? You think you would be dishonoring me if you married me because of a lot of gossip that has only the barest foundation in truth."

Caroline considered this statement, then nodded. "Yes," she said. "I do think that, Raymond. It might not matter if you were an ordinary man, but your name is such a proud one."

"And that is the very reason I am the best man in the world for you to marry," said Raymond. Putting a finger beneath her chin, he gently tilted her face up to his. "It's true we Jeffrieses have a name for being proud," he said. "I won't say it's an unmerited name either. But it's not pride in the ordinary sense, the kind that's only skin deep and takes umbrage at every scratch or slight. The pride of the Jeffrieses goes all the way to the bone." He smiled at her. "That sounds dreadful, doesn't it? But it isn't a negative thing, at least not in the way I mean it.

Pride is one of those words, like sympathy, that has both a positive and negative sense, and I like to think ours is the positive kind of pride. In any case, it's something I've inherited along with the family name and the family nose, and it makes me quite impervious to any small-minded gossip that people might seek to attach to me or my wife."

He looked at Caroline, and she looked at him. She drew a deep breath. "Oh, Raymond, I would like to believe that," she said. "And in a way, I do believe it. But can't you see how much I hate coming to you with such a tawdry reputation? It's so—so humiliating."

Raymond considered, then nodded judicially. "Yes, I can see," he said. "If the situation were reversed, I daresay I should feel the same. But if you will forgive me for saying so, my dear, that is an example of the negative sort of pride, not the positive kind."

Caroline frowned. "I don't see that," she said. "I am only trying to protect you!"

"But I don't want to be protected, my dear. I am quite willing to share in whatever fortune sends us. In fact, to quote the marriage service, 'In sickness and in health, for richer or poorer, et cetera, et cetera.' I do understand your reluctance, mind you. I'm a proud man myself, and it would go against the grain with me to be in your position. But because I am not in your position, I am able to view the matter with perhaps more clarity than you do. What I see is that you are going to have to make a sacrifice no matter what you choose to do. And what I am asking, quite frankly, is for you to sacrifice your pride rather than sacrifice *me.*"

Caroline laughed shakily. "That's all you're asking, is it?" she said.

"That's quite enough," said Raymond. He looked soberly at Caroline. "Believe me, my dear, I know the magnitude of what I am asking. And if I didn't know you for the most generous woman in the world, I would never hope to get it. But I *do* hope, Caroline. I hope it very much."

Caroline twisted her hands. "I don't know," she said. "You truly think it's pride that keeps me from saying I will marry you?"

"Yes, pride of a sort. As I say, there's different meanings to the word. It's another of those cases where the English language comes up short in making a distinction between several very different concepts. In your case, pride might best be defined as an exaggerated sense of concern—in this situation, specifically, concern for me and my reputation. But it's a concern that's misplaced, my dear. If you can bear with me, with all my faults, I will be glad to bear whatever you bring me and believe I got the best of the bargain at that!"

Caroline took another deep breath. "If you're certain, Raymond," she said. "But you're sure you will not mind if people talk?"

Raymond's laugh rang out. "It should be clear by now I don't mind at all! By myself, I've caused enough gossip today to drown out any number of lesser scandals. Indeed, you may find that people will counsel you against marrying a man with such a reputation for eccentricity!"

Caroline smiled weakly. "Not likely," she said. "They're more likely to counsel me to jump at the chance while it offers." Again she twisted her hands. "Raymond, I still can't help worrying. You have not known me for very long. What if you change your mind about caring for me?"

"About loving you," corrected Raymond. Reaching down, he took her by the hand. "I suppose we haven't known each other very long," he said. "But our acquaintance has been fully long enough to convince me of my own mind and heart. Still, I can well understand that *you* might have doubts, under the circumstances."

"I don't," said Caroline quickly. "Indeed, I don't, Raymond! I have never been so convinced of anything in my life as the fact that I love you with all my heart. It's only that I—well, I feel I *ought* to have doubts. At least till I have known you longer."

Raymond nodded matter-of-factly. "That's natural, of course," he said. "But fortunately it's easily provided for too. An engagement is quite in order when a couple plans to marry. I am willing to leave the duration of the engagement up to you. Just so long as you marry me in the end, I don't care how long you keep me waiting."

"Now, that's a reckless statement," said Caroline, a smile beginning to dawn on her face. "What if I choose to keep you waiting ten years?"

Raymond laughed. "As to that, I'm trusting to your generosity and sense of fair play," he said. "I've never been disappointed when I did that, my dear, and I'm sure I won't be disappointed this time either."

Caroline's smile curved a little wider. "I don't think so either," she said. "Indeed, I tell you plainly, I'd marry you this minute if I followed my instincts!"

Raymond laughed again. "Well, that's a course I highly recommend," he said. "Following one's instincts is a wonderfully liberating thing, I find." As though these words had suggested a course of action, he took Caroline in his arms and kissed her. She kissed him back with enthusiasm, but still he could see she was worried.

"Why the furrowed brow, my love?" he said tenderly. "Do you still have doubts?"

Caroline raised her eyes bravely to his face. "Not rational ones, Raymond," she said. "But I can't help thinking of all the mistakes I have made. How can I be sure I am not making a mistake now, or allowing you to make one?"

She spoke these last words in a voice that was barely a whisper. Raymond seemed neither hurt nor offended by the question, however. "You can't be sure, of course—not till you try," he said. "But I have a decent confidence in my own ability to convince you you are doing the right thing. Besides, what's the worst that could happen?" He threw her a mischievous look. "If time goes on and you find you've made a mistake, well, there's nothing to stop you from jilting me!"

At these words, Caroline broke down entirely. "Oh, Raymond, how can you?" she said, half laughing and half crying. "I could *never* jilt you! I *love* you."

"Well, I love you too," said Raymond, taking her in his arms. When he would have embraced her, however, she resisted.

"I've been crying," she explained. "I will get your shirtfront all wet."

Raymond laughed. "Is that all? My dear girl, you much mistake your man if you think I would let a thing like that stop me from kissing you. Tears are nothing but saltwater, and if anything can be said to have brought us together, it's saltwater!"

And having in this manner overridden all her protests, he took her in his arms and kissed her again.